CON

by M. E. White

HARPER & ROW, PUBLISHERS

New York, Evanston
San Francisco, London

FIRST EDITION

STANDARD BOOK NUMBER: 06-014610-9

LIBRARY OF CONGRESS CATALOG CARD NUMBER: 77-181667

For Wild Jack

PART ONE

1 Joey took a drink from his bottle of comfort and waited. A hundred, maybe two hundred rats waited. A lion tamer, a horse, an ancient elephant. Mosquitoes, flies, and tap dancers. Even the warm, moist night air, silent and expectant, waited. *Suckers.*

In the distance lights moved down from the hills, snaked around the underbrush, and fell in line on the road. Dust billows rose, illuminated for an instant in a rear car's beam before disappearing in darkness. It was Saturday night, and they were coming from every direction, from over the old ridge road and the road around by Cott's Corner and The Landing: a parade of dented, rusting Hudsons, four-door Nashes, doorless De Sotos, drag-belly Buick Roadmasters, and broken-down pickups, their running boards half off, their hood ornaments masts for Confederate flags and coon tails, their tailgates and bumpers billboards for the message:

I have faith in the Lord Jesus Christ
THE J. C. KRINGLE RADIO REVIVAL HOUR
12 NOON

And in the rear window, above the message, just behind a driver with a face full of meanness, a shotgun waited.

Hell remained, after the Depression, after the war; it swelled the drivers with fear, swelled them with hunger and hate, made them love to death God and the U.S.A. *Sweet Sister Sue, an angel came down and spoke to me in the ear. What he say?* Fury moved through

3

the parade. *Lord God, but it's true; whispered into my mind, said
. . . but I don't want to sully the holy by speech. No.* Hate-filled,
they moved through the humid night air toward a circle of colored
lights, *Lord God, Sweet Sister,* hoping for release, distraction, and
blood.

Five kids and three starved mangy dogs huddled together on the
bed of a pickup staring out at the darkness. In the cab the father
chewed a new stick of gum and glared; he was thirty years old and
had only twelve teeth left for the gum. He blew a bubble, let it snap.
Beside him his wife sat glumly sucking pink liquid from a soda pop
bottle, her head covered with a bandanna. Last year she had given
birth for the sixth time and lost most of the hair on top of her head.

The dogs in the back began to howl, and the man yelled out the
open window, "You kids shut up them dogs." They were almost
down to The Crossing now. Rats ran across the road, and the dogs
snarled and raced back and forth in the truck bed. The man's hands
tightened on the wheel and his foot stomped down on the accelerator. "Shut up them dogs, I said." He had a sudden desire to race
ahead down the gravel gully into a tree and make an end to it. He
pulled out of line, stomped once again on the accelerator, and ran
down the siding, his headlights picking out gravel, bush, tree, a
curve, then the car seemed to slow of its own accord. He pulled
back into line, mad. "Goddamn dogs, I oughta shut 'em up for
good. Hot," he added. His wife nodded.

Somewhere ahead a gunshot sounded, someone shooting at a rat
probably. Once a reporter had come about the rats, had gone out
and asked the woman, sick in bed then, about them. "Oncet they
bit up one of the babies pretty bad," she had said. "Get into the
food sacks too, but then the dogs go to chasing them and all." She
had paused and looked at the reporter.

"Doesn't that disturb you—the baby's getting bit?"

"Just that way."

"Rats have killed some, I hear."

"Guess so," she said.

4

Red lights and streamers marked out the entrance to the parking area. The line of cars slowed almost to a stop, then men with flashlights moved them into position in one dirt row after another in the empty field, just as they had done last week. J. C. Kringle, child of God, had been there then; he had come with a delta jazz band that could be heard from one side of the hollow to the other announcing the arrival of the child of God and his fifteen assistant pastors, fifteen special representatives of the child of God, fifteen apostles to hear the prayers of the faithful. Fifteen angels. Fifteen.

The child of God had worn an electric-blue suit with purple armpits, and when he got up close enough, you could see that he wore makeup too. A white powdery film covered his face hiding a blackness that began to show through later in the evening when rivulets of sweat ran down from his close-cropped hair striping his face. "Now I know that you have despair," he screamed. "I know you have the agonies," he shouted. "I know that you are all alone and got deep-down miseries."

"Oh yes. That's right."

"I know it's raining *ALL OVER* Georgia tonight."

"Yes. Yes."

"I know it's rainin' *ALL OVER* this land."

"Yes indeed. Tell it."

"And I come to you here with love. Yes, I said *LOVE,* the love cure. Do you feel it?" he cried. "Do you hear it?"

"Yayes," they shouted.

"Do you want it?"

"Yayes," they screamed.

"Love cure. Love cure. Love cure." He was shouting and dancing, and the delta jazz band was backing him up with a beat that made his hips swivel and his eyes roll and pop. "I mean love of God Almighty."

"AMEN."

"Oh yes. You got to love God. Got to sacrifice for God. Got to

5

want God." He let his head roll back and shouted at the tent top. "Do you feel it now?"

"Yayes." Women got up and began to dance. They held up their hands, let their heads fall back, and danced forward to the child of God. They put their hands on his pants. They twitched and jumped toward the fifteen assistant pastors. They all began to shout, *"AMEN."* Everyone danced forward or twirled in the aisle.

"Yes, I'm talking about love of God. Teaching love of God. Preaching love of God. Wha'd I say?"

"LOVE OF GOD," they cried.

The band was silent. The child of God moved slowly forward, whispered; "And to love God, you need . . . ?" The question hung in the air, waited for the response. "I say *FAITH,"* cried the child of God.

"Oh yes."

"You don't vote for God," he screamed, and they whooped with delight. "No, you don't vote for God."

"Amen."

"It's a matter of faith." He paused. "And I'm asking you now: Do you have faith?"

"Yayes," they screamed.

"Yes, and you got faith in who?"

"In God Almighty."

"And are you ready for sacrifice?"

"Yes now."

"Are you ready for the sacrifice of Jesus?"

"Yes yes."

"Are you ready for his blood?"

"Yayes." They licked their lips in ecstasy and waited for the fifteen assistant pastors to pass out the pink water and the crumbs of joy.

"Are you ready for his body?"

"Yayes."

"Ready for his body and his blood?"

"Bloooooood." They seized the word, babbled it. "Bababablooooood."

The man in the pickup followed the flashlight over the loose dirt and into place. Tonight a circus had come to The Crossing. There, one night only, a canvas big top surrounded by a smaller dining tent and a caravan of trucks and trailers. Dust turned up by the cars in the field swept around the tent; then doors slammed, babies cried, and dogs snarled and snapped at the car windows or moaned and strained on their ropes.

"What is it?" the children asked.

The mother shrugged. "Show, guess." Her teeth hurt.

Inside the tent, sitting on the bleacher seats, they were glum and silent. Beneath them rats chewed at gum wrappers and popcorn boxes. Before them dancers twirled and one old elephant dribbled its feces across the sawdust.

Behind the big top there were rats too; rats settled like thick dirt on the tables and counters in the dining tent, rats ran between overturned garbage cans, and rats gnawed at their plunder under the trailers where the performers dressed. In one small partitioned section of the first trailer, an old man sat listening to the rats and making faces in the mirror. Only a few tufts of orange hair remained on his head; the dye had stained his scalp orange too, stained his scalp and left sores. Some scabs had formed now and pus ran from the places he scratched. Joey picked up a stick of makeup, looked at himself, and put it down. He picked up the paper bag with the bottle in it instead and took another drink. But his stomach was uneasy and the drink made his eyes water and pushed a taste of yesterday's breakfast up into his throat; then a yellow stream of bile filled his mouth and he leaned over and gagged into the wastebasket. He put his head down on the dressing table; he was tired and he was sick.

Eighty-five one-night stands since April, and for this he was receiving board and room and fifteen dollars a week. Vaguely, Joey remembered the man in the white suit who had come to his room one afternoon, walked up three flights of steps, looked at him lying there on the bed, and said he had a proposition. Joey could remember the heat, the flies coming in through the open French windows, the feel of his back sticking to the mattress cover as though it were rubber, and the man in the white suit as cool as rain. "Used to be with the circus, didn't you?" the man had asked. "Funny Finney?"

Joey couldn't remember, could remember only beds lined up against a gray wall; apple, mince, and cherry pie lined up under glass in a cafeteria; a little girl dressed like a firecracker for the Fourth of July; and the noise from the street, the heat, the flies.

"A comeback tour of old performers," the man in the white suit had said. One-night stands for a while, then a month at a time in city auditoriums, the best. Everyone loved a circus; kids growing up now who had never known anything but war would love a circus. There was a great interest in the unusual, a great deal of profit in novelty. The man had looked around the room at the pile of old clothes, the old newspapers and empty bottles. Freaks. Joey had remembered the applause.

There had been three clowns at first; one of them toppled over dead before an audience of fifty people who screamed that it was a trick, that they hadn't paid no fifty cents to be cheated, the second was shot to death in Mobile. Now Joey was alone, just as he had always been. He picked up a stick of orange lipstick and smeared his mouth to match his head. Once when he had been alone in New Orleans, he had put an ad in the paper: "Phone Joe 48912." The woman who answered the ad had offered him fifty dollars to take her to the movies. She had been extremely beautiful, and he had done it for nothing. He had worn a white white suit and white shoes; she had worn chiffon and pearls and had outlined her nose in black.

That evening he had told her his life story during the closeups. Staring at an eight-foot forehead, he had told her about how he was inflatable. And she had told him that she had fifty dollars burning

8

a hole in her panties, where she kept big bills. He had told her that, due to the nature of the disease, he had been away for years undergoing a series of shrinkings. During that time he had lost all touch with his wife and child; he was advertising for others, he said. And she had said that the man one seat over was hunting for the money. If he felt in the right places, it was his. He had told her he was a clown. He had made faces in the dark, and when the lights came on he had been alone.

Joey winked in the mirror at the old face, then drew several green stripes down the middle of it. He took another drink from the bottle and arranged again the four flowers of hair on top of his head. When he opened the trailer door, rats scurried away from the light and cleared a path for him as he walked toward the big top. There he stood in the soft dirt under the bleachers and watched the tightrope walker perform. Still agile at fifty, the ropewalker feigned loss of balance, tipped precariously from side to side, and then, as though by chance, righted himself with a wave of his umbrella. The audience booed.

"Old man," a voice in the dark asked, "you ready?"

"Not yet. It's not time yet," Joey answered.

"Get ready. Maybe you can warm them up, make them laugh. They're an ugly bunch."

The lights dimmed, and Joey stumbled slowly into the sawdust ring, stepping lightly in elephant turds. The crowd booed and hissed the darkness, then hooted the emptiness when the lights flickered on again. Joey felt sick; bile rose in his throat and mouth and seeped through clenched teeth into his cheeks, making his head swell dizzily. An empty popcorn box hit him from behind, and he fell to the ground. He thrashed around violently, he foamed at the mouth; he went insane. He had their attention now. He sensed it, smelled it in the air, and ran into the audience with his yellow teeth bared, his orange mouth drooling for more. He seized a woman's hat, put it on, and brayed like a donkey in heat. Part of the crowd moved away in panic; tittering children made faces and screamed

9

after their parents, and Joey was left standing alone between deserted bleachers, a flowered hat on his head.

Now the children stood in the distance braying and catcalling, and Joey charged. Head lowered like a lunatic bull, he ran scrambling after the children, then returned to the ring, pawed at the ground, and charged the audience on the other side. Mad, sick, he ran from one side of the ring to the other, up one aisle and down another, across bleachers and sawdust floor, drawing closer and closer, and the crowd screamed and shouted and ran before him. Still they waited, greedy, expectant, to see the old man's victim, mutilation, or end. They giggled eagerly when a child ran into the ring, kicked the old man, then tore to safety on the other side. There was applause for that.

Joey's face was wet with sweat, and the orange clown lips had begun to run and smear in the dampness until only a gaping bright hollow remained, the mouth of a fool. Blood ran from the sores on his head, streaking his face and neck and ears. Around him frenzy filled the lungs; shrieks of hysteria and joy and delight rose from the crowd. *"BAAAAAAALUUUUUUD,"* they babbled. *"BAAA-LUD, BAAALUD, BAAALUD."*

Joey ran screaming toward the sound. The audience broke and ran too, one woman slower than the others, and Joey grabbed her, kissed her blubbering mouth while the crowd circled around in the distance, taunting, kicking, and beating at the woman. "Whore." It wasn't Della, not his litte girl. Joey released the woman's mouth, unplugging a high-pitched scream that seemed to deafen him. He moved back, away, while the crowd clapped and stamped.

Out of control, the crowd milled in a circle, drew closer, more threatening, and Joey made faces and searched for something to amuse them with, some little thing. He thrust his hand into his pants, then ran toward them again, up deserted aisles, across abandoned bleachers, exposing a finger and giggling with delight. Surprise. But the audience stood dumb before his display. Like a magician sweetening the setup, preparing the audience for belief,

10

he pulled off his pants, his shirt. A little old man with wrinkled skin, he stood nude before them. But they had seen madness before; as had he.

Sitting alone in a house full of dog shit, tied to a clothesline, he had howled and cried and learned. He had escaped wearing camouflage, walked off with a tree on his head. Joe Spruce, he had stood on street corners decorated with wine, crying out that it was the jolly season. A funny man, but the FBI had thought otherwise, the National Guard had chopped the tree, and the police had accused him of playing tricks in downtown Tampa. *Little old ladies, believe me, for only a few hundred I can be restored to normalcy. I can have plastic surgery done on my head. Science will remove this tree and other miracles.* He had gone mad without his star on Christmas Eve and, two months later, fled the local loony bin in clown disguise. Circus circus everywhere. He had sent back picture postcards of Atlantic City and Baton Rouge; he had written on the cards they could not read, on the cards they thumbtacked to the wall along with the calendar pictures of the Rocky Mountains: "Wish you were here."

"Here," a little girl taunted. A fourteen-year-old girl with thick thighs and plump new breasts, she darted from the crowd into the ring and sent Joey in renewed pursuit. "Della," the old man called. "Della." The little girl giggled at the attention and waited while the old man tap-danced forward, flapped in the wind, showed himself how, lost control. She giggled again then, titillated by the nearness of him, teased him closer, and Joey threw himself on her fat flesh, squirming, screaming. The loneliness drew blood. "Della?" the old man cried. He had sat at a dime-store counter eating grease, he had lurked behind *True Romance* in the magazine section, and he had bought picture postcards, hundreds and hundreds of picture postcards, waiting for his little girl, little Della. "Della?"

The child squirmed free, into the arms of other admirers, and the admirers howled and clapped. Joey was pleased. An old man, he needed their applause, wanted to entertain them; he danced, but

11

they circled around him with ugly looks. He pissed a design in the sawdust and sprayed the air, and the crowd scattered, but when he was through they returned, ugly as before, shrieking, "Freak. Clown. Old man." They held up broken pop bottles, and Joey grinned sickly. "Freak."

Blood made the ground slippery; blood made the footing uneasy. Joey could hear their laughter as he ran. Clown, he was making them laugh; clown, he was making them forget. It was not easy. The sawdust stuck damply to his bare feet, and he slipped in the wetness. A pool of blood spread across the edge of the ring, and he fell. Nehi orange bottles glittered above him, a chandelier of broken glass, and blood ran down his arms and legs and over his old body. He was entertaining them now.

In the dark rats ran greedily through the empty tent sniffing at popcorn, dung, and blood. They raced along the empty bleachers and up and down the empty aisles, but blood drew them into the sawdust ring toward the body lying in the rear darkness. They licked at the face and hands and bit at the wrinkled bloody flesh while outside dust billowed around the abandoned tent and pick-ups raced for the exit.

"What kind of show was that?" the children asked.

"Usual, guess," the mother said. Her tooth was hurting again, and she held one hand to her cheek.

"Get on in the back there," the father called. He was in no mood to wait, and he got in the front, stepped on the gas, raced the motor for a minute, and began edging his way through the dirt field and into line on the rutted exit road. In the back the dogs barked and bayed the moon, and the kids screamed. "Shut up them dogs," the father yelled into the night air. Sweat ran down his body, and he licked blood from under one thumbnail. "Just shut up them dogs." The two little girls with their hair done up in pin curls and the three little boys with their black rotted teeth sat silent while the dogs continued to snap at the darkness, their pink gums bare.

12

2 A Negro in a black felt cowboy hat walked down the block, past the gas station on the corner of Chittenden, across Summit, past the waterworks, the beer and pop store, past the bar on this side of Fourth, then crossed the street and disappeared into the Negro bar on the other side. Eddie sat on the curb, half hidden by weeds, and watched him out of sight, envious. He needed a hat or something.

Across the street three cars sat up on blocks in a dirt front yard. A mangy little part collie lay in the shade of one of the cars. Eddie picked up a rock, threw it, hit the bumper of the car; the collie didn't move. Eddie found another rock, threw it; this time he hit the dirt just a little in front of the collie and the dog opened its eyes. After a few more rocks, the dog began to snarl and pull on the length of clothesline that tied it to the car fender. Eddie lobbed another rock in the collie's direction, then grew bored and lay back in the weeds again, waiting for something to happen. His mind wandered off in dreams. He bowed before an enormous audience —Eddie, the Magical Magician with the Wondrous Ways, in a glorious gold brocade coat and a cowboy hat. He whipped off the coat and held up his arms; twelve snakes dangled mysteriously from each armpit. They loved it. Applause. But now they were suspicious, watching his every move for some trick or other; then, just when their attention was diverted for a moment watching him tie his shoelaces, flowers bloomed from his ears. Surprise. More applause.

A motorcycle raced its motor at his feet, and Eddie shot up out

13

of the weeds. "Hey, gimme a ride, huh?" He danced on the curb, pleading.

"Once around the block and that's it."

Eddie strapped his arms around the blue figure, felt the gun and buttons of the cop uniform and the motorcycle's tremor and jerk. Everyone had a uniform now, but Ross was still his hero—he had a motorcycle. "O.K.," Ross said, stopping at the exact spot on the curb where he had picked Eddie up. "I've got business now."

"Take me with you."

"No; girl business."

"Aw." Eddie danced along the curb until he saw Ross disappear up the alley, then slowly sank back into the rubble of the front yard. Eddie, the Magical Magician, had a Gorgeous Assistant there beside him. She let him put his hand on her leg, right on the bare skin, then she let him stick a finger into the hairy dampness between. It was fantastic, he told Fatso and Henderson, but they were dubious. "Yeah, Eddie, prove it, huh? Come on, Eddie." Eddie held up his finger; he had his audience eating out of his hand.

"EDDIE. EDDIE." Always screaming. He lay still, listening to the voice, seeing weeds. "Eddie, goddamn it, get on up here." Eddie flattened himself into the thick weeds, empty beer cans, broken glass, and tried to disappear. "Goddamn it, you get up here, and now!" Slowly he raised himself and started toward the house. Della stood on the front step in her slip, and Eddie began to drag his feet in the dirt. "You going to take all day?"

"Yeah."

"I don't need any smart-ass talk from you, hear?"

"Yeah."

"I have enough problems without you."

"Yeah."

"Get on up here, I tell you."

"Yeah."

"Now take this money on over to the drugstore and get yourself somethin' to eat." She handed him some change, and he started

14

back across the yard in a hurry. "And don't go spendin' it all on candy," she called. "You go and get sick and there ain't going to be nobody here'll baby you. You remember that when you go to lookin' at them sweets, hear?" Eddie turned the corner and was gone, the threat fading in the distance.

Once inside the Rexall, he bought a Baby Ruth and then sat down on the floor at the back to leaf through the comics. Balloons of noise exploded in his mind, and he began rapidly flipping pages and mouthing consonants of destruction, *Zattttttttttttttttttt* ttttttttttttttttt*kkkkkkkkkk*chchchchchchchch*kkkkkkkkkkkkkkkk*ch*k,* oblivious to all else. "Ready to buy that one?" the druggist asked twice.

"O.K.," Eddie said, trapped. He sat down at the counter with the comic and ordered a cherry Coke. Two Negro kids from the other block came in, and Eddie shot straw wrappers at them. Eeny meeny miney mo. "Hey, Eeny Meeny, yawl lookin' for trouble, come messin' in here?" Two heads ducked behind the shampoo counter; in a minute a wad of sticky bubble gum fell at Eddie's feet.

"All right. Outside. Outside."

"Yawl come back," Eddie called after them. He watched them disappear across the street into the black block. Nigger kids always hangin' around grinnin', their mom tellin' him she was goin' to work roots on him if he didn't get along with hisself. He told her he got along with hisself fine. Ha! Some thick cherry syrup still remained at the bottom of his glass, and he shook the ice around for a minute until there was enough liquid for a last strawful, then he pushed the button in the palm of his hand that rendered him invisible and slipped unseen from the counter. Time to go visit his Gorgeous Assistants.

Nurses, they lived above the grocery store. A second-story porch hung out over the parking lot in the alley, a clothesline strung with diapers stretching from one side of the porch to the other. Eddie moved quietly, invisibly, down the alley, between the parked cars, through a maze of garbage cans and old packing crates, then up

15

the wooden steps to the porch. The lights were on in both back apartments, one on either side of the screen door that led into the central hallway and down to the two front apartments and the front steps. This was the first time Eddie had been up there for two months, not since he and Henderson had come up after the Friday night movie and Henderson had dropped an enormous turd in the hallway, right in front of the nurses' door. Jesus! Eddie had been sure they'd be caught then; he'd never run so fast in his life, with Henderson right behind him pulling up his pants and giggling like a crazy. Henderson was always doing wild stuff like that—farting in class, running through the girls' washroom screaming his fool head off. He was crazy for sure. If Henderson were here now, he'd probably muck up the the whole business, but not Invisible Eddie.

Creeping along the railing, his head just grazing a row of damp diapers, Eddie moved even with the window. Inside stood one Gorgeous Assistant in bra and slip, one leg perched up on the edge of the kitchen sink, shaving the hair on her legs. Eddie watched hypnotized as she lathered first one leg then the other and ran the safety razor from ankle to knee. When she was finished, she washed away the lather and began sticking bits of toilet paper to spots of blood. The toilet paper dried on the blood, and she fluttered back to the couch like a war victim celebrating her survival with confetti. Suddenly the girl screamed, and Eddie was shocked out of his trance. Forgetting about his invisibility, he pulled the diapers around him for protection. The line gave; a tangle of wet wash dropped to his feet, and Eddie ran down the steps leaving a trail of footprints behind. Shit!

At the end of the alley he stopped for breath, then crossed Summit and was home. Two old Hudsons were parked in the back yard, and the sound of voices, all of them garbled like a radio not quite tuned, came from the kitchen. Sitting in the darkness of the back porch, Eddie swatted off mosquitoes that hummed through the frayed screening and tried to listen.

"Sweetheart, I got all I wanted from you the first time—out of

16

Wheeling, West Virginia. Now I'm going to have myself some good times."

"Della, Della," a cracked voice pleaded. "I can't take it. I got no home, no place to go."

"Guess you're going to have to make do; I have."

"Della, my little one."

"Touch me and I'll call the police. Have you put away for good. Him too, if it comes to that."

"Whore."

"Shut up."

"You've been runnin' around with your pants down ever since you knew how, but I'm overlooking that fact. I'm offering you one last chance to wear spangles and plumes and sequins, one last chance to be a bird, to fly free."

"Jesus Christ."

"Look," another voice called. "I came over here for a little lovin', not to hear this crazy fucking fight."

"You shut up too."

"Shit. I got more goin' for me at home than this," the voice said, louder now, from the kitchen. "That fat woman's got more folds than you got room for."

"Yeah, honey, you'll be back for tight ass, and you'll be payin' for it."

The kitchen door swung open, admitting a wedge of light and a man, then swung shut again. The man stumbled drunkenly across the porch and out into the yard. He began to puke, leaning against one of the Hudsons. Two blocks away, where the tracks were raised on a mound of earth visible in the distance, a train screeched by, a circle of light probing the night. Softly silhouetted against the sky, shadow against shadow, the train whistled mournfully. It was the New York Central, and it was ten-thirty. The ground rumbled slightly in the passing, and the whistle echoed back over the distance, carrying Eddie with it. Tomorrow maybe he would be up there on the mound at ten o'clock to flag down the train like the

17

Indian in the last western he saw. Then he'd pick up his friends and they'd all go to Utah, someplace like that, just to look at it. The kitchen door opened again, and Eddie shrank into the shadows as Della and an old man moved across the porch, through the screen door, and out into the back yard, where their whining voices continued to argue. In the gloom Eddie could barely make out the two figures; he waited for a minute, then slipped into the kitchen, hunted around for some crackers and opened a bottle of pop.

Upstairs in his own room, he turned on the radio, just in time for "The Shadow." Who who who? Who who who *ha*! The Shadow knows. Heh heh heh heh. Who *ha*. Eddie took a sip of pop, peered out into the darkness, saw shadows. Scary as hell. Who who who? He pulled the covers up over his head. Weird noises. A motorcycle on the roof. Who is it? Heh heh heh. He took another sip of pop, sitting up in a tepee of covers. Heh heh. An ad for a secret decoder and it was over; time now for "Inner Sanctum." A creaking door screeched into an echo chamber, then voices, footsteps, and a light in the hallway went on. Eddie snapped off the radio in midcreak, stashed the pop bottle under the bed, and immediately began to sleep soundly, his eyes pinched tight, his breathing heavy.

"Where's kid anyway?" a blubbery-lipped voice asked. "Haven't sheen him all evening." The words came out like spit over a mouthful of marbles.

"He can take care of himself."

"Not goin' to come bustin' in here now? Had enough already."

"He's probably sleeping out there in the car; does that sometimes."

In the morning, steady, even footsteps clumped down the stairs and bammed through the screen door from porch to back yard. Eddie peeked out at the sun shining around the edge of the blind and listened to the sound of high heels tap-dancing in the kitchen. The half-empty bottle of pop sat on the floor, and he finished it, then pulled on one sock and hopped across the floor to the other.

"Eddie?" Della called.

18

"Yes."

"You upstairs?"

"Yeah."

"Then get on down here."

Eddie shuffled down, hesitating on the bottom step to watch her jiggle around in her cocktail waitress disguise. "Get in here and fix yourself something to eat if you want it." Eddie limped forward, dragging one foot stiffly behind him. "And don't be makin' a mess." Eddie leaned heavily against the sink, relieving his injured foot of the extra weight. "Now what's the problem?"

"Shot in the leg."

"What?"

"Shot in the leg. It's nothing; you should see the others." An officer of the first rank, he looked sadly out the back window over the debris of war.

"A clown like your old man; not worth shit."

Eddie pulled a bottle of pop from the icebox and looked around for something else, a piece of bologna. Once, a long time ago, when his father had come, he had brought him some picture postcards, grease-spattered and dirty from being tacked on the wall somewhere. They were from New Jersey and Georgia and Florida, and on the back they said: "Having a wonderful time. Wish you were here." "Been all over," his father had said as he passed him, one by one, the postcards.

"They've got orange trees in Florida."

"Jeez, Eddie, how come you know somethin' like that?"

"My old man told me; he's been there."

"In Florida?"

"In Florida and New Jersey, both."

"Jeez."

"He's been all over."

"Yeah?"

"Yeah."

"How do you know? You go with him? Ha ha ha."

"He showed me pictures."

19

"No kidding. Jeez, your old man has a camera?"

Eddie looked directly into the bottle of pop. "Naw, postcards."

"Postcards?"

"Yeah."

"Shit, you can buy them anywhere. They've got one of the ocean down at the Rexall."

"These have the stamps on them."

"Big deal. Bet some fuck-ass sent them to your mom."

"No."

"Yayaya, ya ya ya. Bet some fuck-ass sent 'em to your mom."

"No."

"Yeah? Where you goin' to get postcards in the loony bin, huh?"

"My old man had gorgeous assistants; they were there just to hand him things, help him change his clothes, stuff like that. He was famous; he told me."

"Yeah? That proves he was crazy. Ya ya ya."

Gorgeous. This assistant had a beautiful ass on her. Beautiful. Cute little outfit. She picked up a plate, tossed it in the air, and I shot. Turned into a daisy, big yellow daisy. Surprised as hell, all eyebrows. See. Looked like this.

Ya ya ya.

Picks up another plate, tosses it in the air; shoots at it, and it turns into a kite, floats up to the ceiling. More surprise. Noise. A beautiful colored streamer floating across the tent ceiling, waiting to be released into the night; pink, yellow, orange, red, crimson patterned against the stars. I shoot again and . . .

Boom

There was no flower, no kite. Color runs to the floor, red at my feet.

"What are you shakin' for?"

"Nothin'."

"Get up and drink a bottle of pop first thing in the morning. Get your teeth to chatterin'. Got no more sense than a . . ."

Crazy. Mouth begins to foam; tongue lathers, and I begin gettin'

20

the heebie-jeebies right there so as I can't hardly stand up and hold myself together, and they all come down, gatherin' round and workin' their tongues. I don't understand where they're takin' me; don't understand where all the daisies and roses and poppies and rabbits and kites . . .

The Shadow knows. Who *ha.*

"You be here when I get back at noon, hear?"

"Yeah."

"You don't look right today. You ain't been into trouble?"

"No."

"You be here."

High heels tapped across the kitchen and the back porch and sank softly in the dirt yard. It was a hot day. Flies buzzed through the screening, then remained trapped on the porch waiting at the kitchen door. A string of flypaper hung, dry and dirty, from the ceiling. Eddie finished the pop and went outside to sit on the swing and watch the neighbors. When he got bored with them, he walked around to the front, where there was less traffic and the weeds were tall and protective.

He lay in the sun, invisible. After a while, he began to crawl forward stealthily, picking at the refuse—pop bottles, a used condom that he stuck in his pocket as a souvenir, gum wrappers, a hubcap. He reached a path of beaten-down weeds, the path that led to the front door, and hesitated; here was a clearing that he would have to traverse. He stuck weeds behind his ears for camouflage. There was an anthill in the distance; his suspicions were aroused. With a war going on, he could not be too careful. Perhaps it was a trick, the enemy in clever ant disguises. A ruse. Heh heh heh. He threw a piece of broken glass at the hill, but the ants scurried over the obstacle as before. Ah so. More ants were crawling out of the hole now—no doubt Japs crawling up from the underside of the world. He had to be very careful; he inched forward, exposed for a minute in the pathway and then hidden again by weeds. He lay still, watching the ants.

21

He was still lying there in the weeds when she returned. "Eddie? Eddie, you get in here." He got up slowly, a weed sticking out from behind each ear, and walked up the path. "Jesus, will you look at yourself." She stood holding an empty grocery bag in her hand, waiting. "I want you to take this here bag upstairs and put your things in it."

"What for?"

"You're goin' on a trip."

"Where to?"

"I got no time for questions. Just do like I say." Eddie took the sack and started up the stairs. "And remember that radio up there ain't yores so don't be takin' it."

3 Eddie stared out at the old man standing in front of the depot, a yellow, jagged-toothed grin forced over his face like a mask. The old man waved, but Eddie did not acknowledge or return the sign, and when the bus pulled away he did not look back. That was his father. Jeez. What a screwball! All the way down to the bus depot, he had kept mumbling, "I have hidden from the Lord. I have kept my light under a basket, a tree, a rabbit, and other things," while Eddie had pretended to be alone. Now he just sat slumped in his seat looking out at the used car lots and bonus marts that ran along the length of Broad Street until, at the eastern edge of town, motel row began and ended and they were out of Columbus.

Relief, curiosity, and fear mingled, forcing him to clench back tears and sit rigid in his seat, his nails dug tightly into the armrests. Numb with dread, he passed the mile after mile of flat farmland and small towns, startled awake finally only by the bus rolling steeply downhill seemingly out of control. At the bottom of the hill the bus stopped and threaded its way onto a narrow, rickety railroad bridge, not much wider than itself. On the other side of the river, in a larger town, the bus wound up another hill to stop before the A-1 Café.

The driver got out, and Eddie watched him cross the street, enter the café, and sit down at the counter to drink a cup of coffee. When he came back, two women were with him, and he stuck their bags in the belly of the bus with the rest. The two women reminded Eddie of Della; mean and glum, they looked as though they had lost some bit of ugliness in the back of their heads that they were going to bring up and threaten you with one day. He wondered if they were going where he was going; they didn't look pleased about it. The driver eased the bus into motion again, and it slipped and churned and rolled backward before it finally got up enough momentum to climb. At the top of the hill, Eddie looked back over the tall, thin, wood-shingled houses that sprouted out of the hills like trees, hiding most of the city and the river from view. A kid sitting on the porch of one of the houses waved and watched the bus go by as though he had been sitting there all along waiting for it to come, and the bus with increased effort continued slowly grinding its way up and around the old houses past the Wheeling Steel Company until the hills were bare and gravelly and even steeper.

Now Eddie looked down into canyons of emptiness, steep pits of gravel and rock and dirt. A train, its cars heaped high with coal, went by on the opposite ledge, and while Eddie watched it, the bus turned sharply down, plummeting his stomach with it and making his ears pop. The road ahead was even more winding and narrow, at times so narrow that the bus seemed in danger of tipping over on curves and sinking to a twisted metal death on the gravel below. Eddie held on tightly and closed his eyes. Finally, after what seemed hours of winding ascent and descent, the road straightened, and Eddie saw in the distance a series of towns, almost side by side, and beyond them, a sick yellow-green haze and funnels of smoke and fire. But the bus turned right, away from the series of towns and onto a narrow half-paved road that led deep into a tangle of growth. Thickets of mulberry and blue grape and sweet corn grew up to the road and covered the hills, and when, occasionally, another car approached and the bus pulled off to the side to make room, trees scratched along the top and filled the windows with flattened leaves.

After a while they came to a small deep valley and a few houses —shacks with chickens running around in the yard and sitting on the front porch. Every now and then a cow would look up mournfully from a weed-filled ditch or wander across the road, but the animals, even the houses, were almost hidden by growth, in view only a moment then lost in trees. Suddenly the road curved, and they were out of the valley and moving between two lone hills of gravel, nothing growing on them at all, then, just as suddenly, they turned again and entered another thicket of brush and trees—apple and pear and cherry.

They crossed a river, followed it for a while on the other side, then crossed back and wandered along the west bank again. Eddie slid down in his seat and peered out at cattails and swamp grass; this place was different from any he'd seen in the movies, some secret place known only to the bus driver probably. Maybe that was why he had never heard of his grandparents before, never even known they existed. He wished Henderson were here now so he could show him this place where one old bus drove along the edge of a river deep in grass.

Henderson was such a dumb cluck Eddie knew the whole thing would be a big surprise to him. Apples growing on trees all around, Henderson; honest. All these little houses? Hideouts. Bad guys don't want to see themselves in the movies or nothin'. Little wee places stuck up in the hills, cows and chickens and dogs on guard. Every now and then there's this completely bare hill, see; FBI comes in and just tears the place up. They're hunting for bandits, Henderson. No shit. Grandparents scare the hell out of everyone; I'd tell you about them, Henderson, but I don't want to give them away—live a very hush-hush life. School's a snap too; spend all your time picking fruit for lunch. Haven't eaten in a Rexall for days. Place is ideal for The Masked Two.

"Kid?" The bus slowed to a stop. "Kid?"

Eddie looked up.

"Kid, you going to Mount Morris?"

"Yes."

"This is it."

25

From the window Eddie saw one lone side road beside which three or four paint-peeled houses sagged. "How do I get to the downtown part?"

"Post office is in the grocery across from the gas station; they'll probably be able to help you find where you're going."

Eddie got off and watched the bus out of view before starting down the dirt road. At the houses he passed everyone seemed to be home, sitting on the porch or staring out at him from the front windows. Sometimes nine or ten people sat on a porch quietly watching him. It made him kind of uneasy, and he began to walk faster. At a fork in the road—a gas station on one side and a grocery store with a flag and a Dr Pepper clock in the window on the other—he stopped. A boy sat on a folding chair before the one gas pump; Eddie asked him directions.

"Going out there, are you?" the boy said slowly, thoughtfully, as though no one ever did. "That's the old Remley place up on the hill." The boy watched him for some reaction to this information, then went on. "Get there by crossing the bridge here, going up the Little Shannon about a mile and a half, crossing over the bridge there, and following the road on out to the schoolhouse. Turn up the hill on the old road. Can't miss it, if that's where you want to go."

It was three miles or more to the schoolhouse, a square brick building with one old swing outside, and by the time Eddie got there he was tired. Sitting on the swing to rest, he watched four grown men drinking beer and playing cards at the desks inside. One of the men who got up to throw an empty out the window called to him. "Get going, kid." He did.

The road up from the schoolhouse was little more than a path —steep, rocky, almost completely covered over by foliage; only a speckling of light filtered through the leaves overhead. As the road grew steeper and more narrow, the growth became denser, covering the roadbed itself wherever the runoff had left a damp, muddy spot in the gravel. There was no sound, no sign of life, nothing.

Then, just before he had decided to turn around and go back, he heard a dog barking somewhere ahead, and he came to the dog and the house at almost the same instant. A grapevine covered one entire side of the house—big, square, two-story, with four chimneys stuck in the air like dead legs—trellised up the columns of the front porch, and hung back down through open spaces in the roof above. Wild wheat thrust its way through cracks in the porch floor, where two car seats squatted on either side of the front door like sofas. At the side of the house a 1939 Nash, all four doors gone, sat abandoned to grass and loganberries, its gutted interior filled now with an old mattress. Aside from the dog tethered to the porch, the place seemed abandoned. Then, as he stood in the yard carefully scanning the house, he looked up to see an old man at one of the upstairs windows pointing a shotgun at him.

Eddie waved, grinned, tried to appear small, said, "FIN NAY, FIN NAY, FIN NAY," pantomiming the word, the relationship, the bus trip, everything.

Funny.

4 Riles watched the boy's mouth move, watched the glittering teeth, then the widening hollow, the white-toothed grin followed by a tongue of spit, bite spit, bite spit. Sometimes, like this, when he watched a person's mouth, he heard snatches of remembered music coming out. He held his gun aimed at the mouth and heard a fiddle picking and a voice singing: *"Lord, I never should have shot that boy. Never should have strayed so far."* It was a song he'd heard over fifteen years ago when, already an old man, he had taken his one and only trip away from these hills and gone to Nashville. That Saturday night, filled with beer and sweating with Opry heat and pleasure, he'd heard Rod Ahill fiddle, and when Ahill sang, *"Shot a man in Albuquerque just to see him die,"* Riles had stood up with the others and screamed his enthusiasm until he was hoarse; for that one brief moment he had tingled with power and with the tantalizing sound of his own desire to kill, his desire to own a life as his was owned by the man who signed the checks and the union leader who collected them. Now he would never again be caught up in the imaginary power of that song or feel that sweaty communion of desire and blood; he had only memory now and, when his memory failed and the words did not come to him, he had only silence. Riles aimed his gun again, but the boy was gone, just the dog sniffing in the dirt where he'd been.

There was a light tap on his shoulder, and Riles whirled around with the gun to see her standing there, not a tooth in her head, making signals he did not understand. Not much passed between them now—just eating and sleeping and waiting and memory.

28

Riles thought about the first time he had seen her—at a dance where he had played the fiddle and she had stood dreamily in the middle of the union hall, smiling, just as she was now, a part of some other world. She hadn't been pretty, but her strangeness, her bland indifference to the others, her peculiar laughter in the monotonous sameness, had attracted him. He had taken her outside and made love to her in the shadows as easily as if she hadn't understood or known. At the end of the summer he had even married her, but it wasn't until after the boy came that he knew her faceless hilarity and quiet voice for what they were—madness. He looked at the boy the woman led in with suspicion.

Boy was nothing but trouble; left alone two minutes, he would wander off, not enough sense to come home or take care of himself. Schoolkids would bully him, torment him, and Riles would find him hiding in a berry patch with the dogs. Sometimes Riles had tied him up with the dogs, then he would come back and find Sonny barking, imitating the dogs. The sound filled his mind, and Riles turned back to the window.

In the silence a whole history of sound echoed in his head—the sound of fiddling, of church choirs, of dancing, of crickets and bullfrogs and rain, of dogs barking, Sonny too, and the sounds ran together in a deafening crescendo that left his head aching and him in isolation waiting for the explosion. There had been no warning, just the sudden rise of dust that had caused him to cough; he had coughed all his life, but he remembered his mouth filling with phlegm then, choking him, strangling him, until he spit and coughed and choked it out. With wet eyes, his mouth and throat raw with pain, he had looked up and seen the dust settling in a cloud not very far away; then something like a wave hit him, a sea of air and dirt twisting and turning him, dropping him to his knees, throwing him up, violent in its way, but cushioned by silence, a silence that made every stormy motion, every fall, every misstep, every wound, seem remote and distant. He had been waiting for the sound of it ever since—in the hospital and then later at night here, lying awake, his head hurting from the strain of expectation, waiting for the sound that would eventually blow his head off like it had the others'.

Fourteen of them dead. Riles had sat in silence at the funeral not sure which men occupied the closed coffins, not sure which were the dead men's wives among those crying women scattered through the crowd at the back so that the front pews, the places of honor, could be given to the mine owners and union leaders who, arriving late, making an entrance into the unfamiliar church, sat together like vultures in a show of sympathy. Afterward Riles had followed the hearse to the cemetery owned, tended, and gardened by the company whose men could explode to death for nothing, but Riles wasn't dead. Riles wasn't dead; he had only watched. He had been lucky; the papers had come, the newsmen and the photographers, and they had had a ceremony then with Riles standing up on the stage with one of the company men. Coughing soundlessly, he had watched the company man's mouth move, watched the tongue slide out over the lips to lick up flecks of spittle, watched the teeth bite the air, watched bubbles form as the mouth opened wide and heard music: *"Shot a man in Albuquerque just to watch him die."* When he looked out at the audience, he saw hands moving, saw applause without sound like the aimless arm-dancing of puppets. When it was over, the company man, his chin wet with saliva, his suit wet with sweat, had handed Riles a typewritten copy of the speech. Riles had nodded, looked at it; he didn't read. When the check had come, it had been a surprise.

The woman and the boy were gone, and Riles started downstairs. He stopped on the bottom step, looking for some sign of movement, then went to the front screen; they were standing on the porch. Riles held the shotgun uneasily, watching, aiming mentally. Sonny had come home before. He'd had all the hair on his head shaved off then and not been readily identifiable until he began to bark. Then it had been unmistakable. Riles looked at the dog still sniffing in the dirt and saw Sonny on his hands and knees. Sonny had done all the talking.

30

No hair in the eyes is the thing. They are shrinking my head to fit on a postcard. See the mind. Doctor and his assistant do that. It's to be a surprise.

There's a Mrs. Flint, name of Petunia, bald as a billiard ball. Chews gum, spits it on the floor. Like this. Beautiful ass on her. They keep us apart like dogs.

I pick a bouquet of zinnias while she picks her nose with her thumb. So many different colors, blue ones, green ones, yellow ones, red ones. She sticks them to the wall with her bubble gum. That's how they died.

Brown petals fall to the floor, walls fall, clothes fall, people scream. Sirens warn that this isn't a movie.

Fire.

There are no more flowers. No more cards. Smoke fills the air. Everyone bald screams in disguise.

How?

Riles was frightened by the silence; he leaned forward, straining his ears, waiting for the memory to return, but it was gone, still, quiet, frightening, like the stillness before wind whips the leaves and grass into a storm. The woman and the boy were still standing there on the porch, frozen into quiet resignation, their mouths motionless. Riles wondered what they were thinking, but he knew her too well to think she was minding a thing. She was waiting for the preacher to come, and when she lifted her head and began to chew her lips, Riles knew it was prayer. That's how he would like to shoot her, shoot them both. He saw them fall to the porch floor, their bodies twisted and crimson, their mouths bubbling blood, but it was all done in slow-motion silence, so quiet as to be unreal, and he knew there was no point, no point at all. It was too late for that. Clenching the gun tightly to him, he watched her mouth chew silence, thinking that, in their loneliness, they had been attracted to opposite poles for comfort—her to prayer, him to murder— nothing saner than a dog remaining.

Riles went back upstairs. Sitting by the window as he always did, he began again to wait. There was no thought, no music now, only the tense anticipation as he waited and waited and waited for an explosion, an explosion that he could see, feel, taste, picturing the swirl of dust, the collapsing walls, the moving bodies—feeling the noise, tasting the dirt, waiting for the sound of it, waiting for sound.

5 Sometimes, looking in through the front window, Eddie saw them dancing, slowly, silently moving to unheard music; more often the two old people just waited, sitting for hours upstairs by the window as though expecting someone, someone other than the boy who came once a week from town with the groceries or the preacher, who came more erratically, the only ones ever to come. The boy the grandmother paid from a coin purse she kept pinned to her underclothes, hunting through the folds of cloth while the boy waited anxiously by the door ready to escape. Once, shortly after his arrival, Eddie had stopped the boy, asking him if he wanted to see some magic tricks, asking him what they did for fun here, and the boy had answered, "Nothing," and ran from the conversation and from Eddie. Since then they had not spoken. The preacher too was met by the grandmother and paid from the same purse as the grocery boy. The preacher did speak to Eddie, stopping him in the yard, grunting and nodding, asking him on several occasions if he was a believer, if he had been baptized, if he didn't want to get down on his knees and pray, and then Eddie fled with the dog to the hilly glade and the cemetery there that overlooked the south bottom and, just beyond that, the adjoining pasture of the old Indian, Tom Hawk. Here Eddie spent his time.

It was from this vantage point that Eddie had first seen Tom Hawk. The only Indian in the area, Hawk was a lonely, forlorn figure who could sometimes be seen standing out in the middle of his overgrown, weed-filled land as though permanently rooted there, his own scarecrow. Children passing after school on the

33

stretch of road that ran alongside the Indian's pasture would hoot and war-whoop as they went by, but if Hawk was there in his field, they would scatter in all directions, racing past the frightening Indian-painted figure and his land to the safety of the underbrush on the far side of the road. Although Eddie spent a good deal of time overlooking Hawk's pasture, he too avoided it, walking in the opposite direction from the rest after school up the dead end of road, through the tangle of brush and trees that led to the house. There he was met, more often than not, by that thin black ghost sitting on one of the car seats on the porch, staring heavenward, praying, or just waiting to ask him, "Do you believe, boy?" and finally, in order to avoid the preacher, Eddie began to cut through the Indian's pasture on his way to the glade. He had not as yet seen the Indian, then one day as he moved slowly through the knee-high grass, flicking a grass whip before him, scaring a few copperheads out of his way, he was startled by a shadow that fell across his path and looked up to see old Hawk. The Indian's features were sharp, pointed, and he wore his hair in two long braids tied at the ends with bits of shoelace. "Know where you are?" the Indian asked.

Eddie nodded, frightened by the suddenness of the meeting and the Indian's stance.

"You must be new here."

"Yes."

"The boy up at the Remley place?"

"The Finney place."

"That graveyard up there is full of Remleys and Remley victims; that's why it's the Remley place, just as this pasture is mine."

Eddie began to run.

That afternoon, sitting up in the old cemetery with the dog, Eddie examined the headstones. Twelve of them, the writing on them almost but not quite unreadable, belonged to Remleys or to Remley wives; the rest were blank, either worn smooth with age or nameless from the beginning. He continued after that to return from school through the Indian's pasture, but he did not see Tom Hawk the next day or all that week or the next. The Indian's house, an old lean-to, seemed empty, although a small vegetable garden in the back showed signs of care. Eddie was tempted to go to the door, but he did not. This year school seemed interminable, and his fantasy had made the old Indian a mental escape from the nine Doyles, the seven Shannons, and the smaller families of pale, wan children who sat numbly in class with him every day reciting the Lord's Prayer. Sometimes to relieve the monotony Eddie would try some of Henderson's old tricks. Sitting in the back row with his mouth fixed slightly open like a ventriloquist's, Eddie would yelp and bark pitiably, and this would provoke a few titters from the youngest boys. Today he had been kept after school for threatening to send old Hawk after the two oldest Doyle girls. Now he was crossing over to the Indian's pasture on a path he had worn down through the drainage ditch, determined at least to call the Indian's name, maybe even go around to the garden in the back. Then, looking up, he saw the Indian standing out in the pasture in the exact spot where he had met him before.

"School out late?"

Eddie nodded. The Indian's gaze seemed to search past Eddie for someone in the distance. "Have you been away somewhere?"

"No," the Indian said, preoccupied with something else. "This is the only place I know I can ply my profession."

Eddie looked at the overgrown pasture, the weeds, the dead fruit trees. "What profession?"

The old Indian smiled over half a row of black teeth. "Didn't anyone tell you? I'm a professional Indian." Eddie was just starting to formulate another question when the Indian nodded toward the glade. "Dog's hunting for you," he said. Eddie whistled and the hound's head appeared just at the edge of the pasture, bounding toward him, his body hidden by grass. Eddie ran to meet the dog, then turned back quickly, but the Indian had disappeared.

35

Eddie did not see the Indian again for two weeks. That day, while the teacher told the younger children a story about her most recent trip to Pittsburgh, Eddie and the others had written an essay on "Why I Want to Go to Pittsburgh." At first Eddie had tried to listen to the teacher's story for some hints, then, rushed for time, he had written:

Pittsburgh is like Columbus a city full of naked nurses. They take off their clothes and wave to friends in the alley. Sometimes their friends join them. They begin to dance. Some wave diapers and stand on their hands. Some stick feathers in their hair and toilet paper on their legs. They wiggle their rears. I want to go to Pittsburgh to see them. ETC.

After they had finished their essays, the teacher told them all a story about a special class of students she had once taken to Pittsburgh. Ben's Beans had sponsored the trip, and they had gone on a bus tour of Pittsburgh and then toured the Ben's Bean plant. At the end of the tour, they had each been given a little dinner of sample Ben's Bean products: ketchup and pork and beans and pickles. "That is the sort of thing you might have written an essay about," the teacher said. Then she read an essay by a boy who said he would like to find his father, who had gone to Pittsburgh three years ago and never returned, and another essay by a girl who said she would like to see Tex Rinehart at the county fair. While they did an arithmetic assignment, the teacher graded all the papers. She asked Eddie to remain after class again.

For an hour after school Eddie was forced to write, "I pray that God will forgive me for lying," on the blackboard. Outside a few pale children clustered together to giggle and peek through the window. Later Eddie waited in the play yard until the teacher had left and then got into a halfhearted fight with one of the Doyles until five more Doyles appeared. He had been excused from class for a week to pray and, as he wandered slowly through the Indian's pasture, Eddie prayed for another teacher, another school, a trip to Pittsburgh, money, escape, a great deal. In the distance he could see the Indian kneeling in his usual place and, when the Indian rose and started back to his house, Eddie ran to meet him. "Hey," Eddie called, not wanting to miss a chance to ask this time, "who's buried up there on the hill?"

The old Indian stopped. "Indians," he said. "The Remleys and the Indians." He smiled at this as though it were a joke.

"How come they're buried like that, no name or anything?"

"There are more here than that," the old Indian said. "Once this whole valley was summer land for the Delaware nation; the Turkeyfoot came here for their summer encampment, and they were still here when this land"—the old Indian indicated his pasture, the Remley land, and more—"was given to the Shannons and the Doyles and the Remleys as part of their soldier's pay. Some of the Indians moved on then, and some stayed and married Shannons and Doyles and Remleys. Later some of those same Indians or their children or their children's children were accused of being Indian or half-breed; Shannons who hadn't married Indians accused Shannons who had, and Shannons who had married Indians denied it and accused Shannons who hadn't. Any time someone accused of being part Indian died, he was given an Indian burial, dragged up in the hills and buried under a mound of earth that the dogs eventually got at, or left in an unmarked grave somewhere so as not to embarrass the rest of the family."

"And now all the Indians are dead," Eddie concluded, adding, "except you," when old Hawk pointed to his hair, his eyes, and the thin lines of brown, juicelike color that made a finger design on his face and forehead.

"But I'm just an Indian by profession."

"By profession?"

"I was born Patrick Manahan, but there was always some suspicion that my mother, who had thick black hair, very dark eyes, and pronounced features, was part Indian. One day, when I wasn't much older than you, I came home and found my mother sitting with her head on the kitchen table and blood running down her legs

37

and the edge of her chair. There was a tomahawk made from an old ax in her back, splitting her almost in two. Some people thought maybe she had been murdered until an investigation was made and it was proved that only an Indian would make use of a tomahawk and the only Indian around was my mother; therefore, my mother must have used the tomahawk to commit suicide. I was deeply saddened and afraid that I too might be a suicide." The old Indian paused and grinned. "My sisters must have had a similar fear, for they disappeared with my father." He stopped again, gazing out over the pasture. "This parcel of land was in dispute then; I thought I might inherit it, and Remley thought he might expand to the west. It was then I decided that in exchange for my inheritance and a longer life, I would become a professional Indian, confessing my heritage and changing my name, appropriately, to Tommy Hawk. As a professional Indian I was most valuable. Knowing the Indian ways and the natural traits of my kind, I could easily expose other Indians. Thus I exposed Indians to the east of Remley, Indians to the north of Remley, and Indians to the south of Remley. Some of those poor unfortunate Indians also committed suicide and lie up there in the Remley cemetery."

"And what happened to the Remleys?"

"When old man Remley died, there were ten or eleven children —no one knew for sure how many—and they began to feud among themselves. Some of them wanted to sell to the mine owners; some of them didn't. Then, not too long after old man Remley's death, there was the Remley massacre."

"Massacre?"

"It was a professional job."

"You mean Indians killed them?"

"Someone did. Land lay empty for years after that. . . ." The Indian stopped as though there were more that he could tell but wouldn't.

"And now?" Eddie asked.

The Indian smiled, shrugged.

That next week Eddie spent his free time in Mount Morris, the long walk into town rewarded by the radio that played under the counter in the grocery store and an occasional fist fight. Once, when the kid at the gas station was sitting out in front staring down the street, Eddie went over and hung around him for a while.

"Want to see where some Indians are buried?" he asked.

"Aren't any Indians here," the boy replied.

"Twelve of them are buried right nearby."

The boy began to stare down the road the other direction.

"You make much money working here?" Eddie asked.

"Nope."

"What would you do if you did?"

"Go someplace else."

"Why would you go to Pittsburgh?"

"Look," the boy said. "I'm waiting for a friend, O.K.?"

"Let us bow our heads," the teacher said after the roll call and the whispered giggles about his return. "I thank the Lord for these pencils," the teacher said, and the class and Eddie mumbled along in unison. Then at noon Eddie collected nickels and dimes from the children standing in the school yard eating potato chips from their lunch bags and, in return, showed them the piece of Indian arrow he had found. A thin, carefully selected twig with turkey feathers tied delicately to one end, it had been buried in underbrush not far from the river and the old Indian trail. After school he led a small tittering group up to the Remley cemetery and to another lone grave down in the south bottom, small, unmarked, not too old, and perhaps the last resting place of someone's hound. This grave, Eddie claimed, belonged to the father who had not returned from Pittsburgh, and the children all giggled nervously. On Saturday, Eddie led the same willing group down the river path, pointing out the turkey foot markings along the way to one of the old encampments. But his enterprise hadn't quite earned five dollars in lunch

39

money and grocery change when he ran out of material.

Again Eddie lingered longingly in the old Indian's pasture, waiting, without success, almost until dark. He waited the next day too and then, as the dog ran down to meet him, started through the glade to the hill above. Halfway, just beyond the first low branches of dogwood, he looked back. In the middle of the pasture where Eddie habitually met him, the Indian now stood watching the distance, and in that distance, at the end of the Indian's gaze, Eddie saw movement, an indistinct figure coming slowly across the field. Sinking down into the tall grass and hugging the dog near, Eddie watched the woman, her head down, stumble in the grass and loose dirt as she moved gradually into view. It was the teacher, and Eddie saw her reach into her purse and hand some money to the Indian. Then she left as quickly as she had come, angling back through the pasture to the old road. When she was out of sight, the Indian measured off three steps, dug for a moment, and then deposited the money in a Mason jar, which he reburied.

The eyes of the two old people in the upstairs window carefully watched him cross the yard and turn down the road toward school. The dog followed him as far as the first dogwood and then sat down to wait, but today when Eddie got to the upper glade, he turned back on himself. The dog, biting at fleas and rolling in the gravel, did not notice.

From the glade Eddie sat overlooking the Indian's pasture, quietly searching for some sign of movement. When it seemed safe, he walked down around by the south bottom, circuitously arriving at the spot where he had seen the Indian digging the night before. There he lay silently hidden in the wild wheat, jerking up once when he thought he heard something rustle, but it was only the breeze blowing pollen across the pasture. Eddie scratched around for loose dirt and immediately found a movable clump of grass set on bare ground. His fingers poked through the damp earth under the clod to the glass jar, which he then lifted neatly from its grave. It contained twenty-five dollars.

With the money in his pocket, he began to run back across the pasture toward the wooded area on the other side where the teacher had disappeared. A small path led from there to the bridge and the road to town. Once in Mount Morris, he slowed to a walk and then stood waiting at the crossroads for the bus. Just when he had slumped deeper into the grass, ready to give up, a bus emerged around the bend of the river, passing him by at first until, when Eddie ran waving after it, the driver stopped, opened the door, and waited for Eddie's hand to grasp the rail. The bus moved on immediately.

Out of breath, Eddie made his way down the aisle to the rear bench. Ten women in small flowered hats smiled at him from the middle of the bus. The women wore white gloves which they pulled on and off over bright red nails, turning now and then to smile at Eddie in the back. Eddie stared out at scenery grown familiar—the dense growth, the river, and the road that wound along its bank. Then they emerged from the growth onto a wider paved road and, crossing that, started down an unfamiliar highway. Here they passed old roadhouses with dingy signs—DINE AND DANCE FRI. AND SAT. NIGHTS—farmhouses set back on long tree-lined drives, grazing sheep, orchards, hills of identical houses, nurseries, country markets, more identical pastel houses, and then they entered a long tunnel. In the darkness Eddie began to choke; smoke and fumes filled the bus, making his nose and eyes run. At the other end they emerged into a yellow cloud of smoke; not until they were halfway across the bridge over the Monongahela did Eddie see either bridge or water, and then the bus pulled to a stop behind a dozen other buses on a city street.

Eddie followed the women out into the half dark. On the street he had the sensation of the sky falling and dragging its belly over the sidewalk. The air seemed to flatten him to the ground, to smother him; he began to stoop as he crept along under the heaviness. Vaguely he could make out other people; they were short and fat, and some of them wore dark glasses. Eddie followed the direction of the crowd, but his eyes smarted and blurred, and it wasn't long before he was lost. He felt faint.

All the stores were closed, their doors chained shut and their windows covered with plywood. People had written phone numbers and stuck up posters on the plywood, but the posters were ripped and torn and discolored, as though they had been put there a long time ago. An old man standing in an empty doorway blew snot between his fingers and stared at Eddie. "Get going," he said.

42

Now that Eddie was here he didn't know what to do. He wandered around. For a while he pretended to be hunting for someone, his father, gone three years to Pittsburgh and probably up an alley somewhere, then he considered buying a radio, and wandered mistakenly in and out of camera shops. He was an Indian here, among strangers; not speaking the language, he made elaborate hand signals to women on street corners, then he got hungry. Turning the corner into a crowd of office workers dismissed for lunch, Eddie watched as they entered a cafeteria in the middle of the block, bought coffee, and sat down to open their sack lunches. Coffee was probably very expensive, and there wasn't any Rexall. At the end of the block a policeman sat half asleep in a patrol car; Eddie asked him directions to Ben's Beans. "Across the Fifteenth Street bridge there." Eddie nodded; his eyes were growing accustomed to the yellow darkness now and he could see the bridge and the far bank.

On the other side of the Ohio there were stores and restaurants with foreign names. Old men sat on the sidewalk on folding chairs or packing crates, and old women leaned out from upstairs windows yelling down to the people in the street. "You kid, you kid," an old woman with stiff dyed hair called. "You kid." When Eddie looked up, she smiled triumphantly and left the window. "Sophie, Sophie." Sometimes the people in the street looked up and waved; sometimes they stared straight ahead as though they couldn't hear.

It was almost an hour before Eddie got to the plant, which spread in a series of buildings along the riverfront; a long narrow sign that ran the length of the building said: BEN'S BEANS SINCE 1892. There was already a long line of women waiting at the entrance; all of them wore white gloves and platform shoes. Finally a woman dressed like the picture on a can of tomato sauce greeted them. "I am the Ben's Bean Hostess for today's tour," she said. "Welcome to Beanland." Everyone smiled, and the woman in front of Eddie said, "Isn't that an adorable costume?"

The Bean Lady had a list and began to check off names. When

43

she got to Eddie, she asked if he had made a reservation. Eddie nodded and pointed to a name not yet crossed off the list. The Bean Lady smiled. "Are you all alone?"

"Yes."

"No school today?"

"No."

"And how did you happen to come to Ben's Beans today?"

"I wanted to see it today," Eddie said.

The Bean Lady smiled again and began to lead them inside. "Ben's Beans, as you probably know, was started by old Grandmother Ben years ago and, since then, has grown into a million-dollar enterprise. Today the Ben family produces more ketchup and more beans than anyone else in the world."

"Heavens," said one of the women, raising her eyebrows in astonishment.

"We here in the Ben family were the first to can sausage; canned sausage, we are of course proud to say, was a staple during the war." The women applauded. "The Ben family," the Bean Lady said, "tried to do its part."

Eddie watched little cans of Vienna sausage go round and round on a belt while a machine pasted Ben's Bean labels on them. Wandering patiently along, he listened to the story about how old Mrs. Ben had begun by selling homemade ketchup to her neighbors for pin money. "Of course, Grandmother Ben had no thought of actually going into business," said the Bean Lady. "It was just her little hobby." Eddie had an urge to spit into a huge vat of ketchup, but the line moved swiftly down to pickle relish. "Grandmother Ben was famous for her Sunday picnics of ham and beans and pickle relish," the Bean Lady said. "In those days she charged only a quarter for her picnics, and a perfect stranger with a quarter could join the Ben family in the park and enjoy the fun and games and the ham and beans."

"Think of it," the woman ahead of Eddie said.

"Have you ever seen so much pickle relish?" her friend replied.

Eddie was beginning to get bored; he wished the Bean Lady

44

would get to the point and pass out the food.

"Now you probably want to know how Grandmother Ben's hobby expanded into the largest ketchup company in the country, selling thousands and thousands of bottles of ketchup every day."

"Yes," said the women.

"No," Eddie said under his breath.

"Well," said the Bean Lady, "Grandmother Ben had an older sister in California who was quite frail, and one year Grandmother Ben took the train to California to visit her. Since she did not, as you can imagine, want to eat on the train, being a wonderful cook herself, she packed an enormous lunch. She also packed ketchup and pickle relish for her sister, but of course, once on the train, she sold it all. The passengers begged her for ketchup—at fifty cents a serving."

"Think of it."

"Later, passengers wrote her begging for more. People in California wrote. A Spanish prince. Everyone wanted her recipe, but Mrs. Ben kept it in the family, preferring to sell bottles of ketchup by mail order."

The line moved on slowly, but now Eddie could see a cafeteria where two or three employees seemed to be having lunch. The Bean Lady stopped at the edge of the cafeteria to explain. "We here in the Ben family were the first to offer a plant picnic every noon. At first we served only pork and beans, but the employees tired of the same menu day after day. Now we serve some other foods along with pickle relish and ketchup, of course. Today, for instance the Ben picnic lunch is fried chicken and macaroni in ketchup sauce."

"Doesn't that sound good?"

"And now for being such an attentive group," the Bean Lady said, and Eddie swallowed in anticipation, "we would like to give you each a little souvenir." Eddie started to move toward the cafeteria counter, but the women continued to file forward. Eddie followed in line. When he drew even with the Bean Lady, she smiled and handed him a large green pickle selected from a box at her side. Eddie could not believe it. He bit down on the pickle in disgust. A thick nauseating metallic taste filled his mouth and green paint flaked over his tongue and chin as his teeth stuck in the plastic. For a minute he stood helpless, his mouth full of painted pickle. Gagging, he tried to free his teeth, pulling and twisting the pickle until finally his teeth grated across the wet plastic and slipped free. "Fake," Eddie said, holding up the bald, tooth-marked pickle with BEN'S BEANS stamped in gold on one side. "Fake," he said, running toward the cafeteria counter. "Fake pickle." The women stood holding their souvenir pickles, watching curiously. "Fake." Eddie ducked under the counter, where a woman in a white uniform and a hairnet sat reading *True Romance*. "What the hell kind of lousy trick," Eddie said to her, climbing onto the counter. He began throwing fried chicken to the women, who ran screaming away from him. "Fake, fake, fake." He threw a handful of macaroni.

Suddenly two men appeared from nowhere. Eddie slipped in ketchup trying to get away; he could see pickle relish on the floor. He grabbed at another tray of chicken, missed, and then he was lying in something wet and sticky.

7 Eddie sat in the back seat of the car licking crumbs from his fingers and pulling at the spots where dried ketchup stuck his pants to his leg. They were driving into the country, he and the two men; he watched as they passed houses and farms and gas stations. After a while they turned off the highway and drove up a narrow county road, then turned again, past a sign that said, LYNCREST, and climbed a narrow, freshly oiled dirt road to the top of the hill. There an enormous brick mansion sat surrounded by gardens and tennis courts.

"We're here, kid," one of the men said.

Eddie followed the man across the driveway to the door and into a large tiled foyer that had been partitioned into several plywood cubicles. In the center of the hall a crystal chandelier hung suspended above the low roofless cubicles. "In here," the man said, pointing to the first cubicle.

Inside, a man got up from behind his desk and smiled. "Sit down, sit down," he said heartily. The man wore white shorts, a white T-shirt, and a white visored cap, and his face was divided in half by large white teeth set in a grin. "My name's Adam. I'm a tennis instructor." The grin remained fixed on the man's face until Eddie was finally coaxed into an unhappy smile. "That's it," the man said, relaxing. "I know you're going to like Lyncrest." Eddie looked up at the chandelier dangling over his head. "You were running away from home, weren't you?" Eddie nodded. "Believe me," the man said, "Lyncrest will be different. You won't want to run away from Lyncrest."

47

As if prompted to action by the words, Eddie leaped for the door and ran down the tile-floored foyer toward the entrance. Before he had taken two breaths, he was stopped by the man from the car and pinned, momentarily, to the wall. "Now I'll just take you down to your room," said the tennis instructor as though he had not noticed the brief scuffle.

Eddie followed the man down another tiled hall, past huge carved wood doors, and then entered a small high-ceilinged room with a fireplace and twin beds. In one of the beds a fat boy with red hair and thick glasses sat reading. "You don't get enough exercise, Fuller," the man said, and the boy rolled over onto his stomach, his head face down in the pillow. "I want you and Finney here to get acquainted," the man continued, but the boy did not move. "Fuller will explain to you about dinner," the man said and left Eddie standing in the middle of the room.

When the door closed and the sound of footsteps on the tile had disappeared, Eddie looked over at the fat boy. 'What is this?"

"Don't you know?" the redhead asked, sitting up and staring at him.

"No."

"This is Lyncrest; it's a juvenile home. You must be one of the sane ones."

"What's that supposed to mean?"

"I mean you must be one of the ones sent here by the court. I was committed by my parents for setting fire to the house. I've been here on and off for three years; I'm disturbed. After another year I'll be old enough to be transferred to an asylum, and then I'll be insane."

Eddie looked at the flabby white body stretched across the bed; Fuller reminded him of a slug—slimey, sticky, and oozing a snot trail from behind. "Where do you go when you're not here?"

"Home for Christmas," Fuller said, "and for a week in the summer. Last Christmas I set fire to the house again."

"What for?"

48

"I enjoy setting fires, and I don't enjoy volleyball; that's why I'm disturbed. What did you do to get in here?"

Eddie ignored the question. "They can't keep someone here, can they?"

"Not unless they're disturbed."

"How do they know when someone's disturbed?"

"Anyone who doesn't like it here is disturbed."

"I don't get it."

"You're supposed to have everything you want here—this estate some rich guy left the county, love, food, entertainment, a movie every day. Since you have everything you want here, there's no reason for you to dislike it unless you're disturbed. It's very much like my home actually."

"Which you burned down."

"Tried to," Fuller corrected. "The garage was a total loss, all the cushions for the porch furniture burned, but the fire department got there before the house went. I bungled it. If I'd done a really professional job, I wouldn't be here."

"Honh?"

"Insurance. My parents wouldn't have committed me if it meant losing all that insurance money."

Eddie lay back on the other bed and stared up at the ceiling in terror. Tonight after Fuller was asleep, he would get the hell out. It was a ground-floor room, and even without the money they had taken from him, he could probably make his way back to Mount Morris.

"Have you ever had an erection?" Fuller asked suddenly.

Eddie continued to stare silently at the ceiling picturing nurses, clothed nurses, naked nurses, beautiful assistants with soft thighs and bellies who thrust forward sequined breasts, feathered crotches, and thick stiff curly hair. Fantasies mingled, and he thought of his father, and of loneliness, of sitting out on the mattress in the old Nash holding the dog, alone, surrounded by nothing but silence and filled with some deep longing to attack the loneliness, and

49

hearing at the same time cries from some other room, Della heard over the radio and the springs, short cries of pain that made him fear what was to come and desperate to know it. *I have hid my light under a tree.*

"Well," Fuller said, "have you?"

Eddie sat at breakfast with an old man and an old woman, both of them crying silently. He was completely alone.

"Maybe you're still too young," Fuller continued, "although I had my first erection when I was eleven. I took all the bottles out of the medicine cabinet and lined them up on the floor, the big ones on the bottom, the next in size on top of them. For balance, I laid some of the smaller bottles sideways and then, on top of them, added still another row of tall bottles. Slowly I built up this fantastic narrow column of medicine bottles, clear across the width of the bathroom and about the height of the washbasin. Then I knocked them all over; that's when I had my first erection."

Eddie turned to look at Fuller, who seemed to be drooling.

"Another time," said Fuller, "I spent six months building a model airplane; it was a perfect replica of the B-25 bomber—that's what my father flew in the war. When I was through, my mother showed it to everyone, and then the next day I put the plane in the bathtub and set fire to it."

"Why?"

"Why not? What's the point of a model airplane?" Fuller looked at Eddie with disgust. "What did you do, hang all yours from the ceiling of your room or something dumb like that?"

"I never had any model airplanes."

"Oh, right," Fuller said, "you're poor—most of the court cases are." He stared at Eddie curiously. "Maybe that's the reason you've never had an erection. I can get one now just by thinking about the right things." Eddie looked over at Fuller again, prompting him to continue. "For instance, I can think about an enormous automobile showroom with huge plate glass windows and neon signs. Inside, all the latest model cars in all the latest colors, shiny,

50

new. Then I drive up in an old truck, drive through the plate glass window, and bang into the new cars, ramming them into each other, into the walls and steel girders, mashing them with my fenders, tipping them over, flattening them into the cement floor. . . ." Fuller stopped. "What did you do anyway, rob a bank?"

Eddie didn't answer.

"Kill someone?" Fuller was showing him his erection, pumping furiously, and Eddie rolled over against the wall.

At six Eddie followed Fuller down to dinner in a large room filled with a dozen long wood tables. It looked like what Eddie imagined the dining room in a castle to look like. He sat at a table with Fuller and some other boys about his age. At another table some younger boys sat by women who rocked and fed them. One boy sobbed throughout dinner while one of the women sang to him. Aside from the woman's singing and the boy at the end of Eddie's table who talked to himself about pigeons, it was silent. Eddie had trouble eating; every mouthful of food became a sticky paste of saliva that he could not seem to chew or swallow, and he sat playing with the food until the tennis instructor, dressed now in a pair of slacks, came in and began to walk up and down between the rows of tables, then Eddie pretended to eat. When the tennis instructor got to his table, Eddie looked up, his mouth full of potatoes, and the man winked at him.

After dinner, Eddie lay on his bed facing the wall. He felt sick. On the other bed Fuller flipped through the pages of a magazine. How was he going to escape with Fuller just sitting there all the time? Three hours went by. Fuller still showed no signs of fatigue. Then the door opened, and a woman came in and sat down on the bed beside Eddie. "You're new here, aren't you, Eddie?" the woman asked in a soft, friendly voice. Her hand touched him lightly on the shoulder, and he rolled over. "If there's anything you want . . ."

"No," Eddie said. The woman leaned over and kissed him. At

51

first he was too surprised to speak, then he said, "Get away."

"Now," the woman said in her low, soft voice, "I just want you to know that you're loved."

"Get away."

"Now." Eddie began to struggle with the woman, but she lay heavily across him and then, holding him lifeless in her arms, kissed him again. "My poor lonely baby," she said. When it was over, Eddie lay still, listening for the door, then heard the woman again, this time from Fuller's bed.

Fuller screamed, scratched, kicked, and Eddie watched as he struggled momentarily free of the woman's grasp and spit in her face. But Fuller was no match for her, and she weighed down on him like a straitjacket, kissing him on the mouth and loosening one breast, which she dangled above him while he thrashed violently beneath her, trying to turn his face away. "There, there," the woman said. "Doesn't my baby want something to pacify him?" Fuller bit the proffered breast, and Eddie saw a red flash of pain cross the woman's face, but she continued to smile and dangle her bare breast over Fuller.

"Jesus," Eddie said, when she had finally left. "What was that?"

"That was mother love," Fuller said, picking up his magazine again.

"I'm getting out of here."

"I wouldn't recommend that."

"Why not?"

Fuller smiled indulgently. "They have alarms set all over the grounds and guard dogs; they'd get you in a minute. Besides, as I've already said, if they think you don't like it here, they'll think you're crazy."

Eddie sank back down on the bed. "Have you ever tried to escape?"

"I try all the time."

"But you just told me . . ."

52

"What would happen. I know from experience."

"But you keep trying."

"Look," Fuller said, impatiently. "I like it here. Before I came here I was in another institution. There were twenty of us in one room there, no books, nothing to do, one toilet that ran all over the floor. Twice a month, on visiting day, they gave us a bath, dressed us up, and took us down to this nice reception room to see our parents, if they came. I don't want to go back there."

Eddie thought about it, turning the alternatives over in his mind like an argument.

In the morning someone knocked on the door and said, "Breakfast." Afterward Eddie was taken out to see the swimming pool, an enormous cement ocean into which two boys stood pissing. "Would you like to learn to swim?" the tennis instructor asked.

Eddie didn't answer.

"Perhaps you would prefer to play badminton?"

"Yes," Eddie said.

The man led him over to the badminton courts, where several boys stood on opposite sides of a high white net. Eddie watched as one boy held his racket smashed over his face and spit through the mesh.

"I think you'll enjoy badminton," the man said, smiling, "but if you don't, there's plenty more to keep you occupied." Eddie nodded bleakly, and then another man in white shorts came up to give him a racket and a feathered ball. "Just hit the birdie over the net," the man said. Eddie hit the birdie in a high loop over the net, where it dropped immediately before the boy on the other side. The boy stepped on it perfunctorily. The instructor handed Eddie another feathered ball. *Fun.*

By the time Eddie was allowed to go to lunch and then a movie, a kind of numb dread had seized him. They were torturing him; that was what had happened to the others and now it was happening to him. He would go crazy, and they would keep him here forever. He sat sullenly in the private movie theater watching a cartoon. Every now and then, from some seat in front of him, a head would emerge from the darkness, casting a luminous shadow over the screen, and then the boy whose shadow it was would wander down the aisle to the front and stand there petting one of the rabbits in the film. Eddie wanted to scream.

"How did you like playing volleyball?" Fuller asked.

"Badminton," Eddie said. "I didn't."

"That's what it's like every day."

"For how long?" Eddie asked. "When do they let you go?"

"That depends. What did you do?"

"I don't know."

"Bullshit," Fuller said, picking up his book again. "I know you must have destroyed something."

"Why?"

"Because everyone here has. You know that little kid that talks about animals all the time?"

Eddie nodded.

"For his birthday he used to get a new pet every year—a hamster or a turtle or a goldfish or a rabbit or something."

Eddie nodded again.

"Well," Fuller said, "he used to drown them, flush them down the toilet, and then tell his parents that a kid down the block took them away from him."

"He must be crazy."

"Of course," Fuller said, touching his head. "He's disturbed. But do you want to know the best part? Five months after his parents sent him to Lyncrest, his father beat his mother to death with a hammer." Fuller dissolved in a fit of giggles.

Eddie was staring up at the ceiling when the woman came in again. Quickly he rolled over on his stomach, away from her, and then felt her breasts dangling over his back like two soft bags. "Now," said the woman, "aren't you going to tell me why you turn

54

away like that? You're not afraid of me, are you?" Eddie felt her breasts at the back of his neck, loose and wet with perspiration. "Don't you want me to love you, Eddie?" Her arms held him, and Eddie felt her shift her weight, turning him over and then rolling across him. He closed his eyes; her breasts were on his face, smothering him. One wrinkled nipple nudged at his mouth, and he began to suck it, licking the tiny swollen end until, with a crippling sense of helplessness, he felt the muscle between his legs swell and throb and release a silent storm of protest. "Now," the woman said, "isn't that better?" and then Eddie heard her from Fuller's bed, saying, "How is my naughty boy tonight?"

Every day was the same, nothing to mark time by, and when the man who had admitted him called him into his office, Eddie did not know how long he had been at Lyncrest. "Well," the man said as Eddie sat down before him, "now that you've been here awhile, how do you find Lyncrest?"

"It's very nice," Eddie said.

"Good," the tennis instructor said. "Good. That's wonderful. And we're pleased with you, Finney. We think that since you've been here, you've really learned to play and come to have a sense of private property. In fact, we think you've begun to love it, Finney." The man stopped and looked squarely at him. "Isn't that right, Finney?"

"Yes," Eddie said.

"Lyncrest is a little bit like a private club where a few boys get together to have a good time. Only a very sick person would want to tear down the clubhouse, if you see what I mean."

Eddie nodded obediently.

"Only a very sick person would want to tear down a reasonable facsimile of the clubhouse."

Eddie nodded again.

"Unfortunately, there are many sick people in the world—boys who want to ruin and destroy. Here at Lyncrest we try to get these

55

boys adjusted to the world around them, teach them to have fun and enjoy the objects of fun. This is the positive approach and, God knows, there are people in this community who have argued against it, who think we're too permissive up here, but I still think that the positive way is the best, don't you, Finney?"

Eddie nodded.

"You're a sensible boy, Finney, but now let me get directly to the point, let me be personal for a minute. Have you ever seen people on vacation, Finney?" The man frowned as though he were trying to divide some complex problem into its simplest components. "Have you ever seen people go into a store and buy a postcard or some little souvenir—an ashtray with a picture of Niagara Falls on it, a miniature barrel stamped with the words: 'Never go overboard'?"

Eddie shook his head, and the man stared at him in disbelief.

"Surely, you've seen someone pick up some little trinket in the drugstore—a flag or a card or something from a box of Crackerjack?"

"Yes."

The man seemed reassured. "Good. People like those things, Finney. They give them pleasure. Now, you might argue that these little trinkets are meaningless, worthless, that you can't eat them." The man eyed Eddie carefully, underlining his words with his look. "But that would be like arguing that you should abolish photographs or outlaw football games, wouldn't it, Finney?"

Eddie hunted through his mind for some missing link in the conversation.

"Wouldn't it, Finney?" the tennis instructor insisted.

Eddie nodded vaguely.

"Of course it would. It would be ludicrous because football is fun. Football, badminton, swimming, they're all fun. These sports build men. Team spirit. Our team. And if you can't swim, then of course you should get a picture of someone who can," the man said, standing up in his enthusiasm. "The world may not be like

56

Lyncrest, but there are pictures of Lyncrest. That's the point. Put a stamp on a postcard and send it abroad."

"Yes, I suppose so," Eddie said, also standing.

The tennis instructor followed him to the door. "You're very lucky, Finney—lucky that the Ben family is so civic-minded. Of course, they don't like bad publicity." The man chuckled. "Still, they could have sent you to a detention home, and instead they gave you a chance to grow and adjust. You should be very thankful."

Eddie nodded.

"And when you leave here . . ."

"When?" Eddie asked, leaping at the suggestion.

". . . your record will be clear. You will have just had a happy vacation." The tennis instructor stopped, thoughtful. "It won't be long," he said.

"Well," Fuller asked, "what did he say?"

"I don't know. Something about getting a picture of someone swimming."

"Did he ask if you were having a good time?"

"Yeah."

"And you said you loved it here, and now they're letting you go?"

"Maybe."

Fuller peeled the wrapper off a candy bar, methodically smoothing out the bits of foil and lining them up evenly on the bed. "The last kid who was in here said he loved archery, and when they let him go, his parents bought him a bow and arrow. The kid had done nothing but shoot bull's-eyes here. He was a perfect shot, and the first thing he did when he got home was hold up a bank with his new bow and arrow."

"I don't believe it."

Fuller bit into the candy bar. "He dressed up like an Indian, painted his face and everything, then went into the bank with his

57

bow and arrow. At first they just stared at him, thought he was crazy or something. But there was this big clock on the wall, one of the kind with the numbers and the hands right on the wall, and this kid pinned the hour hand to the wall with one arrow and the minute hand with another. They took him seriously after that, gave him all the money. They're still looking for him; I read about it in the paper."

"I don't believe it."

That week and the next Eddie exhibited more enthusiasm than usual in badminton and, finally, the tennis instructor called him in again. "Well, Finney," the man said that morning, "I think you really know badminton now."

"Yes," Eddie agreed.

"Now we hope you'll take something of Lyncrest with you and continue to play badminton."

Eddie nodded, wondering if it would ever be over.

The man reached in his desk. "So that you won't forget your stay with us, I have something for you." He opened a small envelope and handed him a picture of Lyncrest; on the back it was autographed: "To Eddie from The Staff." "Well," the man said hurriedly as though to forestall any thanks, "have fun, Finney." He shook Eddie's hand and, in a minute, Eddie was once again outside, waiting in the drive for the car. When it finally came, he got in the back seat and sat tearing the picture into confetti.

8 Thunderstorms had washed away most of the gravel, leaving mudholes and ruts for long stretches. The car finally stopped only a hundred yards up the old road before a pool of muddy water sunk in a dip at the end of one wash area. The two men got out to check the tires, then the driver got in again and backed the car onto a high spot at the edge of the road. "How much further?" he asked Eddie, looking gloomily out the window at the wet road and the thick underbrush ahead.

"Not too far," Eddie said. He followed the man out of the car and began walking up the steep incline where the road narrowed and the damage had been greatest.

"Are you sure this is the right road?" the driver asked, surveying the area and looking back over the road as though he expected another car along soon.

Eddie nodded.

"Isn't this road used anymore?" the other man asked.

"Every day," Eddie answered. He picked his way carefully over a fallen branch and watched as another, low-hanging branch snapped in the driver's face, spraying him with water. Wherever the growth was densest, water dripped from the leaves in such quantity that it seemed to be raining, and the two men began to mop continually at their faces.

"Car hasn't been up this road in years," the driver said.

"Looks more like a cow trail," the other man agreed.

"Grandparents don't have a car?"

Eddie shrugged, then said, "There's one up in the yard."

"Is there another way up?"

"This is the only road," Eddie said, and the two men fell silent, breathing heavily and moving slowly. Every now and then Eddie had to stop and wait for them.

One of the men stepped in a mudhole and cursed loudly. "Fucking, goddamn riverbed," he said. Kneeling, he tried to wring out his dripping pants leg. "I don't believe anyone lives up here or ever has. Whole area looks deserted. Couple of houses in that little town, that's all. Where did you go to school?" the man called ahead to where Eddie stood waiting.

"Down the road," Eddie said. "We passed it on the way up."

The two men looked at each other. "How many in the school?"

"Enough for a class."

They continued on silently, then the man with the wet trousers stepped into another mudhole, this time with the other foot. Both of his cuffs were muddy now, his shoes were slimy, and water ran down his legs. "I'm going back to the car," he said. "I don't want to catch cold."

Eddie heard branches crack and snap down the road as the man departed. "Many people have cars round here?" the driver asked, stopping for breath. His face was red, and he was beginning to wipe both sweat and water from his face.

"No," Eddie said. "A few people have bicycles."

The man looked down at the few rocks still embedded in the road surface, held in place by weeds. "Hardly even a path for a bicycle."

Eddie started on again, wondering at the new silence, then looked back and saw that the man remained standing where he had been before. "Listen, kid," he said, still breathing heavily. "We'll come back in a couple of weeks, when things have dried out a little, interview your family then."

Eddie watched as the man retreated. Trotting downhill unsurely, he tripped finally over an uneven break in the road where water had left a diagonal rut, and fell flat. Then, without looking back, the

60

man got up and continued on until his mud-covered rear was out of sight. Eddie felt relieved.

In a few minutes, Eddie emerged into the clearing that was the yard and saw the old man at the upstairs window, a raised shotgun in his hand. The dog ran out the length of his tether, prancing on two hind legs and howling with joy, and when Eddie ran to release it, the old man disappeared from sight. "Good old dog," Eddie said, and the dog licked his face and trotted off expectantly.

The house was silent; everything was the same. Eddie ran down the hill after the dog to where summer thunderstorms had swollen the Little Shannon into a fast-moving whirling river. Sitting on the bank, he skipped rocks and watched the dog run to the edge of the river and growl at the foam. Nearby a vine of blue grapes hung heavy, and Eddie picked a few of them, squirting the soft pulp into his mouth and dropping the skins to the ground, where the dog nosed them into the mud and then looked up eagerly for more.

For the next few days, Eddie and the dog investigated all the old places—the clearing where the Turkeyfoot encampment had been, the river trail, the cemetery in the glade, and the hill just the other side of the West Virginia saddle which some people claimed was really an Indian mound. Then, late one afternoon, on his return from the river, Eddie saw a thin black ghost sitting on the porch. When he got closer, the figure turned, and Eddie saw it was the preacher. "Run away, did you?" the preacher called across the yard, and Eddie nodded from the distance, but the preacher said no more, did not mention prayer as he usually did, and in fact did not seem to be waiting for Eddie now. Woodenly, his black suit straight, his face severe, the preacher got up and rattled the screen, then, muttering to himself and staring heavenward, he stood in the yard waiting. Finally he jerked around and started stiffly down the road.

After the preacher had been gone a few minutes, Eddie raced up to the glade with the dog. There on the spot where he had once watched for Tom Hawk, Eddie watched for the preacher on the bit of clear road that bordered the old Indian's pasture. Shortly, he appeared in the distance between trees, and then crossed the pasture itself, leaving the road and tracking slowly through the damp grass. Eddie sank down to watch, pulling the dog with him. The preacher disappeared behind Hawk's shack. Almost an hour went by, then, suddenly, Eddie saw the thin black figure veer back across the pasture and return to the road.

Eddie lay asleep in the sun, the dog beside him playing with a caterpillar, batting it with his paw like a kitten, when the preacher arrived the next day. Awakened by banging, Eddie rolled over to see the preacher rattling the screen, yelling into the silent unresponsive house, "I know you're there." Then he hurried away without any notice of Eddie or the old faces that appeared in the upstairs window.

Day after day Eddie watched the arrival of the preacher, sometimes from the sanctuary of the cemetery, sometimes from the car or the grape arbor, and Eddie watched the old man too, standing vigil at an upstairs window, also observing the arrival and departure of the preacher, day after day. A week went by and still the old people did not answer the preacher's calls, then on Saturday there was a break in the monotony. Eddie saw the grocery boy coming up the road empty-handed and cut diagonally across the yard to meet him. "Postcard," the boy explained.

"For me?"

"For them."

Eddie followed the boy across the yard and stood silently at the screen door waiting for the two old people to come down the steps and out onto the porch. The boy held up the card for them to see. "Says you are informed of the death of your son and of his burial, Montgomery County. August 26, 1951. Doesn't say who informs you."

The old man watched the boy's mouth. When it had stopped, he looked at the old woman beside him. She smiled distantly as though trying to recall something. The boy left, moving slowly across the yard, but the two old people remained on the porch. The old woman turned the card over in her hand, smiling, her face etched with the struggle to remember, and the silence of the house now seemed to extend to some distant and mysterious place, Montgomery County. Eddie's mind conjured up secret sacrificial rites, glorious and heroic ends, mysterious disappearances into fire, water, or foreign ports that, momentarily, gave the little man at the depot and the card meaning.

The preacher came again that afternoon. Eddie watched as he banged on the screen door and wandered out front, looking up at the empty upstairs window, one hand raised to shield his eyes from the sun. After knocking a second time he left, and Eddie returned to the porch. Silence fell like gloom around him. That night the door remained locked, and he slept in the car.

The next day the preacher arrived as he always did, walking like a black wraith up the road and across the yard, his eyes cast heavenward or toward the upstairs window, but the window remained empty. From his vantage place in the weeds on the far side of the road, Eddie watched as the preacher paced the porch, scraping his feet over the board floor, coughing loudly, rattling the screen. There was no response. "I know you're there," the preacher called through the screen, then, looking back as he left, he called to the upstairs window, "God will collect." Eddie returned to the porch and the dog. The hot humid afternoon air made him think the silence had come to smell, and later that night the air was sweet with stink.

In the morning the dog's howling roused Eddie. The air was fresh with dew, clear, bright, but the old dog seemed edgy, and when the sun rose high, sweet stink filled the afternoon and made Eddie wander down to the river, where it was cool and the perfume green moss. The dog returned to the yard first, then Eddie, and then the preacher came. He too seemed to sense the odor, and hesitated in the yard, his nostrils flared in search of something.

With his nose still sniffing righteously, he continued across the yard, but today he did not remain long on the porch, backing away from the screen almost as soon as he approached it. "Goddamn you," he called hurriedly, retreating back across the yard.

Now the stench grew unbearable, and that night Eddie sat with the dog across the road watching the house for explanations. In the morning he could not leave or wander down to the river; his mind was too filled with the silence, his nose with its smell. At his side the dog whined and cried, and when Eddie got up and started toward the house, the dog refused to follow.

Picking through a small hole in the screen with a stick, Eddie lifted the latch. At first the smell inside the house was so heavy sweet that he did not notice it, like a blow too strong to remain conscious under, but before he had got halfway up the stairs his senses revolted. Leaning over the railing, he puked onto the floor below. For a minute the taste of vomit prevented him from smelling as he climbed the remaining steps. He had never been upstairs before; on either side of the hall was a closed door. Eddie opened the one on the right.

At first he saw only the old woman kneeling on the floor as though she were praying. She seemed to rest there naturally, and Eddie felt reassured. "What's wrong?" he asked, moving gently toward her. He touched her skirt, and the body toppled stiffly. Then, looking up in horror, Eddie saw the old man collapsed in a rocking chair, his face and head a bloody pulp, bits of flesh, blood, and brain dotting the wall behind. Eddie puked again. He ran down the steps and vomited still again in the yard, then, still running, he left the dog howling in terror to go into Mount Morris.

It was evening before the doctor came, followed by a perfumed black limousine from which two perfumed and tuxedoed men emerged. Afterward, when the two sheet-draped bodies had been carried down and driven off, the same perfume emanated from the house. It reminded Eddie of Della, the smell of her mornings in the

64

kitchen when her armpits and lips and ears, all freshly scented, gave off a chemical substitute for some real stink. Again Eddie spent the night across the road with the dog, lying on the damp ground rolled in a blanket.

Awake early, Eddie rubbed the dampness from his head and stared up at the sky, trying to reason out the day. Finally, getting up, he crossed the yard to the porch, then stopped at the sound of a broken twig. Someone seemed to be walking up the road; he waited quietly. At his feet the dog now began to whine and slobber and yelp hysterically, racing back and forth in front of the porch. In a minute a man appeared at the end of the road. He wore a Hawaiian-printed shirt and work denims, and when he saw Eddie he grinned. The dog snarled, slowing the man's approach as though he were giving some thought to its manner. He was carrying one old suitcase strapped around the middle with a silver-buckled belt; he set it down in the dirt now and continued empty-handed. The dog, still snarling, cowered halfway under the porch, and the man, mindful of the dog, stopped some distance from it. The slightly off-center smile crossed his face again. "Name's Remley," the stranger said.

"And you would be?" the stranger asked, almost immediately taking the upper hand.

"Eddie Finney."

The stranger feigned an interest. "And you live hereabouts?"

Eddie nodded his head back toward the house.

"But not surely by yourself."

"I do now," Eddie said, just a little on guard although against what he wasn't sure.

"Ah," said the stranger, pulling his hat from his head and lowering his eyes. "I heard the sad news in town. My condolences." There was a silence during which the stranger looked heavenward, twirled his hat in his hands, rounded the brim up and down, and, finally, moved onto the first step of the porch. The dog backed away, crouching warily in a far corner. "I had business with the deceased. I've come some distance." The stranger nodded toward the suitcase sitting in the middle of the yard. "I hate to arrive at such an inopportune, not to mention sad, time. It was a matter of real estate."

"I wouldn't know anything about it," Eddie said, hoping to dismiss the stranger, but his occupation of the porch was now complete.

"Perhaps," said the stranger, "it would not be too difficult to explain. If I might sit down for a moment . . . I've come a far piece. Just but a while ago I was in Arizona—Yuma, Arizona." The stranger slid almost without notice onto one of the car seats. "And what are your plans now?"

66

"Plans?" Eddie backed away from the man—something in his smile seemed both suspicious and mean—until he stood on the step, occupying the position that the stranger had occupied a minute before.

"I wouldn't want to burden you further at a time like this, sad as it is and a crime against nature. I took an interest only because I too have been subject to adversity. I was a, now the only, Remley, and I was like you left alone by death." The stranger nodded toward the glade. "My whole family rests up there to this very day."

"Massacred," Eddie said, remembering.

"It is a matter of indifference," said the stranger, "for the point is this: while I am not one to take advantage of another's sorrow, there are those who would."

Eddie shifted uneasily. "Who?"

"Institutions. Men. Men who, were they to learn of this tragic death, might be asking directions here at this very minute," the stranger said, raising a hand to still Eddie, "but I only guess as much because of my own experience. As a familyless child I was raised in an institution, taken from tragedy to prison by the state." The stranger twisted his hat in his hand and sighed heavily. "My personality has suffered as a result; I am not known to have a sunny disposition." The stranger sighed again as though still saddened by this loss of sunniness. "Since then," he continued, "I have learned that it is well to have plans, alternatives, for overnight—overnight —a person's situation can change, and he should be chameleon enough to change with it."

"I have no plans," said Eddie, trying to hold his own.

"Perhaps you should," said the stranger, smiling his crooked smile. "If I were to continue my story, I might make my argument more persuasive and my business clear."

"Yes."

"I went on a veritable rampage of objection to incarceration, costing the institution in question some two hundred dollars in damage and some five hundred dollars in funds. Then I set off in a borrowed car. I borrowed a car in West Virginia and returned it in Kentucky, borrowed a car in Kentucky and returned it in Oklahoma. . . . Soon I was in Arizona. The five hundred dollars did not last long in Arizona, and I was forced into business—I became what might be called a dabbler in gerontology." The stranger glanced at Eddie as though testing his vocabulary and then, seeming to find nothing amiss, continued. "In fact, I became a spot remover. My uniqueness lay less in the occupation than in the fact that I removed both spot and spotted matter. As the spots I removed were those known as liver spots, those ugly discolorations that appear from time to time on the hands and arms of aged and retired ladies, there were complaints when not only the spots but the flesh itself disappeared. It was for this reason, among others, that I first changed my name from Remley to something less provocative. Like millions of others I became Smith, Joe Smith, but though my name changed, my occupation did not—I continued to dabble in gerontology. Since the old do not want to live alone or die alone—that is, since they have pets—it was my genius to conceive of the Subsequent Planned Burial of Animal, the SPBA. I promised those willing to pay the price that, should they leave this mortal fold, their pet should shortly follow." The stranger paused to sigh again. "While lucrative, my business was short-lived, shut down, as it were, by a group more concerned with the live pet than the dead master, the SPCA." The stranger twirled his hat self-consciously as though reluctant to continue, then went on almost boastfully. "Where I failed in one business, I succeeded immediately in another, becoming the first senior citizen jockey."

"The first what?" Eddie asked from where he now stood in the yard.

"Senior citizen jockey." It was a moment before the stranger explained; he sat silent, his eyes on the broken drainpipe, his mouth moving quietly over various manners of speech like an actor learning his lines. "If you have ever listened to radio, you already know

68

that it is for the young, the very young. I noticed this—a fact especially obvious in Arizona. Thus it was that I became, overnight, a success with my 'Sweet Senility' program—an hour of sweet music and senile jokes." The stranger looked carefully at Eddie. "If you'll permit an example?"

Eddie nodded.

"Knock, knock."

Prompted by the stranger, Eddie mumbled, "Who's there?"

"Jerry."

"Jerry who?" asked Eddie, again at the stranger's prompting.

"Jerry Atrics." The stranger laughed without amusement. "Perhaps one more example will suffice. What did one arthritis victim say to the other?"

Eddie shook his head, grimacing.

"I see you're all doubled up." Again the stranger laughed dryly as though the laugh were a part of the performance. "I'm not boring you, am I?" he asked, looking directly at Eddie.

"No."

"Then to come to the point . . . as Diamond Jim Younger I became a celebrity. I was asked to appear at golf clubs and funerals. At one such event I met my wife, a dear sweet lady sowing a last oat before her death. We went to Honolulu on our honeymoon and then retired to Yuma, Arizona; I to husband her and her funds, she to enjoy the husbanding. Unfortunately, I had more talent for the latter than the former, and the dear old lady began to suffer—first from neglect, then from complications, finally from death. It is to be expected in the elderly; nevertheless, it was perhaps premature, even for me. She had not yet, as it turned out, changed her will and had left all her worldly possessions to her son, an insurance salesman in Nebraska. I was disappointed. I thought success was behind me, then overnight—overnight—my desperate situation changed. Thinking to take another name, since Diamond Jim Younger no longer seemed a propitious one, I hit again upon Remley. Remley." The stranger drawled out the name, seeming to smack his lips over the slow sound. "Remley; the name brought to mind the inheritance so long due me. Where one will left me nothing, another left me everything." The stranger swept his arm dramatically first in one direction and then in the other while the dog snarled at the movement and crouched in the yard beside Eddie. "As providence would have it, I have returned to collect my due at a sad yet strangely fortunate time, when the trespassers have only just taken their leave. Pure Bible," he said. Again the crooked smile passed fleetingly over the stranger's face. "You have, I shall assume, neither plans nor objections."

Eddie was silent, stumbling slightly backward, then he stopped, asking finally, "How do I know you're really a Remley?"

"That," said the stranger, "is a matter of faith. Better to believe than to suffer the consequences of not believing." The corners of his mouth turned up cruelly, and the smile set fixed upon his face.

10 Edna stood at the window waiting until she saw the boy open the screen door and go out on the back porch. Then she took off her glasses and started out her own back door. The door banged shut, and a rat startled by the noise ran in front of her and down the alley. "Here kitty, kitty," Edna called. She opened the low iron gate at the rear and stepped into the alley. Weeds grew up between the bricks, and she walked in a tire path worn into the center of the weeds. Across the way the boy sat on the steps in a dirty T-shirt and low-slung Levi's which made him appear largely an expanse of white knit belly. "Hello," said Edna as though she had just happened to notice him sitting there. The boy did not answer, but Edna felt his eyes on her back as she started across Summit and up the alley on the other side.

Edna turned past the row of garbage cans and packing crates, past the line of parked cars and the stairway that led up to the second floor, and entered the Fourth Street entrance to the grocery. Four little Negro boys ran up and down the aisles, pushing and shoving each other, poking holes in the sugar bags and watching the white granules pyramid over the floor. Edna made her way to the vegetables. "Are cantaloupes out of season already?" she asked the clerk.

"Haven't seen any recently anyway," the clerk said, turning to weigh a handful of tomatoes that a man gave him.

"Are these Florida or Texas grapefruit?" Edna asked as she picked up one of the shiny yellow-green fruits. The clerk nodded his head toward the sign that said TEXAS PINK. "I always think

71

Florida grapefruit are a little juicier, but then I can't resist pink."
The clerk walked to the end of the counter and began watering
down the lettuce.

An old man shuffled up and down the aisle of baby foods, and
when Edna pushed past him, he smiled at her toothlessly, his pink
gummy mouth full of saliva. Edna moved on to the tins of tea and
coffee. "When are you ever going to stock some real English tea?"
she asked.

"I don't work here," the boy on the floor said. "I'm just unloading a truck."

"It's really a hot day to be working, isn't it?"

"Yes, ma'am."

A woman with her hair in huge pink rollers picked up a gallon
carton of ice cream, then changed her mind and set it on a shelf
of paper towels, where it began to melt. In the back of the woman's
cart a baby sat pulling cans from the shelves and dropping them
on the floor. "You stop that grabbin'," the woman yelled and
slapped the baby across the face. It began to cry. "Shut up that
cryin'," the woman said and slapped it hard again. Now the baby's
screams mingled with those of two or three others and with the
shouts of the four racing, shoving boys. "I'd think you'd be a
nervous wreck by the end of the day," Edna said to the butcher.

"Got some nice pork chops on special."

"All right," Edna agreed.

Finally she pushed her cart back to the other side and into a
checkout lane, careful not to get too close to the woman ahead of
her, whose body was a series of oozing puslike sores. "How're you
today?" the cashier asked without looking up.

Edna touched lightly at her hair. "Just fine," she said.

The cashier began to lift the grapefruits from Edna's cart, adding
up the items while talking simultaneously to the cashier in the next
lane. "I said, 'Look, just don't call me. I'll call you.' "

"That's good," said the other girl. "What are you doing tonight
then?"

"Washing my hair."

"Guess who I'm going out with."

"Who?"

"That new stockboy."

"Eddie?"

"Yeah."

"I didn't know he had a car."

"He doesn't."

"Don't forget your stamps," the girl said as Edna picked up the sack of groceries.

"Oh no," said Edna, eagerly collecting the long strand.

The boy was still sitting on the porch when Edna returned. "Don't you have to work today?" she asked, stopping a moment to chat.

"No." A lock of greasy hair fell over the boy's ear, and he began to slick it back, combing the long side hair into a part at the back of his head.

"You're lucky; Saturday it's always such a madhouse."

"Uh."

Edna moved down to her gate and began to fumble with the latch before turning back to the boy. "You couldn't get this stubborn thing for me, could you?" The boy loped indifferently across the alley and lifted the latch with one finger. "Oh, that's wonderful," Edna said, and then it was all over and she was back inside.

Edna put away the groceries, put some water on for tea, and then stood before the mirror in the hall admiring the bright red hair and the delicately arched line of red pencil over each eye. She touched the curls on either side of her face and ran her hand over the stiff, smooth, partless crown. The wig, ordered two months before, had arrived yesterday, and she felt exhilarated by this first outing and by her transformation. The kettle whistled and Edna poured the hot water over a tea bag, then sat down to lacquer her nails a matching shade of red.

When she had finished her nails, she found her glasses and went

73

upstairs. There, sitting at her vantage point before the hall window, she looked out over the alley and the back yards of the houses across the way. Edna thought of the last six years, during which she had been nurse to the two elderly aunts who had raised her, fixing their tea six or seven times a day, washing their soiled sheets, each morning listening to their ceaseless complaints. Then, when it was finally over, both of them dying in the same week, she had been left alone in a strange world from which she had been sheltered for twenty-eight years—never allowed outside alone as a child and kept inside in the grips of death as an adult.

A car drew up in the alley, a small black convertible, and Edna watched as the boy banged out the door and down the steps to get in beside the cashier from the grocery store. His hands and arms seemed to engulf the girl momentarily and then the car backed out and was gone down Summit in the evening traffic. Edna felt a cold chill run down her body like imaginary hands on bare skin. Pulling off her dress and wig, which had begun to itch, she stretched out across the bed and began to read a magazine article: "Ten Hints on How to Bring Out the Sensual You." For instance, the article hinted, "Why not let yourself be completely feminine and soft. Why not give up the stiff restraint of a brassiere while remaining safe from embarrassment and still provocative by covering only your two most precious secrets."

Sunday the house across the way seemed deserted, and although Edna spent the day weeding and hoeing a garden long since nonexistent, she caught no glimpse of the boy. Then, late that afternoon, she heard someone scream, and the high-pitched female cries seemed to go on endlessly, emitted at exact intervals as though on a record. Finally, a woman wearing only a slip ran from the house, her face battered blue, her breasts bouncing. Edna stood up, excited and horrified, to watch, hearing the woman's curses pierce the air like screams. Half an hour later, a police car drove into the alley, and Edna watched as two patrolmen and the woman entered the house. The officers returned with a large heavy-set man who stumbled along drunkenly between them. Edna felt as emotionally exhausted as if she had been a participant, and spent the remainder of the day resting.

On Monday Edna returned to her business career. After the death of her two aunts, she had taken a job as teller at the First National. "Edna," Mrs. Herren greeted her, "what have you done to yourself?"

"Do you like it?" Edna asked. Mrs. Herren did not reply, and no one else seemed to notice. All that week people pushed checks and money toward Edna as though they were handing it over to a machine. Even at lunchtime in the cafeteria across the street no one turned to look at her. Edna was vaguely disappointed. She wanted some new role to play with her new appearance.

On Friday Mr. Adamson from the hardware store down the block came in with his week's receipts and stood in Edna's line. Edna smiled at him hopefully. "Guess this is what they call Indian summer," Mr. Adamson said.

"It's a beautiful day, isn't it?" Edna agreed. "It just makes me feel like doing something exciting."

"Yes, guess this is what they call Indian summer," Mr. Adamson repeated, ignoring her interruption. "It's a good day for a red-face." He guffawed loudly and turned to see if those in line behind him had benefited from his humor. Edna smiled appreciatively. "Now don't rob a bank," Mr. Adamson said as he left.

"I won't," said Edna, but Mr. Adamson was already out the door.

Saturday Edna worked in the garden again, cleaning up the years of debris that lined the back fence—paper and broken glass and tin cans that had spilled from overturned trash barrels and ice cream sticks and candy wrappers thrown there by kids. At noon, when she was just ready to go in for lunch, a car with two men in it drove into the yard across the way. The driver beat out a tune on the horn and called, "Della." Finally, a woman in a bathrobe and slippers came out to stand on the back porch.

"Where's the old man, still locked up?" the driver asked.

"No, drunk." The woman lit a cigarette and sat down on the steps.

"Come on; we're having a party." The driver lifted a six-pack from the front seat.

"I've got a headache; had to work late last night."

"Work at what?" Both of the men laughed.

Something more was said, but Edna could not hear it over the car motor. The woman got up and went inside, and the car backed into the alley. "Hey," the driver called, seeing Edna, "want some beer?" The two men laughed, and then they were gone before she could answer.

Edna saw no one from the house across the way for the rest of that weekend or the next week, as though the occupants came and went now only at night, then the following weekend, as she looked up from weeding, she saw the fat man watching her from across the way. Red-faced, a can of beer in one hand, he clung to the porch post before starting clumsily down the steps, falling finally on his face in the yard. Edna got up and moved to the fence, where she stared over at the fat body spread out in the weeds like a giant slug.

Later, when Edna looked out the upstairs window, the man was gone, but she saw the boy come walking up the alley. The fat man met him at the door, yelling "All right, give me the money. Give it to me." The two of them scuffled briefly on the porch, then they disappeared inside, and Edna was left alone again, just as she had been as a child when, standing at an upstairs window, she had watched her guests, wearing their Sunday best and bearing flowered packages with white silk ribbons, depart in confusion. She had written invitations to birthday parties never held, to Halloween parties and May Day surprises. All drew small clusters of children onto the wide front porch, where they stood idly while old women peered at them from behind heavily curtained windows until they left. Afterward, they whispered that Edna was odd, and they followed her home, curious, wanting some glimpse inside at the two old women and the mystery of her isolation. Sometimes, in the late afternoon, they would turn the bell key on the door, darting onto the porch and then back into hiding where they waited to see an old lady shuffle to the door, calling out, "Who's there?" to the bushes and the plants no longer tended by a gardener or by the brother killed in World War I. "Hoodlums. Scum." They danced on the lawn, tormented her by dashing up on the porch and then disappearing into the lilac bush at the side of the house.

Edna waited two weeks before crossing the alley to the other house. Nervously she knocked on the back door and rattled the screen. When there was still no answer, she pushed the door ajar and called, "Hello." Her eyes slowly grew accustomed to the darkness, and she saw the fat man sitting on a kitchen chair in an empty room. Empty bottles littered the linoleum floor, and behind the man Edna saw still another empty room, beer cans heaped in the middle, the linoleum curling up at the edges. The man turned to stare at her but did not get up. "I wondered if you might have an extra length of hose I could borrow," Edna asked, knowing from the bare rooms, the littered dirt yard, that the question was absurd.

"No hose," the man said, reaching for the bottle at his feet.

"Thank you." Turning, she met the woman crossing the yard, her thin hair pulled back into a hairnet, her green and white uniform stained with ketchup. "Hello," Edna said; the woman did not reply. Edna heard the screen door open and shut behind her, then heard a piercing cry of disbelief. "Jesus Keerist, what is this?" Edna stood for a moment in the alley listening, hearing only the woman's voice: "Get out. Get out. Get out. I'm sick of supporting you, sick of being robbed." A woman two doors down began to yell at a child from an upstairs window; the child, running down the alley without any underpants, screamed wildly. A dog howled.

77

In the morning, while she was fixing her breakfast tea, Edna saw the fat man walk down the alley with an old suitcase. After that there was renewed activity at the house. Cars came and went in the alleyway, and late parties seemed to move from the dimly lit house to the cars parked in the rear yard and then back again. Cars left for a while only to return, and laughter roamed the alley and the yard and the side street. Edna stayed up late to watch, drawn more and more into the vortex of the life across the way. One night figures, only silhouettes in the street light or an occasional car beam, ran past, two of them running together at first, then Edna watched as one of the dark figures turned, stumbled, and tripped, moving awkwardly as though he were dancing in place. Then all movement stopped, and the figure slumped in one sharp crack of sound, falling backward over the noise like an acrobat.

Sirens, ambulances, police moved into the alley, and the next morning a policeman came to her door and asked if she had seen anything, heard anything. "A man was dancing," Edna said, "and then he seemed to forget what he was doing and fall down."

"That's all you saw?"

"Yes."

There was blood in the alley, Edna looked at it. By evening dust had settled over the evidence, and Edna watched for the boy, filled with curiosity. When she saw him finally, two days later, sitting out on the back porch, she took off her glasses and started outside. "Eddie," she called, and the use of his name surprised her as much as it did the boy. "I wonder if you could help me a minute."

"Help you with what?" the boy asked, slowly drawling out the words, taunting her with them.

"I need someone to lift something for me." Edna led the way into the house, conscious of the uneasy grin and the reluctant footsteps behind her. "I can't get into the cupboard behind that rocker," Edna said, pointing to an old horsehair-cushioned rocker on one side of the room and a free space on the other. The boy lifted the rocker up easily and placed it down as directed. "That all?"

78

"There's certainly been a lot of excitement in the neighborhood recently, hasn't there?"

"Is that all you do over here, spy out that upstairs window?"

"I was so shocked to see that policeman walk up to my door," Edna continued as though she had not heard his question.

"He the first man ever in this house?"

"I knew there was a party and a lot of noise, but . . ."

The boy grinned, leaning insolently against the far wall like a threat, and Edna began to rummage nervously through her handbag for her wallet. "I suppose you usually get a little something for doing chores."

"A little something what?"

Edna held up the wallet. The boy moved slowly toward her, then, once in front of her, suddenly grabbed at her hair, lifting the red wig from her head like a hat and dropping it on the floor. Edna giggled helplessly. Perfectly head-shaped, the stiff hair lay between them like a fallen stranger. Edna dropped her wallet beside it and ran upstairs. There, breathlessly, she waited for the sound of footsteps. The door knob turned, and she closed her eyes. She felt herself pushed, shoved, rolled over, felt hands ripping at her clothes, buttons, hooks, then a voice seemed to waken her. "What the hell are those for?" Edna opened her eyes and stared at her two Band-Aided nipples, then she was smothered under a great sweating, heaving, painful weight.

The next day Edna phoned that she was sick; it was several days before she recovered. Then, at work again, the red wig perched on her head, she felt as though people were staring at her. Several times an hour, her hands would reach to her hair suspiciously. When anyone got near her she backed off, and at noon she ate not at the cafeteria across the street as she had, but at a sandwich shop several blocks away. Still people watched her, laughed at her, turned once she had passed to stare at her head, forcing her hands over her red curls again and again. By the end of the day she was a nervous wreck, and by the end of the week, distraught. She stayed inside with the blinds pulled. Sunday there was a knock on the door, but she did not answer; it became more insistent, and finally, she opened the door. The boy, another boy grinning widely behind him, stood before her. "Can we come in?"

"I'm quite busy right now."

"This won't take long." The boy in the rear snickered, and then both of them grinned ludicrously and were inside, standing in the middle of the living room. "I brought along Junior here," the boy said, nodding at his leering friend. "He wanted to meet you." The two boys laughed, then Junior dropped his pants to the floor and stood staring down at his bulging appendage. Edna's mouth moved incoherently over an almost soundless babble as she was pushed to the floor first by one, then by the other.

They came again the next week and the next, and then, as though tired of the same sport, they brought two more, all of them wriggling over her weak, hysterical, perspiring body like a starved herd attacking a lone piece of meat. Edna fainted. When she opened her eyes again, only partly remembering what had happened, she heard them opening drawers and closets, heard them turning over furniture, throwing bottles of makeup against the wall, picking through her underwear, emptying the icebox on the floor, tracking through the wet mess, and finally setting fire to the long red hair that lay on the floor beside her. Then they left.

Edna spent the night in a hotel. In the morning she phoned a real estate office, and that afternoon went to see the broker.

"I think you're making a wise decision," the man said. "Niggers have already moved into the house on the corner. Pretty soon the whole block will go. Of course under the circumstances, we can't give you much of an offer. The near north side is a bad area."

"It just isn't safe anymore," Edna agreed.

PART TWO

11 He took the bus downtown from the airport, getting off at one of the High Street hotels, where conventioneers revolved out of doors followed by corsaged and name-tagged wives. Behind them, reflected in the hotel window, he spotted a strange civilian idling mysteriously on the sidewalk in a print sport shirt, no corsage, no name tag, no Ohio Optimist Club banner; he moved down the block to study the matter further. Stopping in front of a plate glass window, he regarded his image closely. His hair had grown into an awkward post-military baldness; inch-length brown shoots fell over his ears and forehead and covered his head in a flat, straggly, matted crew. A loose, wide-collared shirt in a blinding pagan print of kelly green and chartreuse leaves behind which pink and fuchsia flamingos fluttered permanently hung to various lengths around his waist and over his denims. Eddie smiled, trying to encourage his reflection, and his reflection smiled back. A salesgirl stepped between the happy pair, lifting a mannequin into the display case, and Eddie smiled at her before slinking away in his chop suey shirt and number one hair.

He crossed the bridge over the waterless maze of train tracks and wandered through used car lots, kicking tires, past wholesale furniture warehouses, pawnshops, secondhand outlets, and the Garden Theater, where ten hysterifying ghoul features were showing for fifty cents. He felt lost, but he could remember being lost here before. Two bubble-headed whores lounged on the corner before Square Deal Furniture, and Eddie loitered by. He winked at one of the girls, and she batted fur eyes at him. Maybe tomorrow; now

83

he needed to rest and recuperate. There was the sound of lurking in his mind, bent twigs, falling rocks, cocked guns, and he fell to safety in the doorway of a bar and grill, singing, *"Home, home,"* and arming his teeth. It was a civil mistake; he apologized and turned the corner into the old neighborhood.

Someone had stretched a child's gate across the porch; a baby carriage and a grocery cart sat before the front door. The house itself seemed strangely vulnerable and exposed with the two houses on the corner gone now, replaced by a low brick building with opaque glass blocks for windows. Eddie walked to the corner, standing before the new building to read the list of occupants and the small, neatly printed sign—RESEARCH SCIENTISTS INC.—then he walked back to the house. Across the street there were some changes too—two other new buildings, flat-roofed, two-story brick apartment houses surrounded by paved parking areas. A little girl came out on the porch, and Eddie saw a dark-skinned woman wrapped in a sari standing at the screen watching the child and him. He turned and walked on up to Fourth Street and the bar on the corner.

When his eyes adjusted to the dark, he saw the cook sitting in one of the booths at the back grating cheese. It was not yet noon, and the bar was empty. Eddie ordered a beer, drank it, ordered another. The barmaid stood at the far end of the counter talking to the cook. Eddie finished the second beer and then walked around to the side and started down the alley. Back of the old house, he stopped again. The screen on the porch had been fixed, and the yard fenced with old doors and peeled pink siding from the house torn down next door, all the used timber nailed neatly into a child's low protection. Eddie had an urge to step over the fence and lie down in the yard, then he saw dark eyes with a red dot between them at the door—three eyes, one of them red, watching him. He felt confused, dislocated, and he wandered on. He was home from the war, or whatever the hell they called it now, for crissake. "Fuck you," he yelled back at Three Eyes, goddamn foreigner. "And fuck you too," he said to a dog growling at him from a stretched tether.

Eddie stood for a minute on the corner of High and Chittenden not certain which direction to turn, then he started across the street to a phone booth. A horn honk stopped him. "Eddie, Jesus Christ —you AWOL or something?" It was Junior Burns. For once Eddie was glad to see him; he opened the door to the car and got in. "When did you get back in town?"

"This morning."

"No kidding. Looking over the old homestead?"

"Yeah. Bunch of Hindus have moved in."

"Mmm. A lot of them around; all over at State taking agriculture."

Eddie ran his hands over the imitation crushed leather upholstery of the car seat and twisted his heels into the pile of the carpet. "Where did you get the money?"

"I'm an electrician now."

"An electrician?" Eddie looked over at Junior Burns, at the dumb moony face unchanged from high school—same silly grin, same red hair, same freckles, same pink-white ears. "What do you know about being an electrician?"

"Not much, but I've got a couple of uncles in the local. I'm kind of an apprentice right now. It's good money."

"I can see that," Eddie said, patting the side of the new car. "What do you have to do for it?"

"Just help out. Sometimes I go turn on the lights for the plumbers at new projects; stuff like that."

"That's all? What's the point?"

"Everyone has to have an electrician; it's union law."

"They got any laws about homeless veterans—every plumber needs one to hold the flag?"

Junior giggled. "Don't you have any place to stay? What about old Edna? She'd probably be glad to see you again."

Eddie grinned, his mind slipping momentarily into the past, a

distant dream. "Her place has been torn down; it's a car wash now."

"No kidding, I don't get over this way much anymore."

"Where're you living?"

"Now I'm staying with one of my uncles. Can't help you out much there. I was living in a new apartment out on the east side, out in Whitehall. I got married last year."

Eddie looked over at Junior, surprised. Who the hell would marry Junior Burns and have to go to bed with that dumb grin and those bright pink ears. "Anyone I know?"

"Remember that little sophomore Carol Sears, real cute girl?"

Eddie nodded; he remembered Carol Sue Sears all right, with a kind of deep-felt stirring exhaustion. One of the freshman team's cheerleaders, she had met him at a party once and spent most of a drunken evening in an empty bedroom with him, exhibiting a very fine and practiced hold on the art of torture, letting him fondle her breasts and buttocks, letting him remove her sweater and brassiere while she lay pliably and provocatively across the bed, then, as soon as he was aroused, squirming free and rejoining the party. Later she would return for more of the same, letting him run his hand up her thick, tight thigh, letting him grab at the tuft of pubic hair and cotton pantie in between her legs, letting him poke his fingers under the elastic and into the dampness, before running off again. "Where's your wife now?" Eddie asked.

"She's in the apartment; we're separated."

"How long?"

"Couple of months."

"That's too bad," Eddie said, trying with difficulty to picture Carol Sue and Junior Burns together. The thought filled him with a sense of loss, a sense that in the last two years life had gone on for everyone but him.

"You know, it's just more or less a lot of trouble," Junior said moodily. "You go home every night and there she is and so what? And she's spending a lot of money and complaining, wanting to

86

buy one of those Formica dinette sets."

Eddie wasn't listening; he was picturing Carol Sue alone, her thick tight body gyrating down the edge of a football field. "Let's go see her."

"Who?"

"Your wife."

Junior Burns turned the key in the ignition. "I've got to go over and pick up some more of my stuff anyway," he said, swinging the car around in a U turn and heading back downtown. In the suddenly quiet car Eddie had a sense of tension and excitement. "She may not be there," Junior said. "May be out or have someone up. I don't keep track of her, but she doesn't just sit around at night."

Eddie nodded. "That's why you should introduce her to some of your friends. Keep it in the family."

Junior Burns giggled, then looked over to see if Eddie was serious or not. "You didn't ever know Carol, did you?"

"Not really," Eddie said, thinking back over the attempt again. "Just saw her around, that's all."

"Yeah."

Carol Sue Burns, née Sears, was not there when they arrived. Eddie sat down to wait while Junior went into another room. He came back with an armload of dirty clothes. "Come on; we don't want to stick around here if she's not here."

"Why not?"

Junior shrugged.

"Let's have a drink and think about it."

"I used to have a bottle of Scotch around somewhere." Junior went into the narrow kitchen at the other end of the room, and Eddie stretched out on the slick shiny sofa, his back sticking sweatily to the cushion. "Plenty of ice in mine," he called to Junior. In a minute Junior returned with a plastic bag of ice, two paper cups, and the bottle. "Carol doesn't drink."

"That's a virtue," Eddie said, and Junior nodded gravely. Eddie poured two paper cupfuls of Scotch and leaned back in vinyl luxury. "This is a nice place."

"Carol fixed it up herself; she picked out all the furniture. We were going to buy a dinette set and some leopard bar stools, but then we busted up." Junior looked over at the empty dining area and then nodded at the two pictures on the living room wall. "Carol painted those herself."

Eddie looked over at two sparkle-plenty waterfall scenes; bright blue Niagaras outlined in sequins fell like shimmering confetti over the rocks. "Nice."

"Yeah," Junior agreed. "You get it in a kit. They tell you what to do and everything. Niagara Falls."

"It adds a lot."

"Carol is a real decorative talent."

"And you were helpless before her talent and decorative assets?"

"What?"

"That's why you married her?"

"No; actually we had this kind of pregnancy scare. She thought she was going to have a baby," Junior said, spelling it out, "but she wasn't. Nothing happened. After five months, she wasn't even very big. I thought maybe it was her diet—eating nothing but melba toast and coffee—but it wasn't; she just wasn't pregnant." Eddie looked at Junior Burns's two pink ears and his big dumb face; he was beginning to get on his nerves. "It kind of got things off on the wrong foot," Junior said.

"Mmm." Eddie poured himself another drink and replenished Junior's cup which was beginning to get soggy where he had chewed the plastic coating off.

"Enough of that," Junior said, waving his arm and spilling some of his drink on the beige wall-to-wall. "What are you going to do now that you're out?"

"I don't know. I'm supposed to see a guy I met in Georgia about a job. He and his brother bought an old roadhouse out here on Broad Street; they're fixing it up, putting in live entertainment, turning it into a club, The Down Home. Wet drinks, no cover charge; they think it'll make some money."

"Yeah, but what are you supposed to do?"

Eddie poured out another cup of Scotch while his mind constructed various possibilities. "Sing, dance, do tricks; nothing is too difficult for the veteran of army training."

"Come on," Junior said thickly. He dribbled Scotch from a hole chewed in his cup and wiped it up with a dirty sock. "What're you going to do?"

Eddie pulled out one pants pocket and waved it at Junior Burns. "There is no bird in my pocket."

"I never said there was," Junior said righteously.

Eddie stood unsteadily and went through his other pockets. "There are no birds hidden upon my person whatsoever."

Junior Burns giggled with delight, slapping his hand down on his knee and the coffee table. "Ha! Drunk out of your mind; can't even find your pecker."

Eddie ignored him. "Say a few magic words and produce a singing canary. Watch."

"It's some kind of trick," Junior said before anything had happened.

"Sue Carol, Sue Carol, Sue Carol," Eddie chanted. Junior looked toward the door. "Never take your eye off a magician," Eddie warned. "Sue Carol, Sue Carol," he continued while Junior slipped to the floor along with his head. "Watch." Junior lay on the floor watching. Eddie pulled out his empty pocket again.

"Ha," Junior said. "It didn't work."

Eddie stared at the empty pockets and at the flamingos on his shirt, then he began to whistle and flap his arms wildly. "Birdie, birdie, birdie."

"Jesus Christ!" Junior giggled. "You have to be crazy."

Eddie sat down, looked at the bottle as though he were guaging the remaining number of cups, and then just poured one for himself. "That's the kind of thing my old man used to show me, but then he could fly. It's a better trick that way."

Junior Burns giggled with delight again, raising himself off the floor slightly. "You're more a sitting duck than a singing canary," he said, laughing loudly, banging on the floor, enjoying himself.

"Want to see me dance?"

"Yeah." Junior giggled wetly, his eyes running. "I wanna see a sittin' duck dance." He loved his joke and began to repeat it over and over again.

Eddie poured another drink for himself and a half for Junior this time. "Actually I'm going to see about a bartending job; the entertainment is all female—Carol Sue and her cheerleaders." Eddie began to envision Carol Sue thumping across the stage in sequins, a regular waterfall; he wasn't sure what he was saying.

Junior Burns looked at the door again. "Listen, I've got to get going. My aunt'll have dinner ready. Want me to drop you somewhere?"

"No," Eddie said, lying back down on the couch. He watched Junior Burns retreat into a blur, and then he was asleep, his head stuck to the cushion.

Some time later a wedge of light from the hall entered the dark room. "Carol Sue, Carol Sue," Eddie called out warmly and fell on the floor. His head hurt, and he was too annoyed to get up. He felt hands going through his pockets hunting for birds. He relaxed. There weren't any.

12 When Eddie woke up, he was lying on the carpet alongside an empty paper cup. His eyes wandered around the room; it appeared unchanged from the night before. He got up slowly, sat on the couch for a minute until he had adjusted to an upright position, and then wandered into the tiny kitchen. The cupboards were empty; he opened the door to the refrigerator —two cartons of skim milk, four of cottage cheese. He decided to investigate the other rooms. Pushing open the door to the bathroom, he found a tub full of dirty clothes, a sink lined with cosmetics. He went into the bedroom. Six toasters, some of them still in their cartons, sat in one corner, a pile of dirty clothes and a chafing dish in another. He spotted his wallet lying open on the bureau and checked it for money; it was still there. Then he hunted through a few drawers and a jewelry box for an extra key but couldn't find one.

Eddie lifted the catch on the front door and stepped outside. It was hot and late, and he walked a block to the highway. On the other side there was a restaurant—The Bali. Dark glass and an empty parking lot made it look like a walled fortress with an asphalt moat, but there was an Open sign on the door, and Eddie crossed over and went inside.

"I'll have two eggs over easy and hash browns," he said, sitting in an empty booth near the door.

The waiter straightened his red waistcoat and tapped the menu in his hand. "This is a Polynesian restaurant."

"What do Polynesians eat for breakfast?"

91

The waiter shrugged. "We only serve lunch and dinner. It's four o'clock; we're just setting up for dinner now." He held open the silk-tasseled menu with the gold dragon drawn across the top and pointed to an item at the very bottom—"Special Charcoal-Fired Bali Burgers."

"All right, and a Scotch," Eddie agreed.

He had written the address of The Down Home on the back of an envelope; it was out at the edge of town, probably no more than four blocks away. When he had finished eating, he started walking east on the highway. It was farther than he thought, an old motel on one side, an empty pasture on the other, the club itself a low dingy building with an arcade at the side and parking through the arcade at the rear. Eddie tried the front door, then went around through the arcade to the back. A gravel courtyard lined with garbage cans fronted an open side door that led into a small empty kitchen. Part of the kitchen area had been converted into a flat square wooden stage draped with curtains. Walking around the curtained enclosure, Eddie entered a plush darkness.

At first the place seemed empty, then Eddie saw someone standing behind the bar washing glasses. It was the man he had met in Georgia, whom he had talked to late one night after hearing the border accent and finding him to be from Columbus. The man had told him he was selling the Encyclopaedia Britannica door to door until he'd saved enough money to go into business with his brother. "Hi," Eddie said, now sitting down on a bar stool. The man showed no sign of recognition, nodding warily. "Said you might have a job for me tending bar," Eddie continued.

The man concentrated on the glasses, wiping the soapy water from them and setting them upside down on a folded towel; he was silent. "You union?" he asked finally, eyeing Eddie suspiciously.

"Union? No."

"I don't want any trouble. I'm the owner and I'm the bartender. I can't afford help right now."

"Well," Eddie said, "I was just looking for a job. Thought you might have something."

The man was silent, concentrating on the glasses again. Eddie got up and started to leave, then, just as he started out through the kitchen, the man called to him. "You wouldn't be interested in anything other than bartending?"

Eddie stopped. "Sure." He shrugged, looked around the tiny bar and back at the man washing glasses. "Like what?"

"I need a comedian, a foil for the girls, know what I mean?"

"Yeah," Eddie said offhandedly. "I know a few tricks; old man was a clown."

The bartender stared at him.

"Baggy pants, beautiful assistants," Eddie said, wishing he would shut up. "He was going to be in a movie once, but then . . ." His voice and the story ran down incoherently. ". . . he was in this fire. Old hotel burned down. He lost all his clothes, wandering around the street nude. Police came and picked him up. Sent a postcard from jail and . . ." Eddie stopped.

"A few jokes," the bartender was saying, "just something to bring on the girls."

"Yeah, sure, O.K."

"We're just opening up here tonight. First night. Guy I had lined up for the job got busted in Cleveland. Be back about nine, maybe a little earlier."

"O.K. Yeah." Eddie walked slowly to the kitchen, then he began to run. What the hell did he think he was doing? A car swerved to miss him as he ran across the highway and down the other side. Here is Fanny Fatass, here Miss Bare Bottom; remembering a joke he'd read in the can—What's an ass with a tail on it?—forgetting the rest. He stopped to buy a six-pack, and then he was back at the apartment.

A long low row of doors and windows, an apartment house built like a motel, and Eddie couldn't remember now which door was Carol Sue's. He casually turned knobs as he walked down the covered walkway. Number four opened; it was Carol Sue's and it was empty. Eddie speared a can of beer and then poured out a paper cupful of Scotch; two, maybe three, left.

93

By eight he was back outside The Down Home. The club looked different, better, in the dark, only a neon outline showing in the distance and, closer, a purple banner strung out over the front with the legend: *NIGHTLY ENTERTAINMENT.* Eddie pushed through the two tufted leatherette doors, which showed clearly in a darker purple where the word *Carousel Club* had once been stitched. Inside the swinging doors there was a velvet-curtained entry; Eddie stepped through the opening in the curtains and was back inside the dark narrow room he'd been in earlier that afternoon. Although it was now filled with smoke, there were only four customers sitting at the bar, four men in coveralls with lunchboxes and Thermoses at their feet as though they had been there since getting off work. "Scotch," Eddie said evenly, sitting at the near end of the bar.

"On the house," the bartender said, nodding to him and looking at his watch. He leaned heavily on the bar as he set the drink down, red-eyed and evidently already a few sheets to the wind himself.

Four more men came in, sitting in one of the booths at the side next to an old jukebox, and a barmaid suddenly emerged from the kitchen to take their orders. Eddie waited for the tray of beer mugs to be filled before raising his own glass. The bartender picked up a throated bottle and moved flatly down toward him. Leaning heavily, he poured the Scotch into and over the glass. "Mop that up for you," he said.

Curtains parted and people either came or went, Eddie wasn't sure which. In the narrow space between booths and bar, the barmaid fluttered back and forth with trays of beer. Eddie held up his empty glass again and watched the bartender deliberately make his way toward him, supporting himself on the bar. "Fifteen minutes, O.K.?" the bartender said.

"Mmm." Eddie swallowed the Scotch, tried to see through the smoke to the stage, and then stumbled slowly across the room, bumping into the barmaid, spilling beer, his ears filled with a noisy ringing. From the kitchen he stepped onto the small square box of

94

a stage, pushing his way out through the curtains and then gazing uncertainly into the darkness, a blue blur lined along one side by a series of tiny glowing coals. Cigarettes. He coughed and leaned into the darkness—a row of eyes stared back at him. Now what? He heard the muffled sound of palms beating on the bar. *Plaw plaw plaw.* Then the row of eyes turned to the rear. A man in one of the back booths had wet his pants. There was laughter from that end of the darkness, and four giggling men stood up, evacuating the booth, which the barmaid rushed toward with a mop and a sponge. The center of attraction, a man in denim work pants, pulled at the dampness between his legs and giggled as he headed for the men's room door. Eddie choked, gurgled, made faraway noises in the back of his throat, and the row of eyes turned back to him again. *Plaw plaw plaw.* Someone at the bar farted. Convulsive laughter, whistles, applause; the man farted again. Eddie made another gurgling sound in the back of his throat, lost his balance, and fell. *Plaw plaw plaw.*

Plaw. The sound of a gunshot in the distance. Eddie was afraid; he began to sing. *Shake, rattle, and roll those Yankee bones. Home, home on the range.* He stood up, weaving slightly, into the darkness, out of it. Try to think of another song or something. "Fingerless Powell," he said for no particular reason. Poor Fingerless, dead after first imparting to him the secret of war: they are shooting at each other and we are in the way. That's terrible. Terrible, Eddie concluded. A person could get killed that way. Not if you cover your ass—act harmless, sing, dance. *Ain't we got rhythm.* They don't want to shoot you; it's the others, the Koreans, all of them, and the Chinese, all alike, back and forth across the armistice line. Have to identify yourself, let them know you don't want any trouble; it's all a big mistake; never take sides, just save your Yankee ass. "AMERICAN," Eddie screamed. "AMERICAN . . . OHIO . . . LONE RANGER . . ." Poor Fingerless, his own casualty. Little acts of self-immolation, Americans killing Americans, forgetting to sing, being forced into the middle; it was not safe. Eddie looked into the darkness; they didn't know—no one did —the sheer horrible truth.

"Poor Fingerless. Shot off both thumbs in basic training, put a hole through his foot in combat, and then, a month later, blew off his head. Poor dead dead Fingerless; he never felt at home with his rifle." Eddie choked back a sob; Fingerless had been his friend. It happened all the time, over and over again, but nothing was done.

"They send over more rifles, more ammunition, tanks, portable refrigerators, record players—never fingers or songbooks or explanations: What the fuck are we supposed to be doing? Captain sends in a requisition for fingers. Terrible red tape. Up to the Pentagon. Nothing but red tape, miles of it—and dumb questions. How many? Ten apiece. Also toes. Little ones, big ones, all kinds. How many altogether? Maybe a thousand, maybe more. How about two frozen eyes from a Michigan eye bank? No, fingers, you fool. One little, two little, three little Indians, that kind. They send us a shipment of bazookas—some fairy blows himself up unloading them. Death," Eddie said. "Men are dying." *Plaw plaw plaw,* screams of "BRING ON THE ENTERTAINMENT."

Plaw plaw. More shots. Eddie began to sing again. *Home, home, where seldom is heard a discouraging word.* He crawled down the other side of the hill, came across two abandoned M-1s and a bunch of C-ration tins. Whole place a goddamn junkyard. Keep moving, singing. Come across an abandoned refrigerator, full of empty Coca-Colas, sprouting weeds. Sing. *Home on the range where the deer and the antelope play and John Wayne fucks you all day.*

Shut up.

Shut up while I'm telling you.

"It got rough," Eddie said, glaring into the darkness. "Along with the bazookas they send a new captain. A blond motherfucking climber. Wants to be a general back where it's safe." Eddie didn't like to think about Sturgen. Long meaningless conversations; he began to chant them out from memory:

96

" 'Sir, I have a hangnail. Can I be excused from patrol? Puh-leeese.'

" 'Wise-ass. All you a bunch of no-good wise-asses. This is the worst company I ever saw, but you, you're the worst of the worst, Finney.'

" 'But, sir, I thought you took an interest in our fingers.'

" 'Is this a joke, Finney?'

" 'I don't know what it is. You tell me. And tell my why it isn't ever over, whatever it is.'

" 'Uncle Sam's work is never done.'

" 'Sir, I have exactly as many fingers today as I had yesterday; can I be excused?'

" 'Everyone. Hold out your hands. How many fingers? Count them. One. Two. Ten. That's wonderful. Ten little Indians. Good work, Buffalo Bill. Now let us go over our gun procedures again. Here is our gun, the M-1 rifle. Look at it. Love it. Whose fault is it if it jams or clogs or sticks?'

" 'Ours, sir.'

" 'Should one look into the barrel to see what the trouble is?'

" 'No.'

" 'Stick one's fingers in?'

" 'Never.'

" 'Does the U.S. government issue bad merchandise?'

" 'No.'

" 'Does it train its men well and quickly?'

" 'Yes indeed, sir; we are the best the country has to offer.'

" 'Are we low on fingers?'

" 'Sad to say.'

" 'But our morale is high?'

" 'Oh yes, it is, sir.'

" 'How high?'

" 'We keep the peace and love it, sir.' "

Plaw plaw plaw. Eddie ducked. He was right in the line of fire. A sitting duck, and the captain was pushing him forward, right into the middle, yelling, "Here's our chance for a showdown. Yahoo." Riding off in all directions. Eddie crawled into a broken jeep, alone at last, hiding, but not for long. They saw him. "Hey, rousy fingerress fairy." Eddie sang his song about the deer and the antelope at play, and PLAW. Fired at, for crissake. It was beginning to get really ugly.

Plaw plaw plaw. He was shot. Shirt front was all wet; flamingos were drowning. He stumbled under the impact, looked down, saw a puddle of foam. Christ, look what his blood was doing—foaming. Bubbles of blood. *Plaw.* He staggered again. Blood running all down one side, foaming onto the floor. He began to hallucinate: a nude barmaid with big ugly everything was coming at him, dancing around like a drunken hog. The noise was deafening, and hands were pulling him into the darkness. "I don't want to die in the dark," Eddie said.

"Bum, get out."

"I'm bleeding," Eddie tried to explain. "Foam all over." The door closed behind him. Eddie stumbled, fell to his knees, and began to crawl through the maze of garbage cans. Another goddamn junk heap. Empty beer cans, broken glass, weeds; he came to some gravel, an open space. He tried to crawl faster, but the gravel slowed him up, cut into his hands and legs, then he stopped. What the hell? He'd run into four pairs of legs. He wished he had a gun. Couldn't find it anywhere, the fourth one he'd lost.

"Scab. No one works without payin' their dues."

"Huh?"

A heavy steel-heeled boot came down on his hand, crushing it into the gravel. Eddie crumpled with pain. "American," he whimpered. Feet kicked at his ribs, his back, his gun, his head until the pain in his hand throbbed over his entire body. He clutched at the gravel; it was wet. His mind began to float like a bubble.

Headlights lit up the gravel on either side of his head. Eddie heard a car motor, drunken shouts. They were going to run over him. He tried to move, then the lights disappeared and the car backed away. Dizzy, his hand and head throbbing, Eddie walked down the gravel drive to the highway and began to pick his way over the shoulder, blinded by the lights of oncoming cars.

13 When he opened the door Carol Sue was standing there in a pair of baby doll pajamas; he forgot all about his hand until she asked. "Got roughed up," Eddie said, staring at the quantity of full round belly, thigh, and arm revealed by the pajamas. In the last few years some god of fat had blown Carol Sue up into a plump balloon, and there was something sensual about the plumpness that made his hands reach for it, squeezing two great handfuls of fat. Carol Sue giggled and wiggled free, and Eddie doubled over with pain, his hand a throbbing ache. "Jesus."

"Poor baby," Carol Sue said, and he was suddenly engulfed in flesh, surrounded by quivering fat. With his good hand Eddie reached for the G-string of net pantie, pulling it down and releasing Carol Sue's bottom to its complete fullness. His hand explored its width and then reached for the tent of net that hung from her shoulders, all, he supposed, part of some marriage wardrobe meant to excite Junior Burns to high lust. The thought momentarily unnerved him, and he stood numb before Carol Sue's own attack. She was pulling off his wet beer-soaked shirt, rubbing her belly against his, fondling him, biting his neck. Then the lamp on the table went off, and she was gone.

"Hey," Eddie said.

"Over here," Carol Sue whispered. Eddie moved toward the voice, stumbling over the coffee table and landing next to her on the couch. Some things about Carol Sue had not changed; by now she had dressed again, her bottom once more strapped into the

100

G-string of pantie. Eddie found a prickly bush of hair extended through the net; the net pushed aside easily, exposing the hair and the two soft folds to his hand. Carol Sue giggled again and squirmed out of reach. This time Eddie did not go after her, but he had barely caught his breath when she was back and deftly undoing his pants. While he held his breath, her hands reached through the unzipped opening, exploring him, then she pulled at his pants and shorts. Eddie grabbed again at her exposed bottom and sat her down on his lap: a tingling, shivering, damp weight, positioning itself. He thrust into the opening.

"Carol," a voice called from the back part of the apartment. "Carol."

Eddie groaned softly, disappearing back into himself. "You goddamn little . . ." he said, but Carol Sue held her finger to her lips. He pushed her away.

"Carol, aren't you ready yet?" the voice called in again.

"Howard," she called back in a little-girl voice. "Guess what?"

"What?"

"I'm sick."

Eddie zipped up.

"What do you mean, sick?" the voice, forewarned of doom, called.

"I just got my period," Carol Sue said in a wan little voice.

"I don't care."

"Howard!" Carol Sue said, shocked. "Just for that I'm going to make you go home."

Eddie sat listening to this dialogue with the fatalistic feeling that he was going to suffer for it, but unsure what precautions to take. If only Howard hadn't sounded like such a sap, he would have felt a growing allegiance to him; he had a malicious desire to sit on Carol Sue while Howard finished his encounter with her. But Howard he imagined to be some dog of a Junior Burns hanging around night after night and then being sent home to whimper into his pillow. He probably lived with his aunt and uncle. The poor

101

sucker. The more Eddie thought about it, the less he felt like meeting Howard, not wanting to sit there limp with exhaustion and a broken hand, so that Howard, whoever he was, could return his pity. Carol Sue suddenly pulled him away from this possibility and led him into the kitchen.

"Howard," Carol Sue said, going back to where his voice came from, and there was some muffled bouncing around before the lights came on again in the living room. Eddie heard her giggle and kiss someone wetly several times, and then heard her say, "Mama will wonder where you are." After that Eddie could not resist looking. Howard, his back to the kitchen, was a small, natty little man dressed in a shiny silver suit and cowboy boots. He bore no resemblance to Junior Burns.

The door closed, the lights went off, and Eddie waited. "Who the shit was that?" he asked when Carol Sue's plump body had pressed into him again.

"That's Mama's husband."

"Right out of a rodeo."

"You peeked," Carol Sue said. "Howard says his dress is his signature so his many old fans will recognize him. Howard was once a big country western star and would have been famous if he hadn't lost his voice."

"Yeah. What's he now?"

"He's on parole. Howard says he was in Chillicothe making beautiful music when this man just came out of nowhere and attacked him. Took him completely by surprise and hurt him so bad that he had to go to the hospital. That's where Mama met him. Of course, once Howard saw that he was being attacked he had to protect himself. They shouldn't have put him in jail for that, but they did after the man's wife swore Howard had raped her. It was just her word against his, but they took hers."

"Howard sounds like a real cowboy all right."

"He's been wonderful to me," Carol Sue agreed. "He gave Junior and me fifty dollars for our wedding. I didn't even have to

102

exchange it. Then once when Mama had to work and couldn't go, he took me with him to Dallas on some business. We stayed in the most beautiful motel I've ever seen and had all our meals by room service." Carol Sue sighed dreamily at this beautiful memory. "Sometimes Howard kind of scares me; he has a mean streak, but I never say anything because Mama's just crazy about him. She says he's her little singing dude, and she would love him even if he never had a cent to his name and his voice never did come back after being hurt so bad." Carol Sue's voice choked with emotion, and she leaned desperately against Eddie. "It wasn't beautiful like that with Junior and me. Howard says I just needed more man, and then he says in my case I'm probably always going to need two men; one won't be enough."

His hand was throbbing again, and his head ached, and for one dark moment Eddie thought he was going to faint. In the meantime Carol Sue had lifted the veil from her rotund body and was pushing two enormous stiff-nippled breasts against him and moaning softly. Eddie didn't have the energy to participate or to push her away; he was dizzy, sick. Carol Sue continued her mating call. "Come on," she said, and Eddie followed her into the bedroom. Once his body was stretched across the bed, he knew he was dying. Carol Sue kissed him, her tongue filling his mouth, then his ear.

"It's too late," he said. Home two days and some fucking bastard had already killed him. Waves of pain flooded through his hand and his left arm and his head; then he felt Carol Sue's wet mouth again, rousing him back to life. With some last shudder of energy he rolled over her, almost senseless to what he was doing but aware that the huge shapeless mass of flesh spreading beneath him was perfectly conceived for it.

"Junior says you're a singer too," Carol Sue said later, when it was over.

Eddie passed out.

By morning his hand had swollen grotesquely, and he knew

103

something was broken. Carol Sue was loading a shopping bag with toasters. "What are you doing?" he asked.

"Oh," Carol Sue said, looking around. "I'm taking them back." Eddie held up his swollen hand, seeking sympathy. "You'll have to get Mama to fix it for you."

"Your mother?"

"She's a nurse; she'll get you in for treatment right away." Carol Sue kissed him, and then she and the toasters were gone.

When Eddie got up, he took the name and address Carol Sue had left him and went downtown to the emergency ward. Mrs. Mars, a woman about the size of two Carol Sues, with blue-veined varicose legs, was on duty. She looked at his hand like an authority on hands and led him down to a small waiting room. He had a broken thumb, and the doctor who set it did so quietly while Mrs. Mars kept up an impressive conversation about bones, splints, and calcium deposits. "You're not putting the whole hand in a cast," she observed as though she would never take such a chance.

"It's not a bad break," the doctor said. "Swelling should go down by tomorrow and then there won't be much wrong that won't be quickly healed."

"It's just lucky the whole hand wasn't severely crushed," Mrs. Mars said. "I've seen some bad breaks that didn't look too different."

"If you have any trouble, just call, " the doctor said when he finished.

Mrs. Mars continued her discussion of fractured hands until they were back in the lobby, then she said, "Are you Carol Sue's new boyfriend?"

Eddie was silent, his eye on the revolving door at the end of the room.

"Carol Sue needs someone," Mrs. Mars said. "She gets to depend too much on Howard. Likes to drive Howard crazy. Sometimes Howard just says . . ." Eddie pushed the nearest panel of the revolving door and was outside before she could finish.

It was hot and humid, and he wished he had a car. He bought the morning paper and went into an air-conditioned coffeeshop to read the want ads. There were two pages of job listings, the same jobs listed over and over again, and he didn't understand any of them: tool and die, machinist, lathe operator, assembler. He finally settled on assembler at a plant in Whitehall because they seemed to have three openings and the bus passed nearby.

There were already two men filling out applications in the personnel office when Eddie got there. A woman behind the counter handed him the three-page form and nodded to the table and a chair beside the two men. Eddie went over and sat down. After a set of personal questions—name, age, marital status, health, eyesight, etc.—there were two pages of blanks under the title "Job History" with directions to give "Salary Received" and "Reason for Leaving" for each job listed. The two men beside him, both of them about forty, with thin, drawn faces, were filling out blank after blank. Eddie wrote: "Stockboy Big Boy Grocery—$40 a month," and then, in slightly bolder print: "U.S. Army." He got up and returned the application to the personnel officer, who collected it perfunctorily, placing it on top of a huge pile, and dismissed him. Then, before Eddie had got out the door, she called him back, holding up the blank pages of the application. "But you've never worked as an assembler," she said with amazement.

"No."

"But," the woman said, appalled, "obviously you can't expect to be hired if you've had no experience." She tore the application in two.

The two men were still filling in blanks as Eddie left. Outside he opened up the paper again. There was a listing for a car wash attendant in Whitehall, not too far away, and he walked over.

"Listen," the man in the tiny wet-floored office said, "our turnover here is terrific. You wouldn't believe it if I told you. Come and go, a regular swinging door. Come and go. I won't bore you with

105

it, but see, we get a deal on a three-line ad if we place it by the year."

"You don't actually have a job."

"Believe it or not," the man said, shrugging. "Tomorrow you can't tell, but right now . . ." He followed Eddie outside. "Had an accident?" he asked, looking down at Eddie's hand.

"Mmm. The war."

"The war?" The man stared at him as though he didn't understand. "Oh," he said finally, "you mean you just got out of the army."

Eddie waited for him to ask about the injury. *Plaw plaw plaw.* A moment of glory from an old war movie. *And then two Japs came at me. I picked up a stick.* The man had gone back inside, and Eddie was left jobless in the setting sun. He had exactly sixty dollars; he went back to the apartment.

"Love me," Carol Sue said. She was wearing a fuzzy blue angora sweater and a matching blue skirt, a three-toaster outfit.

"Find a car for me to borrow and I will."

Driving Junior Burns's new car made Eddie feel better. "Fuck you and your goddamn training program," he said to the man who offered him a three-month nonpaying job with a ten-cent store chain. He managed to hold his own in ten similar encounters that day. He did not get a job.

With the use of the car again the next day, he went out to a factory that was looking for a tool and die maker. Sitting at a table in the personnel office with another long application form, Eddie surreptitiously opened the paper to the help wanted list of tool and die makers, then, under "Job History," he carefully copied down the names of all the firms advertising. To accord with this great experience, he upped his age fifteen years to thirty-five. Happily, he returned the application to the man at the counter. The man glanced down at it curiously. "This is quite a job turnover rate, isn't it?" the man said.

"You want someone with a lot of experience, I've got it."

The man sniffed the air, tossing away the application on a pile of rejects. "Actually we have an unwritten policy never to hire anyone with a record of job change more than once every five years."

"What the fuck's the point of all the blanks?" The man backed away as though he thought he was going to be hit. It was tempting.

Eddie drove back downtown to the telephone company; a woman interrogated him about his qualifications for linesman.

"College?"

"No."

The woman closed her book. "Any more we insist upon at least two years of college."

"I had two years of army training," Eddie said, trying to make the two seem equivalent.

"Well, perhaps you could find something in that line again," the woman said.

"Huh?"

The woman stood, dismissing him.

Eddie sat back in the car with the paper. One more and then he had had it. His eye caught a small ad with no headline of capital letters: BE YOUR OWN BOSS, DECIDE YOUR OWN HOURS, OWN A SHARE OF THIS COMPANY AND LET YOUR SALARY REFLECT YOUR BELIEF IN OUR WORK. That sounded more like it. He underlined the address and started the car.

The address led to a small house in the suburbs. A new car sat in the driveway, and when he rang the bell a man answered, squeezing his body into a wedge between the door and the doorframe to prevent Eddie from seeing inside.

"You had an ad in the paper," Eddie said, positive now that he had made a mistake about the address. "A job . . . own hours . . ."

"Oh yes, about the ad," the man said, giving way easily and unlatching the screen. "Come in. Come in." Eddie stepped into the small plain living room. Through an open archway at one end he could see a desk chair pulled up to a large dining room table heaped high with pamphlets and boxes. Around the walls of the dining room were a series of filing cabinets. "I suppose you are interested in Our Work," the man said, motioning Eddie into an overstuffed chair.

"I might be," Eddie said cautiously. "I'm looking for a job anyway."

The man eyed him with a certain amount of suspicion. "How did you happen to answer Our Ad?"

"Just saw it in the paper."

"What have you been working at?"

"Well," Eddie said—he felt more relaxed here, just sitting in a chair in someone's house—"see, I just got out of the army and. . ."

The man slapped his hand down on his knee with enthusiasm. "Isn't that just wonderful. You've been doing Our Work over there, and now you've come back to do it here."

Eddie nodded slowly. "I just saw your ad in the paper and thought maybe . . ."

"Maybe is right," the man said. "You're just the sort of young man this country can be proud of. You've come to the right place because Our Work needs patriots."

Eddie sat silent; he wasn't sure that he was following the man's conversation, but he was pleased by the unexpected flattery and enthusiasm. This might be O.K.

"Now let me just show you something," the man said, going into the dining room and coming back with one of the cartons. He lifted out of the box a small framed picture with an electric cord hanging from it and handed it to Eddie. It was a picture of Christ holding the American flag and standing on a mountain engraved with the words "In God We Trust." "Isn't that a pretty thing?" the man said. "Here, let me show you how it works." He undid the cord and plugged it in. Christ and the flag lit up, and the words "In God We Trust" blinked on and off like a beer ad. "Isn't that something?" the man said and pulled out the cord again. "Brand new; don't want to wear it out."

"You sell them," Eddie guessed with a sinking feeling.

"One dollar and fifty cents apiece," the man said. "Now, this here box holds fifty pictures. I'll sell you the whole box of them for fifty dollars, just about cost—I don't hardly make a penny from this—and it won't probably take you more than a day to sell the whole lot of them. Should make about twenty-five dollars a day free and clear once you get going."

Twenty-five dollars a day. He could probably work seven days a week, maybe do double the business on Sunday; that would be eight hundred dollars a month. Almost one thousand dollars a month. Still, he didn't like the idea of parting with fifty dollars. It sounded like a Remley, something to avoid. Eddie shook his head. "I don't have fifty dollars."

This news seemed to disappoint the man; his face fell momentarily. "I'll tell you what I'm going to do," he said finally, "seeing as how you're a veteran and a fine young man—I wouldn't do it otherwise. I'm going to break up a shipment, give you half a box for twenty-five dollars, then, next time, you can take a whole box. How does that sound?"

Eddie still wasn't crazy about the idea, but then he thought about that twenty-five dollars a day and nodded his head. The man unloaded half the pictures, and Eddie gave him the money for them.

"Now there's one more thing," the man said.

"What?"

"Our Work is Our Religion," the man said piously. "We keep a record of anyone who refuses to buy Trust. Send them all in, names and addresses, to the FBI because in Our Work we have to fight the godless commies who have infiltrated every fabric of American life in their attempt to destroy us."

Eddie nodded, but he found it easier to think about the twenty-five dollars a day.

"That's what some of your soldiers don't know. There's a home front to this war. The commies and their friends, the commie sympathizers, are in the government, the pink pulpit, and even the home." The man was beginning to slur his words, talking fast. "But they're easy to spot—they're godless, all of them—and they're trying to tear down the U.S.A. and force us out of business. Unless we get them first, it will be too late."

Eddie opened the door; he was anxious to get out.

"Say," the man called to him, "I didn't get your name yet—or your number."

"Eddie Sears," Eddie said and gave the old Chittenden address. "Don't have a phone."

When he got back to the apartment, the lights were on and both Carol Sue and Junior were inside, Junior looking somewhat sheepish and uncomfortable. "Did you get a job?"

Eddie nodded, setting down the carton and handing Junior the car keys. "Thanks."

"How much?" Carol Sue asked, getting to the point immediately.

"Twenty-five dollars a day."

"Twenty-five! What union is that?"

"No union."

"Doing what?"

Eddie was not overanxious to talk about that part; he began to fiddle with the bandage on his hand. "Selling some stuff," he said offhandedly. "Pictures."

"That's what's in the box?"

Eddie didn't answer. He tried to think of something to say to Junior.

Carol Sue opened one of the boxes and lifted out a picture. "Kind of a religious thing or something."

"Let me see," Junior said, reaching for it. "You sell these to the Catholics, something like that?"

"Everyone, and if they don't buy one, the guy wants their name and address, says they're communists. He isn't having any of that."

"Oh yeah," Junior Burns said, hitting upon a topic about which he was an authority. "I tell you we don't let them in the union. We got a clause says no electrician can be a communist."

"Then they'd probably like to buy some of these," Eddie said hopefully.

"Well, I don't know about that. If I were you I'd go down to the newspapers or over to the university; there's where you find all your commies."

"But they're not supposed to want to buy them; that would be stupid."

"Even some of those high school teachers, all a bunch of commies," Junior said, expounding on the subject, but Eddie didn't want to listen. He was beginning to lose his mental grasp on twenty-five dollars a day, and that worried him.

It worried him even more the next day and the day after that. By the end of the week he still had not sold a picture. One minister he had gone to see had told him confidentially that it was the sort of thing that only a nigger would buy, but Eddie had doubted it somehow. Besides, he didn't want to be seen hawking Christ over in the old neighborhood. He had tried setting up a street-corner operation in front of a Catholic store with a windowful of Virgin Marys, but the man inside had not looked favorably on the competition and had tried to run him down in his Cadillac. Door to door he had not had much better luck. As soon as they saw he was carrying a box of something, they shut the door in his face. He didn't even find out whether they would or would not have bought one—or anything else about their religion. After he stopped carrying the box up to the door, one woman told him she had never seen such blasphemy, and another woman called the police to come pick him up for selling obscene material. The police took him down to headquarters and finally sold him a peddler's license for ten dollars.

111

He now had an investment of thirty-five dollars; it was costing him money.

Tuesday he tried to return the whole goddamn box and get his money back, but the man was not as friendly this time as he had been on Eddie's first meeting with him, and something pinched and tight in the man made Eddie think he was crazy. He seemed barely under control, almost overcome by some grotesque hysteria, and his face twitched contortedly and then froze in a demented expression. On the dining room table Eddie noticed a half-opened crate of hand grenades. The box still under his arm, Eddie hurriedly professed new determination to succeed in Our Work and left.

That afternoon, taking Junior Burns's suggestion to heart, he went over to the university, walking across a huge lawn filled with lounging students—who, he realized with a kind of shock, were about his age—and into an old brick building. On the second floor he found a row of offices, and in one of the offices, a small pie-faced man with thick glasses and a hat on his head. Eddie pulled out one of his samples, and when the man looked up from his book, stunned speechless by the interruption, Eddie plugged the picture in. "Buck fifty," he said.

"What?" The man did not understand.

"It's a buck fifty."

"I beg your pardon," the man said, leaning back dazed in his chair, "but what might I ask is the meaning of this?"

Eddie was annoyed; goddamn idiot. "I'm selling them for a buck fifty; do you want one or not?"

The man withdrew haughtily behind his book. "If you think I am interested in one of your toys, you are sadly mistaken. Now leave, please. I have work to do." The man continued reading as though Eddie did not exist. Eddie looked at the picture on the desk of a severe hawk-faced woman and two ugly children with mouths full of braces and at an array of pill bottles, then he looked back at the man, whose face was white with fear. There are different ways to be dumb. *Suckers.* Eddie wrote down his name, and then

112

twenty-five other names from the same long line of offices.

That evening Eddie wrote a letter to the editor exposing a number of communists in a certain department of the university and signing the letter E. Sears. "They refuse to hang pictures of Christ or the flag in their offices," Eddie wrote. ATHEISTS TEACH STUDENTS, the paper headlined the letters to the editor column, and for the next few days angry letters of confirmation, demands for explanation, and simple expressions of horror poured in, sometimes enlarging the letters to the editor column to a full page. Several people wrote wondering why their taxes couldn't be spent for flags for the offices instead of salaries for the goddamned commies in the offices. There were continual references to "that great patriot E. Sears," and "E. Sears, a man who could teach the professors something." A radio station with a daytime talk program asked Eddie to come on and entertain the public with more of this controversy.

"I understand, Mr. Sears, that you have the names of certain communists at our state university," the radio announcer began.

"Yes," Eddie said.

"And what do you propose be done about this?"

Eddie had finally hit pay dirt; he explained about the pictures, about how they could be easily converted to plug into a car lighter, about how they were only a buck fifty and could be ordered by mail. The announcer coughed repeatedly throughout this recital and kept trying to interrupt him by saying, "And now, Mr. Sears, let us turn to the problem of . . ." Eddie was not to be diverted. The announcer finally pushed a red button and began talking excitedly about mouthwashes. "Let us remember," the announcer said as though angling for exactly the same buck fifty, "that cleanliness is American, that cleanliness in some circles is thought to be next to Godliness. Let us remember Snell's antiseptic mouthwash."

Eddie found a red button on his side and pushed it. His microphone hummed to life again. Eddie explained that there were only fifty pictures left. "Buy one for a buck fifty and send it to a profes-

113

sor." The men in a glass booth at the side began to wave and signal, and then the program was over.

"You goddamn little huckster," the announcer said.

Seventy-five dollars came in the next day along with a job offer from a club in Cincinnati. "Are you going to be a country western singer now?" Carol Sue asked.

14 Eddie sat on the bare floor of the empty apartment waiting for Carol Sue. It was noon before a horn honked outside, and Eddie went to the door. Carol Sue, sitting at the wheel of a bright red convertible, grinned. "You sure you're not going to miss the furniture?" Eddie asked.

"I was sick of it."

"Want me to drive?"

"No."

Eddie got in on the other side. The seat was hot. "You got a radio too."

"Everything," Carol Sue said. "Air-conditioning . . ."

"An air-conditioned convertible?"

"Why not?"

Eddie shrugged. It was Carol Sue's furniture, Carol Sue's car. "In an open car the air-conditioner would have to cool all the surrounding air—it would have to cool Ohio." This struck Eddie as extremely funny.

"They wouldn't sell them if they didn't work," Carol Sue explained. They were out of Columbus and on the road south now. Eddie leaned back watching the flat farmland go by, the signs alongside thick full fields of grain that said: OHIO STATE AGRICULTURAL EXPERIMENT STATION, the old farmhouses with double doors of colored glass and carved wood, the tree-lined streets of small towns. He was excited. Going down to Cincy—something he'd always wanted to do. He remembered stories he'd heard when he was a kid, sitting nights on the back porch, listening to people

115

talk as they walked up the alley, and that phrase was a refrain—
going down to Cincy—calling up dreams, making music in his
mind. Summer nights, two Negroes lost in the darkness, only their
voices in the air, would talk about going down to Cincy that
weekend, jazzing the words, playing with them, and Eddie would
imagine big sweat-faced blues singers, husky voices shivering with
grief and sorrow, tormented minds enduring just to sing that song,
and afterward, musicians going back to some lonely hotel room,
sinking into emptiness and drugs, surviving more loneliness and
more misery just so they could sweat and sing life into another
crowd. Sometimes two beefy red-faced men in T-shirts would walk
down the alley, drinking beer out of a can and talking about going
down to Cincy; then the words would be like notes plucked from
a guitar, hard and tough, and Eddie would imagine a tent set up
in a vacant lot, a tent filled with tough, hard men and a country
western star who sang hard scrabble and Leavenworth prison.
There would be meanness in the voice, and the singer would be
shifty, scar-faced, and have a way of hitching around at the slight-
est sound as though he were reaching for a gun or a knife, even his
guitar a weapon, letting the crowd know he was a killer, giving
them a thrill just to think about the lengths he'd gone to for
survival. And now Eddie, pride of Columbus, was going down,
going down, going down—a little pigmeat, man, a little geetar, a
little hustle—all for the big count.

The flat farmland stopped, and the country began to get hilly,
then from the top of one hill they saw the river and the city. "Have
you ever been to Cincinnati?" Eddie asked.

"No."

"Just stay on the highway until we see a downtown turnoff." The
highway ran through a Negro district. They stopped at a stoplight
before an old schoolhouse, the play yard filled with Negro kids, and
then slowly, bumper to bumper, went through a small business
district. They were almost to the bridge before they saw the city
center and turned right. "Know where the Cin Cin Club is?" Eddie

116

called out to a man stopped alongside them at a light. The man in the next car shook his head. "Just drive around for a while," Eddie said to Carol Sue. They drove up and down the business district, then through an old part of town, a narrow street lined with by-the-week hotels. "The Cin Cin Club?" Eddie called to an old man sitting at the bus stop.

"See," the old man said. "Down two squares; up the hill."

"They talk funny here."

"They don't want you to think it's Columbus."

At the end of a narrow street lined with more old hotels, small bars, and a few girlie clubs, most of them boarded up, was a large dark flat-roofed club, a padlock and chain across the door. The neon said: C . . . N C . . . N, in broken fragments. "There," Eddie said.

At one time the Cin Cin had been one of the most popular clubs in the city, alternating jazz, blues, and country, Trendly told Eddie. Then, after television, it had changed hands eight times and been closed all last year. Ronald Trendly had bought it a month ago. "The owner had two offers," Trendly said, talking to Eddie in a large room piled high with tables and chairs. "The other guy wanted to put in a parking lot; he wanted to buy the land and charge the owner for removing the Cin Cin. I got the place cheap; the guy was desperate. Now the problem is customers. I've gone into some of the clubs around here on a Saturday night and been alone with the bartender. Unless there's a convention in town, the clubs might as well close down."

"What are you going to do?"

"The club owners are all competing with themselves, hiring expensive talent, big names. For what? None of them have any customers. I'm going to compete with television. That's where I'm going to be smart; I wouldn't pay a nickel for a big name." Trendly slapped his hand down on the bar decisively and laughed as though it were a joke. "I'll tell you my philosophy. You know why people

117

stay home and watch TV instead of going to a club or a movie?"

"Because it's free."

"No," Trendly said. "Because they want to see the ads." He grew excited. "The customer is a consumer; he wants to be sold a bill of goods; it's a moment of belief. You know why women buy cosmetics they never use? They want to think they could be Elizabeth Taylor if they put the stuff on their face, but they don't want to do it and be disappointed. They just buy the stuff; they don't use it—the jars could be empty. You know why they leave their hair up in curlers all the time? Never take it down? They're buying the belief and proclaiming the faith. You get it?"

Yeah, he'd got here too late. He was not going to get to do his magic act—*Here he is, the pride of Columbus. Watch him turn into a singer, a clown, a butterfly. Lonely, winging my way into your heart, birdie, birdie.* "What am I supposed to do?"

"Live TV," Trendly said excitedly. "Think of it. The shows are all going to be free, but you're going to sell souvenirs between the acts. Believe me," Trendly said with great enthusiasm, "today this is the philosophy to have."

While a sign outside read: CLOSED FOR REMODELING, and ads in the Cincinnati paper heralded the "All New Cin Cin Club—FREE SHOWS," Trendly held tryouts and Eddie watched. Girls from the university drama club sang, tap-danced, and played the accordion; bands from one of the local high schools marched back and forth, and members of an adult speech class read dramatically. After careful consideration, Trendly chose eight different acts, approximately one of everything.

"You know how much some of the club owners pay for a headliner?" Trendly asked, sitting down beside Eddie.

Eddie shook his head.

"As much as a grand a week. Now I've got eight acts that would pay me to appear. I may be new at this game, but I'm no fool."

"What did you do before?"

118

"Listen," Trendly confessed, "I'll tell you the truth; I was working for the post office."

Eddie nodded, waited. "And then what happened?" he prompted.

"What do you mean, what happened?"

"What was the truth?"

"That was it. I delivered mail, for crissake. Me, working for the post office. I had no self-respect. Know what I did?"

"What?"

"I lied to my wife. Before we got married, you know. I told her I was in real estate. Then one day she drives by and sees me delivering mail. I couldn't face myself. Fortunately, I'd put away some money and then this came up." Trendly motioned toward the bar. "My wife was about to leave me—didn't want the children to find out, the neighbors—but now, thank God, that's all over. We've moved into a new neighborhood, made new friends."

"I suppose so."

"Funny thing is, I did start out in real estate. It's a touchy subject though—I lost my license."

"Too bad."

"Yeah, but now I'm really in my element. I mean now I can express myself. Once I get this place going I'm going to branch out. Start clubs in Columbus and Cleveland. Louise Enterprises."

"Louise?"

"My wife; that's her name."

When Eddie got back to the hotel room, Carol Sue was, as usual, in the bathtub taking a bubble bath. He had conversation with her:

"Hi."

"You back?"

"Yeah. Taking a bath?"

"Mmm."

Eddie lay down on the bed.

119

"Guess what happened today?" Carol Sue said, splashing around.

"What?"

Carol Sue named a movie star. "She sued for divorce. Isn't that just awful?"

"Yeah."

"He flushed all her jewelry down the toilet and wiped his feet on her fox stole. Of course, he's sick. I knew she shouldn't have married him in the first place. And now right after Tony and Sandra broke up . . ."

Prattle prattle. The bed suddenly tilted, and Eddie rolled downhill toward Carol Sue's fat body, quivering in perfumed readiness. "You'll never do that, will you?"

"Do what?"

"Flush my jewelry down the toilet."

"No. Just forget about it. Try to think of something else."

Friday night the Cin Cin Club finally reopened. Sitting at the bar, Eddie watched the first few customers file in, five-and-dime types attracted by the word "free." They looked at their surroundings suspiciously. "Would you like a cocktail?" Eddie heard the barmaid ask one couple.

"You got any beer?"

"Yes."

"A beer. Nothing for the lady."

Eddie turned back toward the bar; it wasn't going to be easy. The piano player came in and sat down at the bar with him. "You don't look so happy."

"I've had my hand broken for less."

"Yeah?" The piano player licked the end of a homemade cigarette. "Smoke?"

Eddie took the cigarette and passed it back.

"Have you ever seen a more beautiful crowd?" Trendly asked, passing by them.

120

"They're looking better all the time," Eddie agreed. The piano player giggled.

Feeling pleasantly in control of things, Eddie finally walked back to the rear exit and onto the backstage platform. "Ready?" he asked the girl who was to appear first.

"Yeah," she said in a high whine. She was a thin tight girl whose voice reminded Eddie of mice running in the walls at night. She had claimed ten years' experience singing in the Methodist choir and two years' study with a voice coach, but as far as Eddie could tell, the voice coach had done nothing about the voice, just taught the girl to carry a silk handkerchief and fling it into the air dramatically.

"O.K. Here goes," Eddie said. He walked out into the darkness. Halfway across the stage, a blue spot picked him up, temporarily blinding him.

"Hey, you look great blue," a voice at his feet whispered. Eddie laughed so hard he had trouble getting his line out, then decided it wasn't any good anyway. He'd say something better. "Here's another great blue—Georgette Reinhardt." The piano player slapped his hands on the stage; the band giggled. "Another great blue," Eddie said, pleased with his invention. "Another great blue." It cracked him up. The audience tittered uncertainly and finally Georgette Reinhardt fluttered onstage with her handkerchief. Georgette sang "Tea for Two," and Eddie wasn't sure what else, not recognizing any of them. When she was through there was a long silence as though the end had taken the audience by surprise. Finally a smattering of applause could be heard, and Georgette fluttered back into the wings.

"Terrific," Eddie said to her. "They loved it. It's just that they don't applaud at home." Unconsoled, Georgette pushed past him in tears, and Eddie bounced back onto the stage. The spotlight followed behind him for a while, then hit him in the face. Eddie pulled a small piece of rubber from his pocket while the band giggled. Eddie dangled the rubber piece in front of the audience.

121

"This is going to take you by storm." The band began to play suspense music, and Eddie blew into one end of the thing. "No one will want to go home without one." The music reached a frenzied crescendo. "And here it is: the first Georgette Reinhardt balloon." Eddie was convulsed, hilarious. The audience began to laugh uncertainly again. "One buck. Take a Georgette Reinhardt balloon home to the kid."

A bald man who wanted to get up on the stage scrambled forward. "Harry Duncan from Toledo," he said into the microphone. About ten people followed him onto the stage. The bald man blew his balloon up and then stepped on it. There was a loud bang, then loud applause.

"And now," Eddie said when the stage had cleared, "here's Martin Reed to do something with Ping-Pong balls." Martin Reed juggled out, three Ping-Pong balls to his front, then to his side, then to his rear, then between his legs. The audience applauded Eddie's return loudly. Again Eddie reached into his pocket, and there was giddy expectant laughter. "It's a Martin Reed balloon," the piano player called out hysterically. Eddie giggled. Also the band. Also the audience. Everyone laughed. Then Eddie turned his back on the audience and began dramatically removing his coat like a strip artist ready at least to reveal two enormous boobs. The band began a little striptease music. The piano player whistled. Eddie dropped the coat and turned, arms outstretched, to reveal a white T-shirt with MARTIN REED printed in red across the front. "ONLY ONE BUCK," Eddie screamed. "YOUR CHOICE OF COLORS."

By the end of the week they were out of balloons, T-shirts, everything. "I'm ahead of my time," Trendly exulted, then he discovered that he had just broken even. "The problem with this business," he said, "is lack of volume. We'll have to raise the price. From now on everything is five bucks."

"Five bucks! You're out of your mind."

"That's it," Trendly said.

As Eddie walked back to the hotel, he passed the competition, two other clubs in the area, one of them now offering "Souvenir G-Strings; Hot Off the Models," the other "The Secret Underwear of B. Belle—Take It Home to Your Wife." Eddie had no enthusiasm for the evening ahead, and when he got back to the club, the place was still nearly empty. It was nine-thirty before the first show started, playing to a half-empty house that began to boo when Eddie tried to sell them a five-dollar balloon. The second show did not play at all.

"Balloons," Trendly said, "are for baseball games. A penny-ante volume business, that's all."

"Are we going to change the acts?" Eddie asked hopefully.

"What for? I've got no complaint. I just need a new way to sell them."

"Auction them off after each performance," the piano player suggested.

"They're too ugly," Eddie said grimly.

"Listen," Trendly said. "You know how many people attended the Ohio State Fair this year?"

"No."

"Thousands. Millions. And you know who they broke away from their little box to see?"

"Who?"

"The Green Weenie in your bathroom drain."

"Crazy," the piano player said. "Are we going to hire him?"

"He sang a song," Trendly said.

"Crazy."

Eddie sat silently thinking of Martin Reed and his lousy Ping-Pong balls.

"That's the kind of thing people will pay to see. They went wild when Your Diet's Helpmate, the iron concentrate lady, came on. Those are the stars of television. And it's the old movie mag gambit —Lita Lush, glamorous personality, has another side: actually she

123

pines to play Hamlet and is a wonderful cook; her specialty is stuffed grape leaves. Get it?"

"No," Eddie admitted.

"Look," Trendly said impatiently. "Martin Reed, former used car salesman, juggles for you. The woman who sold you a Bayer aspirin sings 'Tea for Two'."

"But they'll know they didn't," Eddie objected. "They won't look the same."

"That's irrelevant. This is art. Art is a matter of illusion."

"Fantastic," the piano player said. "It's all going to be done with magic."

"I've got it—'Surprise All-Stars. From the Bathroom to the Cin Cin. The Talent Behind the Talent. Live at the Cin Cin'."

"I can't believe this," Eddie said.

"I think the guy's a genius," the piano player said. "Besides, it's a job."

The first week of the new show the club was packed. By the second week the audience had dwindled drastically, and by the third it was a disaster. "Basically," Trendly said, "the novelty has worn off. This is a business of constant flux; you have to stay ahead of the game."

"If we could only get rid of that Ping-Pong ball."

"We need surprise. Novelty."

"What do you have in mind this time?"

"It'll be a surprise."

15 Carol Sue lay face down on the bed bored to tears. She wished she had never come to Cincinnati; sometimes she wished she weren't even alive. If she were still in high school, she could drive the new red convertible to school. She would be the center of attraction again just as she had been when she wore her pink angora sweater and rabbit fur collar to class. It gave Carol Sue a little thrill now to think about how she had worn a new outfit every day. Saturdays she would shop with two empty shopping bags, the sales slips still in them, as though she had already made some purchases; then she would try on a dozen skirts, only return eleven, and slip one into an empty shopping bag. She had always looked real cute, so cute that she had been chosen head cheerleader in her sophomore year. Carol Sue saw herself standing on the fifty yard line again in a darling abbreviated version of a football uniform, her two breasts sticking out of the tight knit jersey for the football players to see, kind of hanging out when she bent over or got real excited. Carol Sue chanted some of the old yells to herself; she could remember them all perfectly. After games there had always been a party, and she had always been the most popular girl at the party. A spasm of delight ran through her body just thinking about it: all the boys on the team trying to dance with her, holding her tight then, running their hands over her body and under her angora sweater until she broke away breathless. They'd try to get her to go outside and sit in the car with them; at first she wouldn't, then they'd beg her, and finally she'd go out with the quarterback or one of the halfbacks. In the car the boy would give

125

her a drink of beer and take several swallows himself, and then he'd
be all over her like an animal, pulling at her clothes, kissing her,
feeling her, his hands on her breasts, begging her for it and trying
to do it at the same time. Carol Sue rolled over on the bed shivering
at the memory. She hadn't given in until the end of her junior year,
then one night she'd gone to a drive-in movie with the three most
popular boys in her class. They had a bottle of bourbon and some
Coca-Colas, and they gave her a drink. In the Coca-Cola the liquor
hardly tasted, but afterward she felt warm and happy. Then one
of the boys in the back seat with her had begun to feel her up while
the other two watched and made smart remarks. "Come on, Carol
Sue, you're going to let me be first, aren't you?" They gave her
another Coca-Cola to drink and giggled and watched the movie for
a while, then the first boy got her sweater and brassiere off. They
all had their hands on her breasts, bouncing them up and down,
fighting for them, giggling. The first boy put a nipple in his mouth,
and Carol Sue giggled too. They all sat there laughing. Then, before
she knew it, the boy had got off her skirt and panties. There had
been a stunned admiring silence as all three boys looked at her nude
body, then the one boy pulled off his pants and, while the other two
watched, kneeled over her and stuck himself in between her legs.
The pain, everything, had been over in a minute, and all Carol Sue
could think about was how hot and sweaty and cramped she was.
She tried to get up, but before she could move, one of the other boys
was over her, almost smothering her with his shoulder, and when
he was finished, the third boy, jerking and plunging, and Carol Sue
began to squirm and wiggle beneath the boy, moving herself
against the stiffness of him, tickling the sensation into an explosion,
a great wet spasm. That summer she didn't tease and fight at
parties; then she was voted the most popular girl in her senior class
and was pictured in the yearbook forty-seven times, more than
anyone else. But when the year was over, her mother had nagged
and nagged: "A lot of good it did you. A lot of good. What have
you got to show for it? A yearbook. That's how popular. When I

126

was your age, I was already married for the first time."

It had all ended. That summer Carol Sue had no place to wear her twenty-five sweater sets or her twenty-five matching skirts. She finally got a job, but it wasn't the same—dressing up every day to go to work in the secretarial pool, sitting in a big room full of old women. Then she'd begun to put on weight and had married Junior Burns in desperation. It made her sick just to think about it. She wished she were dead.

Sitting up, she began to flip through *Secret Romance* to see if she had skipped anything. She began to reread the best parts of "Trouble Ahead," a continued story. Beautiful, tall, red-haired Nancy was in love with a brilliant neurosurgeon, but Nancy was not a nurse and that sort of thing never worked out. Carol Sue turned the pages until she found the best part, the moment of conflict, when the neurosurgeon and Nancy were necking in her apartment and the phone rang. Nancy cries and says the neurosurgeon doesn't really love her, but the neurosurgeon says he must perform an emergency operation and leaves anyway. Carol Sue could understand how Nancy felt; she tried to imagine herself necking with a neurosurgeon. She turned over a couple of pages to the end. The neurosurgeon performs a brilliant operation. Afterward, all the assistants and nurses smoke cigarettes and say they've never seen a case like that before. But what Carol Sue liked best was the part where the doctor goes in to see the little boy whose life he has saved and the little boy thanks him and tells him that when he grows up he's going to be a doctor and devote his life to healing Africans. Nancy starts going out with a dumb mechanic. Carol Sue liked stories like that with a moral, where you could see immediately that if the neurosurgeon had slept with Nancy, a little boy would have died and never got to heal any Africans. Maybe she wouldn't sleep with Eddie tonight.

Letting the magazine fall to the floor, Carol Sue rolled over and out of bed. When she was dressed, she walked around the corner to the drugstore and ordered a hot fudge sundae. She watched as the boy stirred up the electrically heated fudge sauce and then ladled it over two scoops of vanilla, shook up a can of whipped cream and sprayed it over the fudge, then put a cherry and some nut crumbs on top. He set the sundae down in front of her, and Carol Sue began to spoon it up eagerly. She didn't know anyone in Cincinnati anyway.

Oh God, but she felt sorry for herself. Of course, if Eddie hadn't come along, she would have gone back with Junior, just because that would have been the easiest thing to do. Then there was Howard. Carol Sue always had difficulty placing Howard in her mind. The first time she'd met Howard was at her mother's wedding, when she and Junior had been the witnesses. Carol Sue had cried and cried then to see how happy her mother was with her fourth husband, and Howard had patted Carol Sue on the arm and held her hand until she'd got herself under control. He had been so sweet. Afterward the wedding party had gone to a motel out on East Broad Street for cake and pink champagne. When they ran out of champagne, Howard suggested that Carol Sue go with him to buy more. Then in the car Howard asked her why she was so unhappy, and Carol Sue broke down and told him about how popular she had been and all. "How popular?" Howard asked, and she told him about the three most popular boys in the class and all the members of the football team, and then, all of a sudden, Howard was making love to her in the parking lot, trying to console her. After that, she and Howard had been real close. She told Howard everything. She even told Howard about one of the salesmen at Mutual, who always asked for her in the secretarial pool and then, when she went to his office, didn't want her to do anything except play with him. That seemed to excite Howard, and he told her she was a love goddess.

What Carol Sue did not like to think about was how Howard seemed to be untrue to her mother. Although, as Howard explained, when a man can't sing or go on doing what he was cut out to do, he needs a lot of diversion just to keep his mind off his

128

troubles. The other thing Carol Sue did not like to think about was how Howard sometime's hurt her, beating her for no reason at all, hitting and slapping at her, kicking her in the stomach, then, when it was all over, telling her it hurt him as much as it hurt her. And sometimes Howard screamed at her, calling her a fat slut, saying she wasn't going to be worth anything unless she lost weight, saying that if she wasn't careful, she'd end up a fat slut like her mother. Howard always explained that he said what he did for her own good, but Carol Sue didn't know about that.

When she finished her hot fudge sundae, Carol Sue bought two peanut clusters for later and then started back to the hotel. In the room again, she took her hair down and then pinned it back up. Some of the hair had slipped out of the curlers during the day. She was still redoing her hair when Eddie came in.

"Want to get something to eat? I've only got an hour."

"Have to watch my diet," she said.

He stood looking at her through the bathroom door, making her nervous. "You think your hair is going to be done for Christmas this year?"

Carol Sue was silent.

"Why don't you give up that diet? You couldn't get any bigger if you ate."

Carol Sue fought back tears, biting her lips, her head down. She heard Eddie walk across the room, heard the door close, then she got back into bed and began to cry. Salt tears rolled down her pink cheeks, and her stomach shook. She wished she were dead; she just wished she were dead.

That night when Eddie returned, she was still lying on top of the bed. Eddie touched her shoulder, and she rolled over to face the wall. He ran his hand down her back, but she didn't move. "Come on," Eddie said. "What's the matter?"

"Nothing. I just don't want to."

"Why not?"

Carol Sue tried to put it in words. "Neurosurgeon," she said.
"Huh?"

She couldn't seem to explain; finally she gave in because she
knew it wasn't going to save a little boy's life anyway. Like everything else she did, it didn't seem to make much difference one way
or another. She didn't know why she went on.

In the morning Carol Sue sat in the dark lobby of the hotel to
the right of four old men who were seated in a circle around a
potted plant, staring at it. She picked up a Cincinnati paper and
read about a murderer in San Francisco who had killed ten people
in a lover's lane. Nothing of interest had happened in Cincinnati,
and she flipped quickly to the back page, where Dr. Heinholz
answered Reader's Queries:

Dear Dr. Heinholz:
   My little boy is 13 and still bites his toenails. What can I do to break
him of the habit?
                                                                Worried Mother

Dr. Heinholz told Worried Mother to see to it that her little boy
wore shoes and took up a hobby. Carol Sue found some comfort
in the fact that she did not bite her toenails. The other letter, signed
"A Fatty," she found vaguely disturbing even though she found it
difficult to identify with anyone who called herself A Fatty. She
decided to write her own letter. Walking over to a desk, she opened
the top drawer and got out a sheet of stationery with HOTEL MUHL,
DAY, WEEK, MONTH printed across the top. "Dear Dr. Heinholz,"
she wrote neatly under "Hotel Muhl"; the rest of her query did not
come as easily. After some thought she added: "Having married
an older electrician who was never much at sports, I am only
. . ." She hunted for the right word and finally decided on "plump."
She read over what she had written thus far, then wadded up the
sheet of paper and took another from the drawer. "Dear Dr. Heinholz," she wrote on the fresh sheet. "Since I was in the yearbook

130

forty-seven times, more than even the captain of the football team, I put on weight." That didn't seem quite right either. She crumpled up the paper and got out still another sheet; she was near tears now. "Dear Dr. Heinholz," she began again. "Not knowing any neurosurgeon intimately since I graduated, I have suffered . . ." Carol Sue tore up the letter in disgust and ran upstairs, tears welling in her eyes. She was still plunged into deep gloom when Eddie returned.

"Look," Eddie said, "why don't you come down to the club with me tonight? You can watch the show; it'll be better than sitting here crying."

At first Carol Sue stood in the wings with Eddie, then, since there were plenty of empty tables, she went out and sat in the audience. The show bored her—some dumb juggler throwing Ping-Pong balls in the air. She turned her attention to a man standing at the bar. The man smiled, and Carol Sue parted her lips enticingly; finally the man started over to her table. "Hi," he said. "Saw you come in with Eddie. I'm Ron Trendly, the owner." He pulled out a chair and sat down. Like the show?"

"It's very nice," Carol Sue said, glancing back at the stage.

"How're you finding Cincinnati now that you've been here awhile?"

Carol Sue moved her chair a little closer and leaned toward Trendly as though she were having trouble hearing him. "Well," she said slowly, "of course, I don't know anyone here or anything like that." She breathed a heavy sigh that pushed her breasts up, out, and almost into Trendly.

There was a pause in the conversation. "Mmm," Trendly said finally; he seemed to have trouble concentrating on the discussion. "Guess it can get pretty lonely . . . new place and all . . ." Carol Sue licked her lips. "But I bet you won't have too much trouble . . ." Trendly swallowed. "Getting acquainted, I mean."

131

Carol Sue smiled. "I think it's just wonderful that you own a nightclub."

"Yeah," Trendly said, sucking in his stomach. "I always looked to be in something creative."

Carol Sue breathed heavily again, squirming slightly in her seat. "I used to be a cheerleader."

"Is that right?" Trendly said foggily, his voice fading. "We'll have to get you for the show sometime." He laughed.

"Howard says I just have a natural talent for movement," Carol Sue said, moving forward until her knees brushed against Trendly's.

"Howard?"

Their knees pressed together tightly. "Howard Mars, the famous country western singer. We're intimate."

"I'd like to have someone of that caliber for the show," Trendly said hoarsely. "I'd certainly like to have someone of that caliber or a cheerleader." His hand dropped to her skirt. Carol Sue giggled, then Trendly's hand moved up under her skirt and she squeezed it between her thighs. "Maybe we could go someplace and talk it over," Trendly suggested. As she got up, Carol Sue's breasts brushed against Trendly, and he grabbed her hand urgently. "Car," he said. "Go out to the car."

Once they were in the car, Carol Sue bit his ear. "Where should we go?" Trendly asked weakly. Carol Sue bit his neck. Trendly pushed her down on the seat, wedging her thick body tightly under the steering wheel. Her legs seemed to fill the air. Trendly squeezed in between, his head and shoulder sticking sideways between her thighs, his face toward the dashboard. "Christ," he said. Carol Sue kicked and tugged herself free of the steering wheel, bruising one leg as she did so, and then Trendly pushed her face down on the seat, mounting her from behind. Just as he began to thrust frantically, Carol Sue collapsed, one knee sliding off the narrow seat onto the floor. "Sit on it," Trendly moaned. "Sit on it." Carol Sue tried. She moved desperately around Trendly, pushing and shoving her

132

hips into place until she collapsed heavily again, her huge weight floundering over the seat. She began to cry.

"O.K.," Trendly said. "O.K. Let's just forget it." Hysterical sobs bawled out of Carol Sue. "Come on," Trendly said. "I've got to get back inside anyway." Carol Sue continued to blubber uncontrollably. She was a has-been. "Look, just forget it," Trendly said. "Maybe some other time." She wished she were dead. She really did.

That night Carol Sue cried herself to sleep, and the next day she spent in the hotel room. Then, late in the afternoon, she asked the desk clerk downstairs for room service. The hotel did not really have room service or a café, but the desk clerk sent the bellhop across the street for her. When the bellhop finally returned and knocked on her door, Carol Sue called for him to come on in. She lay stretched across the bed, naked. After a first glance, the boy stumbled blindly across the room, his eyes averted to the wall. "Sure is a hot day," he said. "Looks like it might rain later though, and that'll be real bad for the Reds." He set the Coca-Cola and the sweet rolls down on the dresser. "Let's see." He paused. "That's a dollar ten." He turned to face Carol Sue again and then fled. Carol Sue asked the desk clerk if he'd like to come up for a while.

"Whole goddamn place smells like sex," Eddie said.

"But," said Carol Sue tearfully.

"But what?"

She sunk her head in the pillow, sobbing, trying to explain. She just never could seem to explain. "I wish I were dead, that's all," she moaned.

"What the hell are you crying for? Aren't you having a good time? Place smells like you'd been having one hell of a ballin'."

"But," Carol Sue moaned, "but you don't understand." Tears rolled from her cheeks onto her chin and down her fat neck.

"Christ," Eddie said, "will you stop that crying." He slammed

133

out the door, and she was alone again. She continued to cry for a while, then she got up and wiped her eyes dry on the bedspread. She felt absolutely desperate. Taking some change from her purse, she started down to the pay phone in the hall.

"Is Howard there?" Carol Sue asked, disguising her voice.

She heard her mother call, then, in a minute, a man's voice came on the line. "What is it?"

"It's Carol Sue."

There was a momentary silence, then a low whirring thud, and Carol Sue knew that Howard had swung the kitchen door shut. "Where the hell you been?"

"Oh, Howard," Carol Sue began. "I'm so miserable."

"So what? That's what you get for runnin' off like that. Can I help it?"

"Oh, Howard," she moaned.

"Where the hell you at anyway?"

"Cincinnati," Carol Sue said. "The Hotel Muhl. Oh, Howard."

There was a long silence. "I'll come down as soon as I can get away." The phone clicked dead, and Carol Sue hung up the receiver.

Turning slightly, she pulled at the door to the phone booth; the door folded halfway back, then jammed into her stomach. Carol Sue drew in her breath, then she pulled the door again, but it wedged tightly against her halfway into the booth. Slowly Carol Sue turned herself around, knocking the receiver off the cradle as she minced around in the small square. In the new position, her back to the phone, she pulled at the door again. It drew halfway into the booth and struck her hip. Carol Sue began to jerk at the door in panic then, forcing it back and forth frantically, rocking the whole phone booth, until, suddenly, in one horrendous jerk, she got the door back, her whole body flattened to one side of the booth. She slipped sideways into the hall, exhausted.

Back in the room, she stared despondently out the window. Howard didn't come. Not until the next day did he come, then he

134

suddenly appeared at the door wearing a Stetson and spurs. "Look at the shape you've let yourself get into," Howard said when she opened the door.

"Love me," Carol Sue said.

"It's enough to disgust a person," Howard continued. "At this rate you're going to outweigh your mother."

"But you love Mama."

"That sow. In a month my parole is up, and there ain't that much of anyone going with me."

"But you said I was a . . ."

"You're fat is what you are," Howard said.

Carol Sue felt dizzy. "If only you'd get your voice back," she pleaded. Howard slapped her across the face. "I just know you could be a big star again," she whined. "I even told Ron Trendly, the famous nightclub owner." Howard stopped hitting her and took off his clothes.

16 The Friday night audience was large, filled with enough out-of-towners to be enthusiastic no matter what, and everything was going well when Eddie started out to announce the specialty act: a former stunt man Trendly had found somewhere who enacted various death throes to a record of gunshots. Eddie tried to think of some reassuring introduction. The night before, at the first burst of gunfire, the audience had panicked, screaming and diving under tables until, finally, someone backstage had taken the record off and Eddie had returned to explain. Now Eddie looked quickly to see if the stunt man was ready; he wasn't there. Eddie looked over at the wing on the other side; a little man in a drugstore-cowboy suit grinned at him. What the hell was he supposed to do? Eddie searched out Trendly in the audience, and Trendly grinned at him from the bar. Eddie searched again for the stunt man and then looked back at the cowboy, who seemed strangely familiar. Even more familiar was the maroon and white bulk behind him. What the hell? The audience was beginning to get restless; hands began to clap slowly, feet to tap. "Now a surprise," Eddie said, his voice dropping into silence. Who? "Former famous," he mumbled. "Famous former western star." He paused. "Howard Mars," he said, remembering Howard's name, but now, staring directly at Carol Sue, he could not think of her name. "And his beautiful assistant," he added.

Not until he got back in the wings again could he remember Carol Sue's name. It was too late; he had a slow sinking feeling as he turned to watch. Carol Sue was wearing what Eddie finally

136

realized was her old cheerleader outfit, maroon and white and at least ten times too small. A roll of fat appeared above and below each breast where the bra cut into her flesh, making it appear that she had six teats. Eddie felt a pained, nauseating desire to rescue her, but Carol Sue was apparently ecstatic. He waited. The audience applauded her appearance wildly, titillated. "Take it *all* off," someone yelled. There was giggling and more applause.

Taking a position at the center of the stage, Carol Sue stuck out both arms jauntily and shook like Jell-o. "H," she screamed suddenly, then, arms apart, fat legs fanning the air in a thundering heavy-footed leap, "O." The audience roared. Leaning over to expose two jiggling fat cheeks of ass, Carol Sue yelled, "W." She jogged back across the floor, the six teats of fat quivering and bouncing with each step. Behind her, Howard Mars strutted back and forth aping her every movement. "A . . . R . . . D," Carol Sue screamed, and Howard Mars stumbled across the floor after her, leaping and bending and screaming in imitation. "HOWARD. HOWARD. HOWARD." The audience began to cheer along with her.

"Take it off, fat lady," a drunk yelled.

"M," Carol Sue called back, bouncing into the air and landing with a thud, then, "A," kicking one leg into the air, "R," lifting the other leg, "S," from a position on the floor. Up in the air again for "MARS." Then, after jiggling from one side of the stage to the other, shrieking, "HOWARD MARS. HOWARD MARS," she leaped into the air, her thighs spread like wings of fat, one last time. "HOWARD MARS." Howard Mars bowed elegantly, and the audience applauded him as though he had just been declared the winner of something.

Howard Mars took a long length of rope attached to his belt and began to twirl it, swinging it out over the floor, stirring up dust, then raising it into the air in a wide loop. Carol Sue stood to one side uncertainly, watching. Suddenly the circle of rope moved toward her and twisted over her head; Carol Sue wiggled across the stage just as the rope dropped over the spot where she had been standing. The audience applauded a near miss, and Carol Sue giggled as Howard Mars drew in the rope and began to circle it over the ground again. The lasso rose and twirled over Carol Sue again as she bounced back across the stage, ducking and running in front of Howard Mars. The audience hooted and clapped. Then, out of breath, Carol Sue again stopped for a minute, and the rope jerked into a knot, just missing her as she danced out of the way, one strand of hair falling over her eye, knocked out of place by the rope. She began to run back and forth in bewilderment.

Howard Mars grinned and drew in the rope. Again he twirled it into the air and out over Carol Sue, following her with it as she danced awkwardly back and forth. Carol Sue stumbled, almost falling, then straightened up to look back at Howard, and in that instant the noose descended, slipping down over her head just as she started to twirl away. Howard Mars jerked the line tight. There was a small strangled grunt which Eddie thought at first came from the audience, but then Carol Sue toppled forward like a dead weight, her hands raised toward her neck, and the audience began to applaud.

Turned into a rose, big red rose.
Plaw.

17 Snow began falling in large thick flakes, floating down slowly and settling wetly on the paved entrance to the street. There was no wind yet, and as the big flakes continued to fall, heavier now, the air grew opaque, white, and tangible, the street barely visible beyond the white curtain. Eddie stood in the open garage doorway watching the snow pile before him, the hot steamy air inside the garage leaving a small wet circle at his feet. Then the first heavy flakes became white pinpricks, and the wind began to blow.

The cars, their lights on now in the afternoon dark, came down the off ramp from the highway a block away and skidded and slid sideways at the corner, not slowing down in time. Eddie waited for two cars to meet at the turn, but then the buildup of snow grew so quickly, drifting all along the street, that even the highway traffic was slowed down; cars began to creep down the off ramp and along the street, almost coming to a dead stop at the corner. Eddie turned his attention back to the garage entrance. Wind had blown snow over the wet patch before him, and a fine powder of white covered his feet just inside the garage. He left a small momentary wet print when he moved. He experimented with this for a minute, exposing a wet footprint and watching the snow slowly cover it again.

The wind blew up around him again, and Eddie looked back out at the street. Drifts of snow lined the road on either side, and now car headlights barely picked out the trail of the car in front before the trail was covered and gone. The snow whirled around the

139

building, around the gas pumps across the way, and circled in the air like a cloud, illuminated now and then over the road by headlights. It was getting cold.

"Look at it. Snow. Ha! It's not a good day for the car wash business, you know what I mean?" Rizik's voice startled him, interrupting for a minute the falling snow, the quiet white. Eddie nodded. "Not a customer. Look at them." Eddie looked at the cars crawling along in each other's tracks. "Their paint is never going to last. That stuff eats right through it. They should get a car wash. Now is the time they should get a car wash. It would be a protective measure, but what do they care? Ha! They'll buy a new car, but they won't get it washed. They won't pay a lousy dollar for the protection it'd give them."

Eddie watched the snow circling in the wind. Patches of snow stuck to the neon CAR WASH sign that extended twenty-five feet in the air to attract the attention of those a block away on the highway. Filtered through the snow, the neon glowed a gentle pink like the mouth of a snow-covered bird perched high out of the storm's way. In the snow everything looked different. The cement that he had stared out over for months suddenly seemed alive; the street and the gas station across the way seemed to have returned to nature; even the cars moving along in a slow close pack seemed alive, and Eddie had a sudden desire to run out into the snow, to let it fall on him, to roll on the ground in the soft whiteness.

"You can't win in weather like this. Who needs it? I should move to California is what I should do. Ha, I should move to California," Rizik repeated. "You know what would happen if I moved to California—and this is the irony." Rizik waved his hand toward the cars creeping along the street. "They'd wash their own cars. Yeah, sure," Rizik said as though Eddie had objected. "Sure; they'd go out Saturday and turn the hose on. Let me tell you, a hose never got a car clean, but what're you going to do about it?" Rizik sighed heavily.

Most of the cars were covered with snow now, an inch packed

over the hood, interrupted then by windshield wipers, and then an inch more covering the top and the rear window. A car just out of the garage and still not snow-covered looked obscene and foreign in the white landscape.

"You have to be crazy to be in this business," Rizik muttered. "Crazy. You can't win. It'll be like this for three months. Snow, nothing but snow. They'll wait until the snow is over before they get their cars washed again." Rizik snorted contemptuously. "Let 'em wait. I'll wait too, and then when they bring their rusty heaps in here again, I'll wash 'em. But I'm not going to stand here all winter watching the snow fall; I can't afford to stay open with no customers. It's killing me. This snow is killing me."

Snow blew up from the street across the drive and into the entranceway. Eddie licked at the evaporating flakes that had settled on his lips and watched the tiny particles flutter delicately up and down on his eyelashes.

"I'm going to go down to Florida for a rest. In this business, what with the turnover and the weather, anyone needs a vacation now and then. Believe me, I wouldn't take a vacation if I didn't need one. You should see what they charge for hotels now. Those hotels think you get rich in this business. Ha!" Rizik snorted with contempt. "It's not funny, not if you're in this business it isn't. Look at them." Rizik kicked a small cloud of snow toward the street. "Don't want to get them washed; want to watch them rust. In the spring I'm going to be washing nothing but rust. A bunch of junk heaps."

Eddie stepped out from under the cover of the doorway. It was closing time. Snow fell on his head. In a minute his head was covered with snow, white with it, and then the snow slowly melted and ran down under the collar of his shirt.

"Wait," Rizik called. "I got your final check here. It includes today," he added magnanimously. "I thought why should I pay him for washing cars today when he didn't wash no cars today, but then I said to myself, 'Is it his fault that he didn't wash no cars?'

141

So," Rizik concluded, "I paid you here for the extra day. You're getting paid here for one day free, for nothing, but that's the way it is in this business."

Eddie stuffed the check into his pocket and began to walk across the snow, sinking deep into the white drifts along the road.

18 Eddie lay on the bed watching the snow fall past the window. The old man in the second floor room across the street was throwing crumbs to a pigeon on the fire escape. Eddie watched him for a minute, then drifted into sleep. When he awoke, the old man was still at his window, still throwing crumbs onto the fire escape, and it was still snowing. Eddie got up and looked down at the traffic on High Street and at the garbage from the old man's window. There were no pigeons now, but the old man was lonely. Eddie had seen him before, setting out the remains of TV dinners for the neighborhood cats. Rats followed him around. Pulling on his jacket, Eddie started down the steps and then headed down the block to the diner on the corner. "Hamburger," Eddie said to the counter boy.

"You want that on the dinner?"

"Yeah."

"Want gravy with it?"

"O.K." Eddie watched the boy scoop up the mashed potatoes with an ice cream dipper.

"Hey, Elroy," the boy said, still intent on piling up mashed potatoes. "You workin' or robbin' now?"

"Both," a thin, pasty-faced kid at the far end of the counter answered. The kid, his back against the wall, grinned, letting the ketchup from his hot dog dribble down his chin. "Old Elroy does it all." He began to punch nervously in the air as though he were boxing someone seated on the next stool. When he saw that Eddie was watching him, he winked, and Eddie turned back to the counter boy, who was squirting gravy over a plateful of potatoes, peas, and a hamburger patty.

"Thanks," Eddie said as the boy set the plate in front of him.

"Somethin' to drink with that?"

"No." Eddie buttered the roll, the bottom of which had already slid into the gravy, and then put it into his mouth.

"Looks like puke, don't it?"

The remark rested in the air for a minute before Eddie realized that it was directed to his meal. He looked over at Elroy, who jabbed at him from the distance.

"Look at this," Elroy said, pulling his half-eaten hot dog from between the bun. He held up the black, wizened bit of frankfurter. "That's been cooking a year. Looks like a turd dipped in ketchup."

"Will you shut that guy up," called one of the two men at the other end of the counter.

"Shut up, Elroy," the counter boy said.

Elroy grinned, his mouth full of hot dog. The two men, wearing overalls, continued drinking their coffee, ignoring him. "Let's go across the street for a couple of beers," one of them said.

"Naw," the other answered. "I've got to get home for dinner."

"Come on. In weather like this, she can't possibly expect you to be on time."

Eddie looked out the front window. The fluorescent light in the diner made the snow on the sidewalk look green.

"Where you workin' now?" the counter boy asked Elroy, sitting down on one of the ice cream bins.

"Around," Elroy said, punching in his direction.

Eddie pushed back his empty plate and stood up. He stacked some change up on the counter and nodded at the counter boy. "Bye now," Elroy called after him. Eddie stood out on the sidewalk for a minute and then started back to his room alone. There he watched the snow and the old man.

In the morning Eddie lay looking up at the ceiling. He counted each flower in the wallpaper pattern, then counted the strips of torn paper, then the water spots; then he just lay there counting in order, saying the numbers to himself, trying to entertain his mind. At noon he gave up and went down for breakfast. After eating, he wandered down the next block to the pool hall. It was empty. He played around for a while, then walked on down to the Garden Theater. Its two shows for adults only didn't open until five. He went back to the room. His feet were wet from the salt slush on the street, and he took off his socks and hung them over the register, then he lay down on the bed and stared up at the ceiling until he fell asleep.

When he woke it was dark. He got dressed and walked to the corner; the diner was empty except for the counter boy. "What's the special tonight?" Eddie asked.

The boy opened one of the stainless steel canisters and looked in. "Stew, I guess."

"O.K."

"Gravy?"

"Yeah."

Eddie was almost finished when Elroy came in. He looked older than he had the day before and, standing, was about the size of an overgrown jockey. Eddie watched him in the counter mirror as he sat down and began to jab the air, throwing his shoulders forward, twisting, and ducking. Eddie put the last of the stew in his mouth and pulled out his wallet. He was down to the check from the car wash now. "Want to cash this for me?"

The counter boy looked at it dubiously, then shrugged. "O.K."

Eddie put the change in his pocket and left. Halfway down the block, a voice stopped him. "Hey." It was Elroy. "It's payday, huh?" Elroy said and winked. Instinctively Eddie reached for his wallet, touching his back pocket. Elroy laughed, jabbed him once lightly in the ribs, and laughed again. "Old Elroy's got a proposition for you." Eddie waited uneasily while Elroy punched at his shadow in the street light. "Just a little short of cash, but long on

145

everything else." Elroy grinned. "If I knew where I could get some cool change though, I could repay it double." Eddie shook his head, and Elroy fell in step beside him, brushing his shoulder. "Look, I just need enough to get into this game tonight," Elroy said in a low voice. "It's a sure thing."

"How do you know that?"

Elroy jabbed at the night air, then turned to display four aces. Almost as quickly as they had appeared, the aces disappeared somewhere in the perpetual motion of Elroy's body. Next Elroy held up the king of spades. "It's a sure thing," he said again.

Eddie was beginning to get the idea of the punch-drunk role. "For you maybe, but not for me."

Elroy grinned. "You come with me. Stay there the whole time." He headed down a side street and Eddie followed, entertaining himself with the deception now.

After they had gone two blocks, Elroy turned into an alley where there were no car tracks and the snow was deep. In the next block, the alley was lined with small dilapidated garages on either side, a series of mud trails crisscrossing the snow. Eddie slipped once in the dark slush and then moved to higher ground, tracking along in a low drift at one side, stepping through the snow crust to the garbage can rubble below. "In here," Elroy said finally. He turned into the back yard of an old frame house. The back porch had either collapsed or been torn off; someone had laid boards across cement blocks for steps. Elroy knocked, and an old man opened the door as far as the chain latch permitted and looked out. A narrow line of light fell across the snow; otherwise the house appeared dark.

"We want to go upstairs," Elroy said.

The old man made no reply, pushing the door shut and then reopening it free of the chain to admit them. Elroy nodded, then started up the stairway on the left. Halfway up, he stopped. "Better let me have that loan now; don't want this to look like a two-way deal." Eddie hesitated, and Elroy winked, punching the air. "It's

146

a sure thing, a sure thing." Eddie handed over the money.

There was only one room upstairs, the windows painted black and the walls lined with old furniture—a bedstead, a bureau, and, in one corner, a roulette wheel; in the middle of the room five men sat at a table playing cards. "Old Elroy's here," Elroy said, flaying the air, sitting down, winking, all at the same time. There were grunts all around and the shuffling whir of cards. Eddie leaned back against the wall and put his hands in his pockets; then he leaned forward and folded his arms across his chest. He began to wiggle his ears. "What's he supposed to be doing?" one of the men asked finally, jerking his head toward Eddie.

"Nothing," Elroy said. "Friend of mine." Eddie rocked back on his heels, a faint smile flickering over his lips. He began to hum quietly.

"He can't just stand there like that; he's making me nervous." The man threw his cards down angrily.

"Listen," Elroy said, "maybe you could go downstairs and wait." He winked, and the five men laughed. Elroy winked again, and the five men laughed harder. It was a big joke.

Eddie started back down the stairs, then, not wanting to meet the old man again, sat down on the steps. The room below, what he could see of it, was empty, but low voices came from the front of the house, and he heard a woman laugh in a high brittle voice. Like scratched glass, it set him on edge. Twenty, thirty minutes went slowly by; then there was a soft knock on the door. Eddie saw the old man open the door a chain's width, heard someone ask, "Where's the action?" and then watched as the old man pushed the door shut again and bolted it. Eddie stood up uncertainly. Outside he heard car doors open, voices, people running. He started up the steps two at a time. The room was deserted; lights flared in through the open windows, and Eddie saw two men squatting on the roof of the porch below. He crawled out the window to join them. Two others had dropped to the ground and now stood in the front yard handcuffed together. Elroy was not to be seen. Slowly Eddie crawled forward over the wet asphalt, trying to get out of the light beamed up from the squad cars below. From the corner he saw a cop lead from the house two women with underwear showing under their open coats, and then he noticed a faint shadow cast over the snow from the next roof. Eddie leaped across, landing on all fours on the flat tar paper just as one of the cops looked out the upstairs window. "Hey, you," the cop yelled. A small circle of light followed Eddie across the flat roof and then picked out Elroy on the far side. "Hey," the cop yelled again.

"Shit." Elroy said. "If you had any smart . . ."

Eddie suspended himself full length from the ledge and let go, dropping soundlessly in the mud. The beam from the flashlight shone overhead, searching the air, and then Elroy dropped to the ground behind him. Eddie ran down the line of houses first, then across the front yards, behind a row of parked cars; he had almost forgotten about Elroy when his voice stopped him. "Come on; the keys are in this one." Eddie hesitated, then remembered his money and started back. He lay flat across the rear seat until Elroy backed up and made a squealing U turn that threw Eddie to the floor. When he raised himself up, he saw a cop running down the street after them.

Eddie sat by the window watching the lights from farmhouses along the road shine on the snow, white and clean in the open country, then he looked down at his mud-caked shoes and pants. "Let's have the money."

Elroy lifted both hands emptily. "I dropped it."

"All of it?"

Elroy nodded.

"What the hell happened? All those aces . . ." Eddie punched the air. "I thought it was a sure thing." He looked out the window, not really caring. "You're holding out on me," he said out of the side of his mouth, tough guy.

"Old Elroy hasn't got a cent. You could search me."

148

"What were you doing in there, for crissake?"

"Losing."

"Bullshit."

"Look, I got to set things up, you know. If I win every hand there's going to be some suspicion, so early I drop everything. Early in the evening I just drop everything. Now they believe I'm a loser, but then my luck turns; at the end I win a bundle 'cause I'm so lucky. Now, like tonight, I didn't have a chance being interrupted like I was. If I hadn't been interrupted, I would have won a bundle later." Elroy reached for something in his pocket. "Don't you worry though, sweetheart, 'cause old Elroy has these." He held up a stack of credit cards.

"Where did you get those?"

"Easy. I was hired to look up the addresses and then send these out to the customers. I just addressed them all to myself and quit. They came in the mail this morning, all ninety-two of them."

Eddie wondered why someone with ninety-two credit cards would be desperate for money, but he did not ask, preferring to look out the window. It had started to snow again; the wind blew a light powder across the highway. In half an hour they were over the Indiana border, and Eddie could see lights in the distance, a twenty-four-hour café. "Let's get something to eat."

"No money."

"You can't charge food on those things?"

"They'd never believe I had a credit card."

"Show it to them."

"They'd get suspicious, ask for identification. I got no identification, just cards."

Eddie thought about that for a while, then asked, "Where are you going to get identification?"

"Look, I don't need any identification once I get some money. Like in New Orleans one time, I had thirty dollars on me, had myself dressed up like a king, and I went into this fancy French restaurant there, ordered wine, big five-course dinner, the works.

149

Now," Elroy said, savoring the moment, "here's where I really played it smart. Left a twenty-buck tip; that immediately established me as no bum. That was all the identification I needed, then I just casually turned the bill over, signed 'Harry L. Walters the Fourth' on the back, and walked out. Nobody said nothin'. That's how much faith they had in me. You got to play it right. Got to be professional."

"Yeah," Eddie said. He wanted to ask how much the bill was, but didn't.

"It's all in the way you do a thing; like with a game, you got to set it up. Old Elroy's been around for a while."

Sleepy, Eddie slipped down in the seat, his head back. Hours later, the sun hit him full force. He yawned. Elroy was driving through the business section of a town. At a downtown stoplight, he turned onto a side street and parked. "Now," Elroy said, "We'll get some clothes here and get rid of the car."

Eddie stood up stiffly in the morning sun. He brushed at the mud on his pants and stomped his feet, sending dry cakes of dirt cascading to the sidewalk. "Let's say we had trouble, had to change a tire on our way in, something like that."

"Look, anyone with a credit card would call a garage. Just leave it to old Elroy; I'll think of somethin'."

They walked around the corner and down to the middle of the block, then pushed through the glass door of a men's store. Eddie ran his hand down a long line of sleeves while a salesman at the back watched edgily and disappeared behind a rear curtain. He returned with another man, obviously the manager, who stepped politely between Eddie and the row of suits. "Something I can do for you?"

"My friend here needs a new suit," Elroy answered, "something for television; he's going to be a guest." The manager looked down at the carpeted floor and at Eddie's shoes. "Publicity stunt," Elroy said. "Must have taken a million pictures running out there in that field."

150

"Well," the manager said, warming up, "and what is your specialty?"

Eddie looked around, waiting for Elroy to answer, then realized that Elroy was silent, and said, "Birds," as his eye swept over the cover of a man's magazine, a hunter and two quail.

"Birds?"

"Mmm." The man seemed to be waiting for more. Eddie began to make noises, blowing through his teeth, his nose, blubbering out of the corner of his mouth. "Bullsprong, tigerthroat," he said, identifying the noises.

"Isn't that interesting," the manager said.

"Mmm."

"Guess you were out calling birds this morning?"

"Mmm."

"Took a million pictures, you know," Elroy said. "A million of them."

"I think I have just the thing for you." The manager held up a heavy gray suit, then picked out a blue shirt and held it alongside.

"That looks all right," Eddie said.

"I don't want you to get into anything too dark . . . I mean for your purposes."

"No," Eddie said.

"I think it will be a perfect fit." He led Eddie back to a small room with a full-length mirror. "What show are you going to be on, 'The Olney Hour'?"

"That's right."

" 'The Olney Hour' is the only hour," the manager said. He chuckled, and Eddie stared at himself in the mirror without satisfaction. He was putting on weight, even his nose looked fat, and his stomach, hanging out over his pants, brought back memories of Carol Sue. He winced. "This will slim you right down," the manager said.

Eddie stripped, baring his teeth toughly, wiggling his ears, then just stood there in a pair of dirty shorts and two different socks.

151

"Maybe I could get some shorts and socks to go with it."

"And shoes?" the manager asked, glancing again at his feet.

"Yeah, those too."

When he had finally changed, he felt uncomfortable. He bent over, stiff and awkward, and gathered up the old clothes. "Maybe you could put these in a sack or something."

"You'll never be sorry," the manager said. "It's a perfect fit."

Eddie walked back out of the dressing room, and Elroy handed him a card. "Joe Reilly," Elroy said in a low voice.

"I'll tell you what," the manager said, returning with the package and stepping behind a desk at the front. "I'll make a deal with you. I'll give you everything a third off, if you'll mention my name, Indy of Terre Haute."

"Half off," Eddie said.

The manager grinned. "That's a little steep."

"For half I'll talk it up big, not just mention it."

"Well," the manager said, "Indy of Terre Haute—I suppose you could work it in several times."

"Every other sentence."

"You won't forget."

"No," Eddie said, sliding the credit card forward.

"This is from an Ohio firm," the manager said, hesitant for a minute, then all smiles and grins. "But of course I know it will be all right, Mr. Reilly," winking.

Eddie nodded. He picked up the package of old clothes and the card and pushed out through the glass door.

"I'll be watching you," the manager called. "Indy of Terre Haute."

"That's right," Eddie called back.

"Now you have credit card written all over you," Elroy said admiringly. Eddie looked at himself in a store window. "And more attractive, a lot thinner, you know what I mean." Elroy brushed beside him as they walked, talking closely to him. "Why don't we go to Hawaii and live it up? Take a vacation." Eddie looked at

152

himself in another window, suspicious.

In the next block, they entered another men's store, going through the same routine. Then, when Elroy stepped behind a curtain with another gray suit, Eddie started for the door. Once outside, he began to run, his new tie flopping in his face and his new shoes pinching. He turned the next corner and headed down a side street, running ridiculously.

19 Only two days ago Wakingi had been stopped by the RCMP and searched; the trunk had been opened, the back seat slid out, everything in the glove compartment thrown on the floor. When the RCMP found no liquor, they threatened him, promising him that there would be a next time and that next time it wouldn't go easy, telling him that he was one Indian they'd remember, one Indian that looked different; and when he still didn't confess, they began to hit him, one of them holding him and the other hitting him back and forth across the face, furious, punishing him for the empty search until he fell senseless into the snow. Now, with his treaty check cashed at the BA station on the highway, Wakingi headed for Kenora to get drunk with friends, to celebrate the only thing he had to celebrate—this month's treaty money—in the only way he had to celebrate. Not more than thirty miles out of Winnipeg, the RCMP stopped him again, searched the car and then him. This time two different policemen found the treaty money and grinned. "And where would you be going with this?" one officer asked, leering at Wakingi, who did not answer. "Were you going anywhere in particular?"

"We know an almost drunk Indian when we see one, like."

"Any Indian that isn't drunk is almost drunk," the other officer said. "Those are the two kinds of Indians."

"Maybe we should arrest him now before he gets in trouble."

Wakingi waited for it to be over, wondering if they would dare take the money from him, but they didn't and finally let him go, following him for fourteen or fifteen miles before making a U turn

154

and heading back to Winnipeg. Wakingi felt faint. All his life he had been holding his breath, filling with hatred like a grotesque balloon. He needed a drink. His mouth was parched and dry, and he licked his lips, but he did not go to Kenora. He drove on another ten miles, and then, impelled by some impulse for survival and freedom, turned off the Trans-Canada onto a narrow paved road and headed toward the border, and dreamland.

There he would be free to get drunk, many times, do many things. He had seen the movies. Last week he had watched an amputee with no legs and only one arm become President, and Wakingi had cried, blubbered drunkenly in the dark, for this brave man who had once been the surgeon of the poor and then had lost both legs and one arm by heroically falling on a bomb in order to save the others in the field hospital. When the old surgeon got back from the war, everyone advised him against running for President, saying that an amputee could not be elected, but the old surgeon had said; "In these perilous times, the nation needs a war hero, not legs and arms. Should the people elect a centipede President?" Wakingi had laughed at that one. The old surgeon was elected President, of course, and the nonbelievers had knelt on the floor and stuffed his empty pants legs with American flags and then wheeled him out before a huge crowd, who had cheered and cheered and cheered. And afterward there had been a cocktail party and a celebration. Wakingi knew it would be better there; he was a believer.

Wakingi looked in the rear-view mirror with the two knit dice hanging from it; the road was deserted. In the back window a plush puppy waggled its head with the movement of the car and blinked its flashlight eyes at the snow; Wakingi watched the puppy in the mirror. The old Ford was Wakingi's only major possession, his home; he had spent a long time decorating it and fixing it up, and he was proud of the way it looked. He had put thick blue seat covers on the front and back seats; he had got a small rug for the floor, and he had bought the little plush puppy and the knit dice

155

and a decal that just said "Stampede" now, the "Calgary" worn off.

Wakingi checked once more to see that the road was clear, then stopped, not more than fifteen miles from the border, before the yellow gate of a forest preserve. The dirt work road was frozen hard now and coated with a light snow. Wakingi walked quickly down a slight incline, opened the gate, drove into the preserve, and then got out again to close the gate. The work road ran for several miles and then ended in a half circle in the center of the preserve; there a narrow footpath led from the work road to the far side of the preserve and Wakingi carefully guided the little car through the low brush and thick foliage of the path. At times he could see nothing through the front window, and he ducked instinctively at the oncoming branches, but aside from one torn windshield wiper and some scratches, the little Ford lugged along unscathed until Wakingi turned it into a narrow space between two trees where it was almost entirely hidden from view. Even if someone were to walk down the path, the little car might go unnoticed. He hated to leave the car, but he could not drive across the border without being stopped and questioned.

Making a knapsack out of an old jacket, Wakingi filled it with a few clothes and trinkets that he kept in the glove compartment. He took a knife and then, looking once again at the plush puppy in the back window, decided to take that too. Then he locked the car and started on foot down the remainder of the path. The car had left tracks in the snow, but it would snow again soon and the tracks would disappear.

At the other end of the preserve was a long, flat prairie expanse, treaty territory, enclosed by the forest in its own emptiness. Wakingi had once brought a girl in here, but she had immediately run away from him and the camping idyll he had planned, and although he had heard her screaming and hysterical as she ran through the woods, he had not run after her. They and the others did not mix; he knew that she had come out of curiosity and would report herself raped. No reason for him to identify himself by going after her.

156

Wakingi turned south again, and by nightfall he was a lone figure walking along the frozen North Dakota prairie almost in reach of the Red River. In an hour he was at the bank, and at a narrows dammed with branches and refuse and frozen solid, he finally crossed to the other side and to the north-south highway. His feet were wet, and he was cold, but it was easier now walking on the cleared highway. There were no cars, and Wakingi saw no lights in the distance; the landscape was barren. Late that night, he came to a roadside turnout. There he built a fire in one of the trash barrels and then bedded down in the washroom, warm for the first time since he had left the car.

In the morning Wakingi took the penknife from his knapsack and walked along the flat fields beside the highway hoping to come across a jackrabbit or a squirrel. He saw one rabbit in the distance, moving along the horizon, and wished he had a gun; everything else seemed to be in hiding against the cold. He had almost decided to give up and go back to the dry footing of the road when he came to a windbreak. A squirrel halfway up one of the trees clung motionless to the bark, listening, its head cocked, and Wakingi moved forward silently, his knife open and ready. In one quick arclike motion, his wrist suddenly propelled the knife toward the target. At almost the same instant the squirrel moved, but the knife caught its fleshy side skin, landing with enough force to pin it to the tree. Wakingi finished the job with a rock, then built a fire and skinned the squirrel; he took a certain pride in this meager activity, forgetting momentarily his hatred, remembering his grandfather, who had told him animal stories as a child and shown him the tracks, the breeding grounds, and the winter places of the animals when those places still existed. Only later had he learned to be embarrassed by the old man and the old ways, the mysterious love of the hunt against the science of death, and then finally to hate himself and his people, even the food he ate. Now the food tasted good, and Wakingi felt happy, free, no longer helpless. And here in the snow, away from their world, he knew the senselessness of it, knew that the treaty money did not buy squirrel meat, only the

157

liquor that was not allowed. Today he would celebrate this moment, using the treaty money as nature intended it be used—for liquor.

With the tail meat in his pocket to chew on later, Wakingi headed back for the highway and then turned south again. Some time later a car came along, blowing up snow dust, and he could see a farmhouse in the distance. Then the farmhouses became more frequent, and he saw the outlines of a granary against the sky. It was another hour before he reached the town, a small northern town with an IGA, a Penney's, a hardware store, but not, so far as he could see, a liquor store. Wakingi lounged against the front steps of the post office wondering if he should ask someone, but a few more buildings along with the granary on the other side of the tracks decided him against it. He continued down Main Street. Alongside a feed store was a small clapboard building housing the local liquor store. A pale, thin girl sat alone behind the counter reading a magazine.

"Whiskey," Wakingi said.

The girl's voice was toneless. "What kind?" she asked.

"Rye whiskey."

The girl dropped out of sight for a minute in a back room and then returned with a bottle. Wakingi pushed a roll of pink, blue, and purple bills toward her. "What's that?" the girl asked, pointing to a two-dollar bill, and moving away slowly as though she thought he was offering her poison.

"For the whiskey."

"It's fake," the girl said in her small, flat voice.

"Take it."

"No."

A tense, desperate anger slowly returned to him; he picked up the money and the bottle and started toward the door. "Here," the girl said. "Here, you can't do that." Wakingi stepped out onto the narrow sidewalk. "Thief," the girl screamed.

"Shut up," Wakingi said, holding the door slightly ajar and

showing his knife to the girl. She ran into the back room, and then Wakingi began to run too, hurrying down a side street until the side street led into a field and then loping across the field, farther and farther into the flat distance. He avoided the road now, moving instead along a post line in the snow.

He wasn't sure how long he had been running or how far he was from the town when he came to a partially dry gully, protected from the wind and hidden by brush. Wakingi sank to his knees and opened the bottle. He held the warm liquid in his mouth a minute, rolled it over and under his tongue, then let it flood his throat, hot and comforting. He had almost forgotten the feel of it, the taste. He took another drink, tipping back the bottle, filling his mouth, remembering another time in Kenora two years ago. He and a friend had gone to a movie and, after the movie, to the diner next to the Shell station at the edge of town, and after that had started walking back along the water's edge. Not too far from an old private dock, they found an abandoned canoe with a broken paddle alongside it in the weeds. It was just after the spring thaw, still cold, and the cottages on the big island had not been opened for the summer yet. With the broken paddle, it had taken them almost an hour to cross the lake, guided by the light from the buildings along the highway.

They docked the canoe in the brush on the island and then walked up a steep path to a cottage hidden among the trees. It was boarded over and shuttered for the winter, but they found one shutter battered loose by the wind and broke in there. Inside they found the furniture drawn together in the center of the living room and sheeted over, and, in a low cupboard, they found a small supply of liquor. Wakingi filled his mouth with whiskey now, remembering that luxury, his first experience with it, remembering how they had built a fire in the fireplace, burning the sheets, and how they had sat there late drinking whiskey from water glasses.

When the fire had finally smoldered out, they had ransacked the house for treasure, taking two beer mugs. Then, in high spirits and

159

loaded down with the liquor and the mugs, they had returned to the canoe and rowed drunkenly back toward Kenora and the highway. Not far from the shore, they lost the little stub of a paddle, and then had sat drinking from their supply and singing happily until the OPP picked them up and took them to jail. This Wakingi remembered with renewed bitterness; he took another long drink, clouding his memory, another, sinking him slowly into sleep.

Wakingi did not notice anything again until he heard the dogs. They were baying in the distance; they were tracking him. Gathering his knapsack, Wakingi moved unsteadily through the underbrush and began to run; the sound of the dogs seemed to encircle him. They had his scent; if they found him, they would hold him until the men came with their guns. Wakingi took out his knife and, holding it open and ready for the dogs, ran again with all the energy he had, following a zigzag path through the field. He hoped he would run into water again, but the land seemed to spread out flat, even, dry, and treeless. He could not lose them here, and there was no chance that he could outrun them; he was beginning to tire. He stopped for a minute, but the baying of the dogs did not let him linger long. Sweat beaded on his forehead, and his mouth and throat felt dry.

The farther south he went, the more sparse the brush, and Wakingi was now running out in the open snow. He could still hear the dogs, but they seemed to have dropped back some, their sound a little more distant. Wakingi relaxed; then he heard a shot, a high echoing whistle like the sound of the wind changing direction, and he knew that they were closer than he thought. He fell flat, crawling across frozen ground for a while, his hands ice, and his mind filled with rage: it was the same everywhere. An uncontrollable hatred pushed him on, out in the open again, running desperately. He still could not see the dogs or the men, but two more shots rang out in the distance, and Wakingi fell flat again, ready to cry. He was being hunted down like an animal to be shot in the snow. A

160

haunting silence seemed to sneak up on him and fill him with fear. Then, looking back, he saw something red far in the distance; they wore red uniforms and they were almost on him. Wakingi felt like screaming for help, crying out in terror, but instead he began to run again, running without any thought at all, just running.

After a while he thought he saw a building, several of them, barns, a house. Wakingi changed direction slightly, heading for the buildings. He moved in a crouch, darting this way and that, reminded of the urgency by the dogs. As the house and the barns came closer to view, he saw that there were no cars or trucks in the yard, no sign of life to the house; and he began to run openly toward the back door. Perhaps he would find a gun and some food. The dogs seemed more distant; he was gaining on them, and now he could arm himself. Relieved, he ran up the gravel road and into the rear yard.

The porch sagged under his footsteps; the back door swung open easily. Wakingi stood for a minute looking back in the direction he had come, half expecting the men and the dogs to appear; when they didn't, he locked the door behind him and turned to hunt for a gun. He pulled out all the drawers in the kitchen, took an apple and some cheese from the icebox, and then began to search the rest of the downstairs. The house was sparsely furnished, almost empty, and Wakingi found nothing. Finally he started upstairs. There, in the first bedroom on his right, he pulled out the drawer of a small nightstand; it contained a Bible and a small revolver. Wakingi checked; it was loaded. He started downstairs, then, hearing a noise from another of the upstairs rooms, stopped. With the gun out, he moved slowly down the hall, pushing open doors. In the end bedroom a little girl, maybe twelve years old, sat on the floor, a rope around her waist tying her loosely to the bedstead. The girl bubbled like a baby, her lips barely under control.

161

"Daddy," she said, looking up at Wakingi.

Outside the dogs began to bark in a close pack, and Wakingi thought he heard voices now. "Come on," he said to the girl, who was crawling toward him, drooling.

20 Eddie walked backward, waving at cars as they approached, swerved around him, and continued on. Finally a car slowed down, then pulled to a stop on the shoulder several hundred feet ahead. Eddie ran to meet it. The back seat was stacked with sample cases, and the driver, a red-faced fat man, seemed to fill the front seat. "You a salesman?" Eddie asked, squeezing in beside the fat man.

"That's right. One of those traveling salesmen. Just like in the jokes." The fat man giggled, snorted through his nose, and then winked at Eddie. "I guess you've heard the jokes." His head was bald except for a fringe of baby hair in the back, and he began to mop the freckled bald spot with a bandanna, sponging up beads of sweat. "But I've lived them," the fat man added. "I am a living joke." He giggled again, and again began to mop his head. "Whole life has been a dirty joke. I should write a book. I got a million stories. A million. Once in Indiana I ran into these two twins, Fora and Afta. Course I didn't know then they were twins, see, and the one of them says, if I step out to the barn she has a lot of somethin' I might be interested in. You're telling me. I jammed her in the hay there until I'd gone through both ends twice. Go back out to the car, and there's the other one, ready to go, been priming herself on the aerial, and she says, 'I got a lot of somethin' you might be interested in,' and I say . . ."

Eddie looked out the window, only half listening as the fat man continued through an endless series of jokes. "Tell you about a beautiful redhead I met. I mean this girl was beeeeoootiful. I'm

163

telling you. And refined. She was Lady Beautiful. Come from a real good family there in Indianapolis, went on to school there, studied history, but had a few quirks, know what I mean?" He giggled. "Well, I met her one night in one of those clubs, got her back to the motel, and, so help me God, she was tattooed, right on the belly. A beautiful girl like that tattooed on the belly. But listen, you know what she had tattooed on her?" Eddie shook his head. "Abe Lincoln. She had a picture of Abe Lincoln tattooed there on her belly and—get this—she tells me she goes to a barber every week and gets her pussy trimmed into a beard. Had her pussy all done up like Lincoln's beard; tattoo has a beard. I'm telling you, every time I see a five-dollar bill, I get a hard on." The fat man snorted and mopped his head. He smelled like sweat.

"What do you sell?" Eddie asked in the moment of silence.

"Ladies' lingerie. Lawnjeray," the fat man repeated as though that were the best joke of all. He giggled excitedly. "Wanna see a sample?" He laughed until he choked, then rolled down the window and spit a huge gob of phlegm onto the highway. "Here," he said, unbuttoning his shirt. Eddie watched as he revealed a black net brassiere stretched flat across the two hair-circled nipples on his otherwise hairless chest; the two black net tits hung down limply. "There are bikini panties to match," the fat man said, winking. "I model the stuff. Some of my customers get a kick out of it."

"I suppose so."

"It gets their attention; that's the whole story to success. Little gag like that is sheer genius, a real good come-on, and that's salesmanship, that's the whole story. I remember the time I was selling novelty items." The fat man nudged Eddie with his elbow. "Novelty items," he repeated. "'Know what I mean? Rubber novelty items." He wiped his head and blew his nose like a horn. "I'm telling you I always tested the product, then, see, I'd go up to a prospective customer and say, 'Listen, I'll tell you what I did with it. Ran into these two twins the other day, Fora and Afta, and . . .'"

164

Eddie was tired; he slipped slowly down in the seat, his head against the cold window. "Then he'd be begging me for it, begging me for it," the fat man was saying. "Begging me for it." Eddie's eyes closed for a minute, his head nodded, and the fat man's voice droned into a silent hum. When he opened his eyes, some time later, the man was still talking. "That was about '59, and I was both selling and delivering. I'd drive out to some old farmhouse, and the wife would come out, ask me what I wanted. I'd say, nice as you please, 'Got a little business with your old man. Don't suppose you could tell me where to find him?' Then she'd get suspicious. 'What kinda business?' she'd ask. I'd smile at that, say, 'I was just out here to demonstrate this here new product. Don't suppose you'd like to see the demonstration yourself?' " The fat man whooped with laughter, and Eddie began to nod again; his head dropped, slid against the window, then away from it, rocking back and forth with the movement of the car. He heard the fat man giggle once more, and then he was asleep.

Several hours later, the car stopped suddenly. Eddie woke, blinded by the snow and the sun, slightly confused. Nothing but empty highway ahead, snow on all sides. He looked over at the fat man, who was watching something in the rear-view mirror, then turned back to see a small dark figure running down the edge of the highway toward them. The stranger had a knapsack and looked Mexican, or maybe Indian. Pulling open the back door, he pushed aside a stack of sample cases and slumped down. "Somebody sure to hell left you off in the middle of nowhere," the fat man said.

The stranger grunted.

Eddie put his hand up to shield his eyes from the low sun, then turned around in his seat. "Where you from?" he asked the stranger, but the stranger just stared out the window, his hands shoved in his pockets, absorbed in his own sullen thoughts.

Eddie faced front again, his hand still shielding his eyes. The fat man had begun to tell his stories to the stranger in the back seat, and Eddie fell silent, oblivious. He stared at the road ahead shining

165

like tinsel in the snow; then he began to nod sleepily. Something cold and sharp woke him. Shifting sideways, he saw a gun just behind his ear.

"Take off your clothes," the stranger ordered.

" 'Listen,' I said to her, 'I've got a little item here that'd make Lincoln's beard stand on end.' "

"Shut up."

The fat man coughed nervously. "And this'll kill you—she says . . ."

"Shut up." The fat man began to mop his head frantically. "Just drive," the stranger said, giving the fat man a poke with the gun.

Eddie sat silent, hesitating, then felt the gun again at his neck and heard the safety flicked off. He began to take off the new suit, first the coat and then the pants. "Give them back here," the stranger ordered. Eddie dropped the suit behind him. "Everything," the stranger said, nudging him with the gun. Eddie took off his shoes. "Everything." He took off his shorts and socks, then he sat naked staring out the window at the snow. Beside him, the fat man was gripping the wheel in panic, working his lips silently. They drove on for another hour before the stranger said, "Here. Stop here."

The fat man slowed down, mopping his head and hiccuping. "I won't say a word about this," he whined. "Just drive on like nothing happened. Won't say a word. Just let you two off to settle your . . ."

"Shut up," the stranger said.

"Mupp," the fat man burped.

The stranger nudged him sharply with the gun, and then the car came to an abrupt halt. Eddie slid forward into the dashboard. "Get out." Eddie waited for the gun to single him out, then he opened the door. His bare feet stuck to the pavement like adhesive, and his body grew numb immediately. As the car started back down the highway, Eddie began to run, moving both his arms and his legs to keep warm. It was getting dark now, and it was fifteen

166

minutes before a car, its low beam on, passed him without notice. There was nothing again until a station wagon slowed down suddenly and four grinning faces bared their teeth and yelled obscenities from behind closed windows. Horn emitting one long blare, the station wagon moved on. Finally a car coming from the other direction flashed its lights, passed him going fast, then made a noisy U turn through the center divide and started back toward him. Eddie waved sheepishly and began to run backward, but when the car slowed down, creeping along behind him at his speed, he started to run in earnest, moving onto the shoulder, ready to move into the snow in the drainage ditch. A siren stopped him, and he turned and waited for the two highway patrolmen to draw even.

They drove in silence past the edge of a town and then to a police station where, after three hours of waiting, he was led into a small room. At the far end were three dark shadows in the bright light; Eddie squinted at the policemen. There were two hours of questions, then someone brought in coffee and sandwiches, the first food he had had all day. He relaxed a little. The three men smiled at him, watched him chew. Afterward, there were more of the same questions.

"All right, now what did you do with the little girl?"

"What little girl?" Eddie asked again.

"The little farm girl."

"What little farm girl?"

"Little girl about twelve."

Eddie shook his head sleepily.

"Did you rape her?" The policeman smirked.

"No. I haven't raped anyone."

"She was simple, you know; whatever you did to her will be considered rape under the circumstances."

"I didn't do anything," Eddie protested tiredly.

"Were you impotent?" One of the shadows smirked. *The Shadows know. Heh heh.*

167

"No."

"You didn't try to rape her?"

"No."

"But you thought about raping her? You conspired to commit rape?"

Eddie shook his head. "I don't understand."

"In your mind," the policeman explained. "You did it in your head." He leered and licked his lips. "Suppose you tell us all about it. You dragged her out from the house at gunpoint, then what did you do?"

"I didn't do anything," Eddie said in a voice that was barely under control.

"What did you think about doing? What did you feel like doing? What did you want to do? What did you do in your head? What did you do to her in your mind?"

"Nothing!" Eddie shouted. "Nothing."

"But you did drag her from the house and into the weeds?"

"No."

"We have an eyewitness account. Two hunters saw you take her from the house at gunpoint."

Eddie shook his head; he was too tired to reply.

"They got a good look at you too; we have a complete description—an Indian dressed in Levi's and carrying a . . ."

"An Indian? I'm not an Indian, for crissake, and I wasn't wearing Levi's . . ."

"Yes," the policeman said, smiling crookedly. "If nothing else, we can hold you for destroying evidence."

"What evidence?"

"Your clothing."

"It was stolen."

"Suppose you tell us about that." The three shadows licked their lips, waiting eagerly.

"I was hitchhiking, I told you. I hitched a ride with this traveling salesman and rode with him all afternoon."

168

The three shadows exchanged glances. "Could you describe this salesman?"

"He was fat," Eddie said, trying to think of something more distinctive, a tattoo, something. "And he was wearing a black net brassiere and a matching pair of bikini panties."

The three policemen snickered. "Go on."

"He sold ladies' underwear," Eddie explained, "and modeled it himself."

"And was it with him you conspired?"

"Conspired to what?"

"To rape this little girl. Did he hold her down while you had intercourse? Did he watch you have sexual intercourse with her? Did you both take her? You before and him after? Force her to . . ."

"There was no girl. The salesman stopped and picked up another hitchhiker, male, maybe an Indian. This guy, whoever he was, pulled a gun and took my clothes, then they left me at the side of the road. This hitchhiker forced the salesman to keep driving."

"Well," one of the policemen said, smirking, "there are good Indians and there are bad Indians."

"I am not an Indian," Eddie repeated forcefully, gritting his teeth.

"But you were barefoot."

"All my clothes were stolen, I've told you."

"And I suppose you do drink?"

"Yes."

"Then, by analogy, you are an Indian."

Eddie controlled himself. Through clenched teeth he said, "No."

"There are only two alternatives—either you are or you aren't. Either way, we have enough to hold you. If you're an Indian, you are guilty of destroying evidence in order to disguise yourself. If you are not an Indian, then you're not in disguise and are guilty of exposing yourself in public."

169

"This must be some kind of a joke."

"It's no laughing matter. You'll need a lawyer."

Eddie lay on the cot in the small square cell, staring at the ceiling and waiting for the lawyer. Finally footsteps echoed down the length of the cement block, and a man dressed exactly as Eddie had been the day before, in a gray suit, a blue shirt, and a striped tie, was admitted to the cell. Eddie stared at him. "Where did you get those clothes?"

"What?" the lawyer asked, sitting stiffly on the cot.

"That suit? Where did you get it?"

"I bought it."

"From whom?"

"I don't really remember."

"I had a suit like that once."

"Mmm," the lawyer said. "Actually I don't think this discussion is getting us very far. I'm quite busy, so suppose you just answer a few questions. Job?"

Eddie shook his head.

"You're unemployed?"

"Yes."

"That won't make things any easier. What was your last job?"

"Car wash."

"How long did you work there?"

"About a year."

"And before that?"

"Nightclub MC."

"How long did that last?"

"I don't remember. Not too long."

"Haven't you ever been steadily employed?"

"I guess not. I was in the army for a couple of years."

"We can't use that. That makes you sound like a trained killer, someone who knows how to use a gun." The lawyer shook his head. "Well," he said, "under the circumstances, I think the only thing we can do is plead insanity."

"Are you crazy?"

"You appear to be completely unstable; it'll be an easy case to win. The jury will think you are completely unstable, I know that. An insanity plea is our only hope."

"But what about the girl? What about the rape business? What about all that?"

The lawyer nodded. "She was found late last night in a bus depot in Nebraska."

"Well, then," Eddie said, relieved.

"She was wearing a wedding ring and a corsage."

"So it's all right. She just ran off and got married."

"When the doctor examined her, he found she was two months pregnant. She had no idea how she got to Nebraska; she's an idiot, you know."

Eddie shrugged. "I don't know anything about her. All I know is that now there's no reason to hold me."

The lawyer smiled patiently as though he were dealing with a child. "Raping a pregnant woman," he said, "that's brutal. They'll hang you."

"But no one was raped. I wasn't in Nebraska; I don't know anything about this farm girl; and now she's gotten married. I'm innocent of everything, and I'm not insane."

"I'm afraid," the lawyer said, "that you don't understand. You were found walking down the highway stark naked, and you confess that your clothes were stolen by a traveling salesman in a brassiere and panties. No jury in the world would believe that. They'll think you're insane."

"So what?"

"So that's what we'll plead."

"I think," Eddie said, "that I'd like to have another lawyer."

"Well," the lawyer said, "you may be able to get another lawyer, but you won't be able to get another opinion. Insanity is the only obvious plea. We all went to the same school; we'll all tell you the same thing." The lawyer smiled sympathetically. "I'll tell you what —just have faith in me. Insanity is going to be a snap to prove, and you'll be out of here in no time, just as soon as you're well. Believe me."

"I'm not sick."

"Just have faith."

Eddie felt sick. He watched the gray-suited lawyer depart, then watched him through the bars as he went up the corridor before calling, "Where did you get my clothes?"

"You wouldn't ask questions like that if you weren't sick."

"That's my suit," Eddie called. "I was going to wear it on TV."

"You must be completely mad."

PART THREE

21 Eddie sat contentedly in the sand not very far away watching them change the tire. Their words were lost in the quiet desert air, but he knew they were fighting, and that if he went over to help with the tire, he would get involved, be asked to take sides. In the distance the purple mountains looked exactly as they had in the old calendar pictures his grandparents had saved and pinned on the wall, proof of something they had never seen. Some sand blew up around him, then settled down again, and the hot still calm returned, lonely and peaceful. Eddie looked back at the car again; they had finished changing the tire now, and he got up and started back to the road.

"A lot of help you are," Honey greeted him.

"It looked like you two were doing all right. I didn't want to tamper with success."

"Success!" Honey snorted. "Charles has never been a success at anything—even changing tires. I had to stand there and tell him what to do. I've always carried him. I'm the only one in this group that's ever been on top."

"And she was too, right up there with the best," Charles said obediently.

They were back in the car now, headed again for Reno. "That was six years ago, and I got a gold record for 'Lie, Mama, Lie.'" Honey turned around in the front seat to look back at him. "Did you ever hear my original version of that?"

Eddie shook his head. It was her stock remember-me number, and Eddie had heard it and the falsetto jabber that was her singing

175

style more times than he cared to think about. He hoped to hell he never got booked with Honey again.

"I always liked the original version, but things have changed now, and if you want to stay on top, you have to change too." Honey looked meaningfully at Charles. "What I need is a partner who's not afraid to swing with the times. I'm sick of being dragged down by someone else."

"Honey, now you know none of this can be blamed on me."

"Two months in eastern Oregon and western Nevada singing to the local sheepherders and a couple of tourists on their way back east. Christ! But if it weren't for me, you couldn't get booked at all, couldn't even play the bars; it's my name they remember."

Eddie listened to them bicker, watching Charles pull himself into a sullen shell while Honey attacked. Honey was about twenty-eight, a has-been since she was twenty-two; Charles was a little older, about his age, and too old to stand much chance of ever being a pop idol again. Their voices, high-pitched and staccato, continued to lick back and forth with accusations, and Eddie stopped listening, turning his attention to the horizon, a distant, level calm. Then, in a moment of front-seat truce, Honey turned back to him. "Were you in Hollywood before?"

The question startled him. "No, I've never been in California."

"I thought maybe you used to be in a western series."

"No."

"What did you do? You've never said."

"Not much. I washed dishes for a while, night-clerked, bartended." Eddie shrugged.

"How come they call you Crazy Eddie?"

"Just a nickname."

"Something from the past?"

"I don't think about it much."

"Who's the guy that books you, Tony Montana?"

"Yes."

"I once heard that Montana made a mint by hiring ex-cons and lunatics and palming them off as entertainers."

"Honey, for God's sake, it's none of your business."

"That's what I heard," Honey said. "I heard he was a real slick operator. I didn't make it up." She looked back at Eddie. "How did you meet Montana anyway?"

"I was bartending in a hotel in Elko. I used to do card tricks, play off the customers, clown around. Montana saw me and offered me a job."

"Clowning—is that supposed to describe your act?"

"Honey!"

"Well, let's face it," Honey said bitterly. "Being booked with him is about as much help as being booked with an animal act."

"Any animal that heard you sing would probably revert to nature and tear you limb from limb."

Honey smiled. "And what do clowns do when they revert to nature?"

The question went unanswered, and they lapsed into silence behind a car and trailer transporting a sheepherder's hut to better pasture. The trailer swayed back and forth across the narrow road, forcing them almost to a standstill, then they were creeping slowly across a sea of salt, a blinding white in the sun. "Go ahead and pass," Honey said. Charles pulled into the left lane, just beyond a small DUST HAZARD sign posted on the shoulder. Ahead the road was entirely lost in a cloud of salt and sand, the air as white as the ground. Instantly they lost sight of the trailer and the hut, blinded. "Jesus Christ," Honey said, as Charles eased slowly back to the right in the white darkness. One tire hit gravel, pulling the car, making them spin out a little, momentarily out of control, then they were back securely on hard surface with something moving slowly toward them from the other direction. Charles again veered to the right away from the oncoming car, again hit gravel and threw them forward in a sudden lurch as he applied the brake and bucked back onto the concrete. "Jesus Christ, will you watch what you're doing?"

177

"I can't see a damn thing. Maybe you'd like to drive for a while?"

"No."

"Then shut up."

The dust settled and they were in the clear hot sun again, not more than a car's length ahead of the sheepherder's transport. A pickup truck driving over the salt flat passed them, the three men in the front seat covered with powdered dust and looking as cadaverous as bones bleached in the desert. Charles stepped on the gas and in another ten minutes they were in Salt Wells—four old sheds, five cars, and a Coors beer sign.

"Can you imagine anyone actually living out here?"

Eddie looked at the lone gas pump and the old bar-café. "There are probably worse things."

"When I was on top, we had a Roman villa with two fountains, a heart-shaped swimming pool, a barbecue pavilion, a Japanese teahouse, and an artificial waterfall on the grounds."

"Sounds like a Reno motel—except they have wedding chapels too."

Honey looked at Eddie with contempt. "You've never been on top, and you'll never know what it's like."

"On top of what? Not you, Honey. Never."

"Will you two shut up?"

"Oh, Charles, you're so strong and commanding," Honey said in mock awe, then she looked back at Eddie. "Charles is my accompanist. He even accompanies me to bed." She smiled sweetly. "But right now I could use a new accompanist, some clown who could get it up again."

"I said shut up!"

"I wasn't listening."

Eddie turned back to the window. They were just outside Fallon now, a narrow strip of irrigated valley, lush alfalfa, and a few fruit trees. They drove past several blocks of farm equipment displays, an old fairgrounds, and a series of trailer parks, then they were

178

through town, on the other side of the valley, and moving faster.

"You know, someone told me you were once charged with rape."

"Don't worry; I'm very particular about who I rape."

"They said you were accused of raping a little girl."

"Honey," Charles cautioned, "I'd leave well enough alone."

"Don't worry; I can take care of myself."

"You don't even know whether he's armed," Charles said as though Eddie weren't there or couldn't hear.

Honey giggled. "Are you armed?"

"Want to search me?"

She giggled again, and there was another silence as Charles sped up, his hands clenched tight on the wheel. Eddie pulled at his shirt; it was hot, and the material was sticking wetly to him.

"Ragtown," Honey said, reading a road sign. "There's no town there; why don't they take down the sign?"

"There never was a town there."

"Then what's the sign for?"

"It's supposed to mark the spot where wagon trains first hit the Carson River; women got out there, washed their clothes, and hung them on the brush to dry, so they called it Ragtown."

"How do you know all that?"

Eddie pointed back at the marker. "I read that once."

"What were you doing out here?"

"I don't remember—hitchhiking or something." Eddie watched a man sift through the garbage cans at a turnout, looking in paper sacks for a discarded lunch. Maybe that was him, a scene from the past.

"I'm getting hungry," Honey said.

"We'll be in Reno in plenty of time for dinner."

"I'm hungry now. Let's stop at one of those Basque restaurants outside of Carson."

"That's the long way around. You can eat in Reno."

179

"No," Honey said, smiling indulgently. "And it's my money."

Eddie said nothing as they bypassed the shortcut and continued on in silence. In an hour they were in Gardnerville, stopped before The Pyrenees, an old frame hotel. Inside there were two rooms, a bar in front and a long narrow room with two long tables in the back. Honey put a quarter in one of the two slot machines. "Ask him when they start serving dinner."

Charles went over to the bar. "In about ten minutes," he called. "I'm going to have a beer; want anything?"

"A Picon."

Eddie sat down at a poker table alongside the crowded bar and shuffled an open deck of cards. In a minute Honey joined him. "Playing solitaire?"

"That's not my game."

"What is?"

"I thought you already knew all about my preferences." Charles came back with the beer and the Picon, and Eddie got up to go to the bar. The bartender, slightly drunk, joked in French with two old men at the other end of the counter, then switched to a heavily accented and slurred English to call to a man in overalls next to Eddie, "Hey, didn't you go out today?"

"Naw," the man in overalls said, giggling. "Yesterday the crew got drunk; today I'm drunk. That road's never going to get surfaced."

"Yesterday his crew gets drunk here; today he gets drunk here," the bartender repeated. The men at the other end of the bar laughed, and Eddie laughed too, sharing for a minute the sense of irresponsibility and freedom. "Picon," he said when the bartender looked at him.

"Everyone is drinking Picon tonight; that's good. Tomorrow no one will do anything. Let them drive up and down their driveways." The man next to Eddie giggled again as everyone else, Eddie included, toasted this sentiment.

One of the men at the other end of the bar shouted something in French, which the bartender translated while the man nodded eagerly at each word of the English version. "He says, 'The roads lead nowhere; only the insane use them.' He would rather walk behind sheep in the mountains."

"He doesn't drive because he's never sober."

"And he doesn't walk behind the sheep either; he rides them."

"He is the true animal lover."

The Frenchman laughed with the others, even before the bartender stopped laughing long enough to translate for him. Eddie let the last of the amber liquor drain down his throat, happy, then held up his empty glass. "Another for the road," he said. The head of the road crew clapped his hands on the bar; everyone else laughed. Eddie twirled his fresh drink, trying to think of another toast, then, turning sideways in his seat, he noticed Honey and Charles still sitting at the poker table. He had easily forgotten them. Now Honey caught his eye and motioned to him. He did not want to leave the bar—he was having a good time—but when it appeared that she would join him if he didn't, he reluctantly went over to the table.

"Charles has stopped speaking to me."

"I have not."

"Well, I wish you would; I'm sick of listening to you." Honey moved her chair near Eddie's and smiled conspiratorially. "Where are you booked next?"

"I don't know. I think I have a couple of days' vacation due me."

"Sounds all right. Where do you stay in Reno?"

"You wouldn't like it."

"Tell me about it."

"A flophouse—ten to a room."

"I guess it would depend on the other nine."

A woman of about sixty came out from the kitchen ringing a bell with one hand, holding a drink with the other. "See," the bartender called out happily, "everyone today is drinking Picon." Two old men came down from the rooms upstairs and four or five more people came in the door, then the crowd at the bar, the bartender, everyone, moved into the dining room, sitting at one of the long tables. Eddie was between a Spanish kid and an old sheepherder, across from Honey and Charles. He looked down the table at the road crew, the other sheepherders, a couple with two children, then at Honey and Charles, as artificial as dolls abandoned by their manufacturer for some new novelty. A bowl of soup made the rounds along with a bottle of wine, and Eddie ate while half listening to the conversation between the Spanish kid and the father of the two children, a dark man tense with hate.

"Where do you go now?" the Spanish kid asked.

"Bishop. The guy there at the Shell station; he's the organizer for Inyo County."

"How many there?"

"Not so many, but they have nothing so they are very strong. You know, even our food has been destroyed; it doesn't grow here anymore. Before it wasn't a desert, not to us, not to the Indian."

"You don't like this? You don't like the food at The Pyrenees?"

"Yes, of course; that's not the point."

"Why so silent?" Eddie looked up from the bowl of soup. Honey was watching him. "Aren't you speaking to me either?" Eddie shrugged. A plate of steaks was passed to him, along with some french fries and a bowl of vegetables. "I've been working on some new numbers; maybe you'd like to see them?"

"Why not show them to Charles?"

Honey laughed. "I'm beginning to think it wasn't a little girl you raped."

"Honey, that's enough."

"I guess so; I'm not getting anywhere with it anyway."

Eddie looked back down the table. The bartender had finished quickly and gone back to tend bar; now the old woman sat at his place, eating and smiling. When she caught Eddie's eye, she winked as though there were some joke in just being there, as though she knew that he understood this too. "Finished?" Charles asked.

Eddie nodded, pushing back his plate and following the two of them outside. Now that the sun had gone down it was cool, and they drove the winding valley road without speaking.

"I'll get out here," Eddie said when they stopped for a light. He dodged traffic and cut quickly across the street, leaving behind a sullen unfinished silence. Eddie pushed through the milling crowd in front of the two big casinos, turned the corner, and, at the end of the next block, entered a small bar. He gave the bartender room money and enough for a can of beer. Upstairs, he took the room on the right, where one of the three beds was already occupied by a drunk. Eddie lay down on the cot in the corner, listening to the drunk snore as he drank his beer; in a few minutes he was asleep himself.

When he woke up, the man in the other cot was still snoring loudly. One small neon light flickered on and off outside, turning the room and the drunk pink and green at intervals; it was still dark. Eddie closed his eyes again, trying to force sleep, but he had had enough. He got up and started down the back steps. The bar below was empty, and the street almost deserted. He went around the corner to an all-night cafeteria and ordered breakfast. Ten lonely people were dotted around the fluorescent-lit room; Eddie sat with his own tray against the wall watching their mouths move silently, speaking to no one, the mad hum just barely competing with the fluorescent buzz, and he had been bartender long enough to know that they were boasting to themselves about enormous losses, about families they would never see again, about the lives they had gambled away; they talked of losing things they had never had. He had heard the same stories over and over again. Gambling was not their disease but their rationale, the crux of their belief that it might all have been different.

Eddie pushed his tray away and wandered outside and down the street. Two blocks away he entered an empty casino; the last show was over and the band sat at the bar. He ordered a beer and waited for it to hit the powdered eggs and grease in his stomach. He burped, walked over to a row of slot machines, and played his change. When the band left, he was alone with the cocktail waitress, a long coat sweater pulled on over her dancehall costume now. Eddie eyed her from a distance. She was a tall cream-puff blonde who had probably started out as a showgirl and with age and use finally worked her way down to the late shift in the bar and grill; still she wasn't too bad. "Made any plans for the rest of your life?"

"Sorry. I've got nothing but breakfast and sleepy-bye on my mind. Beyond that I don't make plans."

"I've got nothing against breakfast."

"What are you doing, waiting around for the morning shift?"

"No, I'm waiting for you to offer me breakfast."

"What do I get out of it?"

"Ample praise and encouragement of your domestic skills."

"You local?"

Eddie nodded.

"I figured. O.K."

Her apartment was only three blocks away, a new high-rise with a fountain in front. A redhead greeted them at the door. "Sorry," she said. "I overslept."

"That's Didi. She works days and I work nights; we share the apartment." Eddie followed her into the kitchen. "How about waffles?"

"Fine." Eddie watched her put two frozen slices of dough into a toaster and turn the heat on under a kettle of water.

"What's your name?"

"Eddie. Yours?"

"Tina," she said, giving him the same baby-doll name that every whore in Nevada assumed. "I like great big country breakfasts; do you?"

Eddie hesitated. "Sometimes."

"I'm just a little old farm girl from Nebraska. We used to have our own cream, and I'd go out and pick eggs."

184

"They grow on trees there?"

"Silly. There aren't any trees in Nebraska."

"And what's a little old farm girl like you doing here?" Eddie asked, wishing he didn't always have to sit through a story of wounded innocence or latent virginity or whatever it was.

"After my father left," she said, her eyes registering The Big Hurt of My Life, "I had to quit school and go to work."

"And I bet you were really good in school too," Eddie said. "Planned to go on to college and everything."

Tina looked pleased. "How did you know?"

"You have an intelligent face."

Tears came to her eyes momentarily. "I was the oldest, just fifteen; I had to help at home. There were the younger kids to think of. But I was just a kid myself; it was pretty rough."

The redhead came out in a black wig and a pair of stretch pants that were tight enough across her ass to show the lines of elastic underneath. In the wig her face seemed dwarfed and immobile, and her tiny little expressionless eyes, nose, and mouth seemed to have been painted on. "I'm out of the bedroom," she said.

"Bye-bye, Didi, have a wonderful day," Tina called. "Then this gorgeous man came along," she continued as though there had been no interruption. "He was a traveling salesman, and I was working in the drugstore. He stopped by every week. Of course, he promised me everything, then, after I got pregnant"—she sighed —"I never saw him again. I just couldn't tell Mama—it would have broken her heart—so I came out here." The waffles popped up. "I don't have any syrup, but I just love peanut butter on waffles. Want to try it?"

"Actually I just like them plain."

"Oh, isn't that terrible. You'd rather have syrup, wouldn't you?"

"No, I really like plain waffles."

"Have you ever tried them with peanut butter? The peanut butter melts in all the little squares and gets all warm and everything."

185

Eddie smiled weakly, remembering happier times. Once he'd gone into a change booth in one of the downtown hotels, and when he'd closed the door behind him, the light hadn't gone on; then when he'd reached around to find out what was wrong with the light, his hand had grazed the nude body of a woman. She hadn't said anything, and he had screwed her against the wall and then zipped up his pants and gone on down to the next booth for change. No make-believe little girl, no talk, just straight screw; he wished he'd looked in that booth this morning. Maybe the nude woman was still there. "This is the way I like waffles," he said, "plain." He ate a bite of cardboard. "Sometimes I like to dunk them too," he said, sticking the waffle into his coffee. He got it down in three bites. "Well," he said, his mouth still full, "let's get started."

Tina giggled. "I'll just have to slip into something else."

Eddie waited for her to return. When she did, her makeup was gone, her hair was up in curlers, and she was sporting a pair of baby-doll pajamas that looked like they had been blown up by a hot-air jet. "Fine," Eddie said, following her bloomer-puffed ass into the other room.

Once in bed, she snuggled up to him. "What's the big tough man going to do to the little girl?"

"Probably nothing." He pulled up the bubble of net in front, and her breasts slid like two pancakes onto her stomach. Christ! She was closer to forty-five than thirty-five. He tried to prop up one breast so he could suck the tit. "Maybe you'd rather do this later," he suggested hopefully.

"Do what?" she asked in a breathless little-girl voice.

Eddie wondered what Honey was doing; he could see now that he had made a mistake. A nice tight ass like that—he should have gone for it. She had certainly laid it out for him. The thought helped, and he was up and, with one quick thrust, entered into the abyss. Jesus, she must have had ten children by now or rutted herself into a grand canyon. He slid back and forth in the void for a while and then gave up. "Sorry, I don't feel too well."

186

"Oh," Tina said sympathetically. "Did him have an awful day?"

"Yes," he said.

"Tell her about it."

"I don't want to talk about it."

"And I bet you just had an awful life too."

Eddie was silent.

"Tell Tina all about it. What did your father do?"

"He made artificial flowers," Eddie said, staring at a vase of plastic roses on the dresser surrounded by pink plastic curlers. "Red ones, blue ones, green ones."

"What did he do with the flowers?"

"Every day he gave me a flower to wear to school," Eddie said in a choked voice. "When I got to school, the kids would beat up on me and take away the flower. When I got home at night, my father would ask me where the flower was and I'd tell him I lost it, then my father would beat up on me. Gradually I lost interest in my surroundings. I turned to God."

"That's beautiful," Tina said. "We have a lot in common."

For a long time Eddie was aware of sunlight coming in through a window in the living room, then he fell asleep until he heard movement in the room and looked up to see Tina, fully clothed. "I'm off at four," she said, "and then we'll just talk and talk and talk." She cupped her hand and wiggled her fingers like a baby. "Bye-bye."

Eddie gave her ten minutes, then he was up, dressed, and gone. Crossing the apartment parking lot, he saw the roommate in her wig and stretch pants coming in with a load of groceries. It was about four o'clock. He wandered around, sat in the bus depot for a while, then, when it wasn't so hot, moved out of the air-conditioning and sat in the park. After a while, he walked over to a hotel, ordered a drink in the bar, and then went into the back room to play blackjack with a couple of shills. When the bar began to fill up with divorcées, he returned and ordered another drink. The

187

divorcées eyed him hungrily and he looked them over trying to pick out a nice piece himself. He settled on a small, well-groomed woman in a tailored suit sitting at the back; he caught her eye and smiled. She didn't return the smile, but he knew she had seen him; she looked nervous. When she got up to leave, he waited for her to get out the door, then started stalking her.

She watched his reflection in a store window and then began to run her hands through her hair. After they had gone three more blocks, turned two corners, and started down a side street, the woman stopped and looked back. "Are you following me?"

"Yes." Eddie grinned. The woman smiled. She was young, pretty, expensive looking, the sort who hung around cocktail lounges for six months hoping to meet a cowboy. Instinctively, Eddie bowed his legs and looked bashful.

"It's rather a long walk," the woman said.

"Are we going the right direction?"

"No." She laughed, her small, carefully shaped mouth showing a perfect row of tiny teeth.

Back at the hotel, they got a taxi, and she gave directions to a guest ranch, a motel with horses out on the edge of town. "Do you do this often?"

"What?"

"Follow strange women around."

"Are you strange?"

She showed her teeth again, and then the taxi stopped at a lodge and dining room behind which was a series of cabins fronting the river. Her cabin was at the very end—rustic simulated log on the outside and elaborately western on the inside, with knotty pine furniture, Navajo rugs, a lot of leather. "Why don't you fix us a drink?" she asked, waving Eddie toward a small bar alcove.

"What would you like?"

"Vodka." The woman took off the jacket of her suit, and Eddie saw beneath the sheer net blouse her bare breasts, two tiny perfectly formed tits. "You know, I didn't use to be able to do this."

"Do what?"

"Accept immediate casual relationships. Now, of course, I think it's perfectly natural and beautiful. It was just something I had to learn. Always before I was too tense and nervous; I simply could not cope with myself. I had to learn to accept the fact that I have a beautiful body and that to deny it is to deny beauty." Eddie looked at her legs; they weren't bad. "Harold was actually my main problem. He was not artistic and so inhibited—it affected me. Of course, group was my salvation."

"Group?"

"Then I was totally unselfish; I gave myself to everyone—even the group leader. It was so beautiful. I was like an artist expressing my genius. But Harold didn't understand; he had never done anything meaningful himself. He sold drainage ditches and steel culverts. He never related to them; he didn't even *donate* them. He used to say that his life's dream was to sell a million steel culverts before he was thirty. Can you imagine? That was his *dream*—just to sell a lot of steel culverts, not to *create* them, or *be* one. I was very young when I married Harold, just a baby really. I didn't know. I thought he was rich and handsome and wonderful, but Harold was a boor."

Eddie had finished his drink, and now he shifted around uneasily, uncomfortable. The woman did not seem to be talking to him but to herself, admiring herself as though her words were a mirror. He watched her tiny mouth and teeth, her pointed almost birdlike tongue, sucking, biting, licking on some private satisfaction, her whole body taut with pleasure as though in the throes of some lone sexual experience. Watching her was making him horny; he wished she would stop talking so they could get started, but she seemed completely divorced from him, so caught up in some purely personal sex experience that even when he opened her blouse and began fondling one tiny tit, he did not interrupt her ecstasy. Then, suddenly, the woman moaned and stood up. "I must learn not to intellectualize," she said. "It's compulsive. Around someone like you I know I don't have to explain everything. It's so natural. I have this great feeling of freedom; I must let myself go, feel, be."

She leaned over and kissed him, her tiny sharp tongue darting in and out of his mouth with precision. "Just one minute." Eddie's hand grabbed after her departing figure, then he began to tear off his clothes, throbbing with anticipation. "All right," she called.

She was lying naked and strangely rigid across the bed. Eddie fell on her tight body, forcing himself between her legs, which were clamped together like an empty vise. With one great thrust he tunneled into her, feeling the effort he made in the swelling of her stomach, but she still did not give an inch. She remained perfectly rigid. "I'm a steel culvert," she murmured.

"What?"

"I'm a steel culvert, and you're the rain."

"Huh?" Eddie continued his attack on her unrelenting body, but some of his enthusiasm had gone.

"The rain is falling softly on the culvert," the woman murmured. "Pitter patter. Pitter patter." Eddie was losing depth and one ball was sore. "Pitter patter."

"Jesus Christ, what the hell kind of act is this?"

"You're really extremely inhibited, aren't you? Afraid to let yourself be."

That did it. "This the kind of game you and your husband played?" Completely limp, he looked down at her stiff tight body. Lying like that, she seemed somehow sexless, a steel rod. Still he was tempted to make one more try before she turned him off completely.

"Actually, I can only truly relate to others who have gone through creative therapy and are sensitive to my needs."

"Yeah," Eddie said. As he dressed in the other room, he heard the bed moving slowly and heard her whispering over and over again, "Pitter patter, pitter patter."

Outside it was a dusky dark. His body ached, and he began to run. When he got back to the highway he started walking into town, oblivious to the highway movement and the lights until a car pulled over onto the shoulder in front of him. When Eddie drew

190

even, a woman rolled down the window and asked if he wanted a ride.

"All right." The woman had long straight hair tied with a scarf at the back, and when she smiled she revealed a stretch of missing teeth. They drove in silence. Once they were back in town and stopped at a light, Eddie looked over at her blank, impassive face. "I'll buy you a drink."

"No; I have to get home," she said as though there were some urgency about it.

"Just a short one; it won't take long."

"No." There was a blank silence. "You can come out with me, if you want."

"All right."

The woman drove on through town, then turned off the highway and drove out to a trailer court on the north side of town. A few children ran around in a fenced play area beside the entrance, and the woman slowed down as she drove past them, scanning their faces carefully, then she steered between two rows of trailers and pulled into a carport extension alongside one of them. Eddie followed her up the makeshift steps and inside. "I'm home," she called. Eddie stood back hesitantly. Somewhere in the back a television clicked off, and then a young girl about fourteen appeared. "Four dollars," the girl said. The woman opened her purse and counted out four dollars in change. "See you tomorrow," she said.

"Sure," the girl answered, looking at Eddie with a smirk.

"Baby-sitter," the woman explained after the girl had left. "She probably makes more money than I do." She opened a cabinet under the sink and got a bottle. "You stay out there at the lodge?"

"No."

"Didn't think so. Weren't dressed right, but then I seen you comin' down the drive there so I didn't know. Work out there?"

"No." Eddie made a brief attempt to explain, then gave up.

"Yeah," the woman said. "Out beating the bushes. I know how

it is." She poured two drinks, drank hers in three short swallows, and then refilled her glass. "I needed that. I just got out of the hospital two weeks ago, and I'm about ready to go back already."

Eddie looked at her thin face and neck, her skin the greenish color of makeup turned ghoulish under fluorescent light and the black toothless hole in her mouth surrounded by a few gray and discolored teeth. She was ageless, the sort of woman who had probably looked the same since she was sixteen. "Have you been sick?"

"Yeah, I sure have." She pointed to her head. "Those goddamn kids drove me nuts. Screaming and yelling all the time; didn't do nothin' but watch the TV and scream." She took another drink, her eyes vacant as though they had turned back to look at some memory. "First word they learned was 'coke,' then they'd pick up and yell, 'Potato chip, potato chip.' Got on my nerves. We'd go to a grocery store there, and they'd scream and yell and grab things off the shelves, and I'd hit 'em. Even the little one, just a baby. I beat the shit out of it. And then they'd come around to see me about it. Come to investigate." She poured them both another drink. "The government don't do nothin' but spy on a person. I told 'em if it was my kid, I could beat the shit out of it if I wanted to; if it was theirs, they could have it. I'll tell you that baby was a mess time I got through with it—looked like it had been run over, head all black and blue, arms bent the wrong way. It didn't look like no baby then."

"My god," Eddie said, and the woman looked at him, her face contorted.

"It wasn't no baby. It didn't have nothin' to do with me. Neither of 'em did. Didn't do nothin' but scream and yell, just gimme, gimme, gimme, that's all I heard." She finished her drink and was silent for a minute, looking down at her hands and through her open fingers to the floor. "I started workin' two shifts," she said softly, her words slightly slurred now. "I like to never saw them. Get home and there'd be potato chips and Coca-Cola bottles all

192

over the place, and they'd be yellin' for more, minute they saw me. I didn't have no control over them; they wasn't mine. They was that's." She nodded toward the back of the trailer, and Eddie knew she meant the TV. "They was them's children, them Coca-Cola and potato chip people's." She laughed. "They said I wasn't a fit mother, but I wasn't no mother at all. They belonged to the devil. I went to the preacher over it, and that's what he tole me. Said you have to beat out the devil, sister, don't matter none where it appears. You have to beat it out. I did, and then, last time, they come took 'em away and put me in the hospital."

"And then they brought them back when you got well?" Eddie looked toward the back of the trailer; there had been no sound from there since the baby-sitter left.

"They wasn't mine; they was the government people's. They come and took their own. Tried to blame it all on me, but when I saw them little battered bodies, I knew it wasn't none of mine. I said I didn't recognize them nohow, said it was someone else's doing, not none of mine." She finished her drink and stared blankly at the floor, nodding her head with grief. "Them two little little babies are gone to hell."

"But the baby-sitter?"

The woman didn't seem to understand his question. "Them two little babies were the devil's own. You couldn't even beat it out of them; they'd have gone and said 'potato chip' with their last breath. They wasn't mine; mine's different."

Eddie wanted to go, to get up and run, but something desperate, almost frightening, in the woman made him think better of it. "Why don't you fix us another drink," he said, his voice calm.

The woman poured the rest of the liquor out, emptying the bottle into the two glasses but giving herself the most. There was a long silence. "I need to get me a husband now," she said finally. "I'm half back to the hospital already for worrying about it." She nodded disconsolately, swallowing her drink and picking nervously at her face and hair with one hand. "Got to get a father for my baby;

I'm like to kill myself if I don't." Her face twisted with pain, and she began to pick at the skin, scratching herself. Eddie slowly emptied his drink into her glass. "Kid's got to have some father aside from the devil; don't want it to turn out like them others." Her head nodded nearer and nearer the table and then she was out cold. Eddie picked her up and carried her into a tiny bedroom at the back. On the table beside the bed, there was a wedding picture of the woman looking no younger than she did now, wearing a white dress and carrying a small bouquet, beside her a boy in a tux and a bow tie, a dumb grin on his face. As he went back down the narrow hallway, Eddie opened the door to a still smaller bedroom, almost entirely taken up by a crib. The crib was empty.

The night air was clear and cool, and he walked back down the row of trailers, each of them lit an eerie television blue, and then into town. By the time he got to the bar, he was tired, the last twenty-four hours a mental blur. He took a key and went up to the same room, again occupied by only one other person, this time an old herder who lay silently facing the wall listening to "The Basque Hour" on a transistor radio. For a while Eddie listened too—mostly music, the talk in French or Spanish or maybe Basque, only the Boise station break in English, but the volume was turned full, now and then blaring away a staccato of interference or drifting off into incoherent noise. It got on his nerves, made him feel lonely and frustrated, and finally kept him awake to think of what he did not want to think of. "Hey," he called to the old man, "I want to get some sleep." There was no response. "Hey, could you turn that thing down a little," he called again, louder this time, but the old man still made no response, did not even turn to look at him. "TURN IT DOWN, WILL YOU?" The old man did not move. "Christ, can't you hear? TURN THAT GODDAMN GIBBER-ISH OFF." This time his words drowned out the radio altogether, but the old man was too deaf to notice. His hands clenched, Eddie rolled over toward the wall as the room filled with nonsense. In an hour it would be over.

194

Montana's office was a broom closet off the gym, big enough for a small desk, two chairs, a phone, and some pictures: *To Tony, a great guy, with best wishes from Lucky L. For Tony, the two-armed bandit—A bandido friend.* Eddie looked around the empty office for a minute, then walked down to the other end of the gym, where some men in sweatsuits were working out. "Tony around?" One of the men nodded back toward the office, and when Eddie turned, he saw Tony coming up the steps.

"Crazy Eddie," Montana called as though he were drawing a conclusion. "You were supposed to be in a couple of days ago."

"I took some time off."

"Yeah? I hope it was a nice piece, because you could be off permanently."

Eddie shrugged.

"I had a job all lined up for you starting Monday night. Not only did you not show, but I lost the booking. It was a place up on the south shore too, so don't come bellyachin' to me about being back on the cowboy circuit now."

"Yeah. O.K." Eddie walked with Montana to the office, sitting down to wait while Montana flipped through a file on his desk. A kid with an electric guitar and one long braid of hair down his back looked in at the door, saw Eddie, and said, "Sorry."

"No," Montana called, motioning to the kid. "Want you two to meet. This is Eddie Vegas. This is Wichita." Montana's clients were all easily identifiable by name if by nothing else. Eddie nodded

195

and the kid, tall, thin, and confused looking, nodded back. "Be with you in a minute," Montana said, dismissing the kid and looking at Eddie again. "Here it is. The hotel in Tonopah for a week. Can you get down there by tonight?"

"I'll take a bus."

Montana wrote a name on a piece of paper and then stamped his own name on the other side. "I'll have to let you know about next week later."

Eddie grunted. With the address and name in his hand, he walked down to the depot and got an almost empty bus. Two couples who looked as though they had just got married sat totally absorbed in each other in the rear; Eddie sat in front, where he could stretch out. "Tonopah, huh?" the driver said after they had been gone about an hour. "I've picked people up in Tonopah, but I've never taken anyone there."

The comment seemed to require no response, and Eddie remained silent. Sinking down in the seat, his feet up on the rail in front, he watched the sand whirl up in small dust clouds, then disappear in the stillness, a fine invisible powder. Every now and then he could see tracks in the sand cutting across a rise maybe a mile away, left there yesterday by motorcycles or a hundred years ago by wagons, but cut into the desert crust permanently, freeing the loose sand underneath to blow over the surrounding crust and lie there to twist and twirl in even the lightest breeze, killing forever in those two narrow ruts the desert's delicate protective cover. Eddie liked the desert, vast, foreboding, and sensitive, a power not easily tampered with, seeming at times almost a link in history, its past traced across it for centuries. He had heard on the radio about a prehistoric fish found somewhere out there in salt ponds, preserved by the desert, not yet killed. It gave him a sense of eternity.

In Fallon they turned south over a road he had not been on before. At first the landscape was the same, an endless stretch of desert broken once by a small silver lake shimmering like a mirage in the sun, but then the landscape turned ominous, an enormous

196

burial ground, grave mound after grave mound stretched along behind several rows of barbed wire. "What's this?" Eddie asked, leaning forward.

"Ammunition depot. That's where they bury it." Eddie looked again over the rows of cement graves. "Over there's the bomb," the bus driver said, nodding his head toward the distant desert. "It's underground now too."

"The bomb?"

"Week after I first started this route I got a day off on account of that bomb there. They should have dropped it on the commies, should drop it on those Viets; that's what they made it for, isn't it? I knew then there was a trick to it. See this?" The driver held up a black death's head.

"What is it?"

"Gas mask."

Eddie saw then that the hose for the thing was hanging over the emergency brake. "What's it for?"

"I've seen things die."

"From the bomb?"

"Now I wouldn't know about that, but I see them out there— dead. See those buzzards?" Eddie looked up at a dark cloud, saw it descend, black birds circling. "There's something dead there; that's what it means. Once I saw some buzzards die too; birds were in a frenzy, no direction to them, then one of them would just stretch out its wings, glide a little like that, and plummet to the ground, dead. You can draw your own conclusions." The driver put the gas mask away, thoughtful and silent for the moment. "I'll tell you what I think though—I think it's a plot. How can you win a war by blowing up Nevada? Poisoning a few birds? It doesn't fool me any; I know why we're losing. Couple of weeks ago my canary died. That was no accident; it was a healthy bird. And the post office, they're in on it too. The postmaster made a little mistake, one little mistake, but I caught him right up on it." The driver laughed. "Said something to me in Russian."

"How do you know it was Russian?"

"It wasn't English; I didn't understand a damned word of it. Oh, it's big; it's big. They're all part of it. People next door bought a brand-new car; brand-new. First time they drove it, the right front wheel fell off. Then while they were just sitting there in the car with the air-conditioning on, waiting for the repair truck, the air-conditioner goes haywire and it starts to rain. Starts to rain inside the car. I asked them did they think that was an accident and just laughed. I knew it was planned. Half of it is psychological warfare, that's all; they're trying to drive us crazy. If you don't believe me, just think about it. Pay attention. You can't make sense out of anything anymore; it's all a trick. They are trying to drive us mad. One of these days I'm going to get just mad enough to shoot a couple of them." The driver laughed maniacally, pulling a gun from his pocket and showing it to Eddie. "That's how mad I'm going to get."

Eddie turned around to see if the others were watching. They were, peering curiously over and around seats, looking down the aisle at the bus driver, who was waving his gun and laughing. Then, suddenly, caught up short, the driver put the gun away and fell silent. Looking out the window again, Eddie saw an ocean, shimmering illusively in the distance, moving farther away as they approached, surrounded by salt and sand and barbed wire. Danger signs were posted every few miles now, and planes circled in the air like buzzards.

"Here you are," the driver said finally as they climbed to a high desert plateau and then stopped in what appeared to be a ghost town. Eddie got off across the street from the hotel and stood looking at it uncertainly. He wondered if Montana had done this deliberately, sent him out to nowhere to wait for a return bus. Walking over to the hotel, he found that the door was boarded over, but when he kicked it, it swung open easily, admitting him to a small lobby where three old men sat before a color television. Eddie walked through the lobby to a café and a bar at the back; both were empty. He pushed open the door to the men's room and

198

stood before the urinal reading the small print on the prophylactic dispensers:

Pinkies, the original pink prophylactic.

Korona, not wet, not dry.

Tops, cover only you know what.

Gentries with Genitrol make you feel as close as natural.

Teasers with that added something.

The men's room was dark and wet, and when the smell of deodorant became overpowering, he went back out to the lobby and sat in a chair on the other side from the three old men. He could hear the television; someone was giving a speech, saying, "Let me make one thing perfectly clear, perfectly clear, perfectly clear, perfectly clear, perfectly clear, perfectly clear, perfectly clear; make no mistake about it. . . ."

"They're all dubbed now, you know," one of the old men said to his companion over the sound of the television.

"What?"

"I said they're all dubbed," the old man shouted. "All the speeches are dubbed. It's the same picture, but they play different records with it, different speeches."

"Is that right? I thought it was the other way around—the same speech but different pictures. What's the point to it anyway?"

"Haven't got the bugs out yet, but once they get the bugs out it'll be technically feasible."

"It'll be what?"

"TECHNICALLY FEASIBLE."

Eddie slumped down in the chair and closed his eyes. "You vote?" the old man asked. "I used to," the other old man answered, and then Eddie was asleep.

At six, when Eddie looked up again, the lobby was silent, the television off, and the three old men gone; someone was mopping down the entranceway. "You don't know where I could find Porter

199

Hall?" Eddie asked, walking over to the man.

"That's me."

Eddie held out the note from Montana, and the man stopped mopping long enough to read it. "They sent you?"

"Yes."

"Well," the man said as though he had no particular interest in the matter one way or the other, "show starts in half an hour. In the bar there."

Eddie walked back to the bar, which was still nearly empty, only the bartender and four customers, three old men and one old woman. Eddie sat down at the bar and ordered a drink, swinging around once to look at the four old people and the empty tables. On a small platform beside the bar was a theaterlike marquee with the word PRESENTING; underneath it on a small blackboard someone had written: *Comedian Ed Vegas.* A larger sign on the far wall advertised: *The Three Shillers. Next. Straight from their hit engagement at The Jackpot in Winnemucca.* After twenty minutes, when still no more customers had come in, Eddie ordered another drink. "Is this all the crowd you get for the first show?"

"You Vegas?"

"Yes."

"Make enough noise, Vegas, and maybe someone will come in from the café to see what's going on."

Eddie sipped at the new drink while watching the door. "I suppose there are more for the second show?"

The bartender shook his head. "This is about it."

"They hire an entertainer every week for this?"

"That's right. Got to keep the faith."

Eddie ordered another drink and finished it hurriedly. Finally, at six forty-five, fifteen minutes late, he was actually standing up on the little platform behind the lighted PRESENTING, looking down at the bartender and the four old people. They applauded, laughed, whooped. It was contagious. Eddie opened his mouth. *Funny. Haw Haw.* Screamed, "*Ooooooooooowah.*" Again "*Ooooo*

200

ooooowah." Sounding inner abstractions. "*Hooooh*ooooh*oooo
hooooo*hawh*oooo*haw."

Hi, Tonto. Haw haw.

Goddamn Indians on the warpath. Old ones. They came running
to see, peeking at him through the door, from around the corner.
Four more Jerry Atrics. He stared down at them blankly, blurring
them. *Haw.* Something to distract them, a little noise. "Ooooohoo-
waw. Indians," he said, winking at an old lady, maybe at the
bartender. Nothing was clear. "There are two kinds of Indians—
professional Indians and amateur Indians."

That was the truth. Eddie stared out between bars watching his
clothes disappear. Hey, that's my suit. "Goddamn Injun took my
suit. Went on television, said, 'How!' "

Haw.

Very funny. What the hell was he going to do? A person could
be convicted. A public nuisance without, a costume party with.
Two more Indians came up, real professionals. Hired by the court.
They exposed him. Exposed him right there in front of everyone.
Exposed him to the left, to the right, to the jury. Jesus Christ. It
was terrible. Terrible. "Lone Ranger," Eddie screamed.

Hi, Tonto. Haw haw.

"Indians. Everywhere you look."

"How many?" the judge asked.

"Ten little. Enough for a conspiracy."

"A conspiracy to what?"

"Overthrow Nebraska."

Eddie objected. "Ohio," he said.

"Honh?"

"Ohio."

"That's a nice state."

"Yes, it is, sir. Beautiful."

"Wife is from Cincinnati. Ever been to Cincinnati?"

"Yes, sir. All the time, sir. Go down often."

"No Indians there."

"Right. Nobody there but us Reds." A little joke. Smile at the people. Applause.

Haw haw haw.

Two more Indians came up, sat in the seat. One after the other. Smiled at the judge. Said confidentially, "He am one crazy Indian."

Who who who.

Who? *Haw.*

It was all a big mistake. *Ohio. Lone Ranger.* "Listen, in this country, what chance does an Indian have?"

Haw haw.

Eddie saw them laughing, all standing around whooping it up. He watched their mouths. *Haw haw haw.* They had brought notebooks with them. If he wasn't an Indian, what was he? they asked.

"An ant," Eddie said, making merry. It was all a big joke.

They tittered into their notebooks, rubbed their noses on their sleeves, peed in their pants. They were convulsed. "An ant?"

Eddie held out the palm of his hand, looked in the mirror, stuck out his tongue. He didn't look like an ant. Too big, for one thing. For two thing, for three thing. "It must be a disguise." *Haw.* He was an ant in disguise.

They giggled and giggled. "Why an ant?"

It was the kind of question that drove him buggy. "Why not?"

More questions. More laughter. *Haw haw.*

A person could go crazy. Eddie discussed it with a Mrs. G. in the next ward. Mrs. G. chewed gum and sat in his lap telling him about the late Mr. G. "I've been here before," she said. "Once after each husband."

"How many husbands?"

"One little, two little, three little, four . . . or . . ." She could not remember. "My attorney has told me so much about you," she whispered in his ear. "So much." Smoooch.

Eddie decided to leave while Mrs. G. picked her nose. It wasn't safe anywhere. Bugs. Boogers.

Hoo haw.

HAAAAAAAAAAAAAAAAEY. More Indians. Screaming, bawling. A regular goddamn warpath. "RAPE," Mrs. G. screamed. "RAPE. RAAAAAPE."

"Who was it?"

"An Indian."

"An Indian?"

"Or an ant." She could not remember.

Eddie began to sing. *Lie, Mama, Lie.* Who, him?

"Once an Indian always an Indian."

"This must be some kind of trick."

"You better believe it."

Haw!

Things were getting rough. Thoughts of escape. He had to get out of there quick. They were coming to get him now. He fell forward. Stumbled on a table. Looked down and winked. *Hi, Tonto.* Escape. *Haw haw haw.*

23 Victor Simmons believed he was being entertained; he guffawed loudly at every pause and stomped his foot appreciatively whenever a word seemed to be emphasized. Sometimes he choked and wheezed with laughter unexpectedly when everyone else sat silent, seeming to get a joke that no one else did; then a few of the others would turn to look at him admiringly and Victor Simmons would laugh fit to die, enjoying himself at the top of his lungs. He nudged his wife with his elbow, shaking his head, making a helpless effort to speak. "This guy," he said, choking on the words, his eyes running with tears, his hand pounding on the table, "this guy." He shook his head again, gasping for breath. "I don't know when I've laughed so hard." As if to prove his words, he sent up a loud guffaw that exploded through the bar and almost tipped him off his chair and onto the floor. For a moment he was the center of attraction, drowning out the comedian altogether as he righted himself in the chair and hung on, helpless with laughter, to the table.

He was having the time of his life, and the show was free too. Come in here, sit down, buy yourself a drink and one for the wife, even though she didn't usually drink a drop. He whistled loudly at something he thought was dirty and winked at the man at the next table, slapping his hand on his leg, titillated by whatever it was. Not so many people that you couldn't get a good seat either or hear the show. He tried to think what the show had been last year; seemed to him now it had been a little better, with some music and color to it. This fellow he couldn't quite make out; part of the time he didn't seem to make any sense, acted kind of weird, crazy or something. Of course, it was real different, never heard anything like it before, and sometimes, too, the jokes just came so fast he could hardly keep up with them. When he got back to The Dalles, he'd sure tell them about this. He guessed he was really seeing a show, and not just the stuff they had on television either; this guy . . . Victor Simmons let out an ear-shattering shriek and began to giggle crazily until his throat hurt from all the whooping and he quieted down a minute.

Maybe he'd sit in on the show tomorrow too, see if he could piece more of it together, remember something he could repeat when he got back to The Dalles. Used to be a comedian just came out and told jokes, just one, two, three, four, and you could almost sit there and write them down, go home and repeat the whole lot of them; now it all seemed so complicated, and he didn't even get the point of half of it. It was probably drugs. That was how Victor Simmons saw a lot of things. Any time he didn't understand something, he would shake his head and say to himself, "Drugs." Now he shivered with pleasure at the thought of being this close to the problem, an actual witness to depravity. This guy did look funny too. He wasn't fat actually, but he was a beefy guy with a big round face, a big nose, and baggy eyes. Wearing an old T-shirt like that, he looked more like a truck driver than a comic; he was a real peculiar entertainer. Victor Simmons had seen him sitting there at the bar earlier and hadn't even guessed that he was going to appear, had thought he had just made a delivery or something like that. Victor Simmons could remember when a clown looked like a clown. A comic in those days wore a fright wig and baggy pants, and you knew right off that he was funny, just naturally. Now this guy screaming his head off, saying weird incoherent things, it made him uneasy, just made him kind of uncomfortable. Of course, if he wasn't funny, he wouldn't be there and they wouldn't be paying him to perform. He was smart enough to know that. They didn't pay out a whole lot of money to someone for nothing. This guy was funny. Victor Simmons beat his feet on the floor and leaned over to wheeze loudly, doubling over with laughter. Raising up for breath, he winked at Emma, who was laughing just as hard as he was; then he began to choke and Emma giggled and slapped him on the back and then they both winked at each other.

He was glad Emma was having such a good time. They had been coming down here for ten years now, ever since he had sold a half interest in the pharmacy and started to take things a little easier. They had scrimped and saved for this, and now that they were doing it, taking the month off again, he was glad they were having such a good time. They had saved a little on the heat bill one month or gone without meat for a couple of days, talking it all over and anticipating the golden month of freedom and abandon to come. Ten years ago they had gone to Las Vegas, but there uniformed men had followed them around the casinos, forcing them to play the fifty-cent slots, making it impossible for them to watch the others without feeling like cheapskates. Most of the places in Vegas didn't have nickel machines and neither he nor Emma knew how to play craps or roulette or anything like that, and then the people in The Dalles dressed different or something, and they just generally felt kind of out of place. It had been pretty much the same thing in Reno the next year, but they could come down here to Tonopah and see all the shows free and just sit in the lobby and watch television with the others. It didn't cost them much at all. The hotel here was no great shakes, of course, but it was all right for a month. They still told people in The Dalles that they spent the month in Reno, but that was just because Reno was better known in The Dalles; besides, it was about the same thing.

Sometimes he thought they'd spend their vacations differently if they had family close by, but the kids had their own lives, and he and Emma didn't want to baby-sit for a month anyway. They wanted to kick up their heels, have a few laughs, do some of the things they'd missed out on. Still, the best part was getting home; then, when he was back behind the counter, everyone who came in would say they guessed he must have had a great time looking over all those showgirls, didn't look like he'd had a wink of sleep for a month, and did he win any money this time, just kidding him along and laughing. He always said that he had seen a couple of real good shows, and he guessed he'd pretty near laughed his head off at this one fellow. Emma had hit the jackpot once and almost fainted dead away when the buzzer rang, he told them. Then he'd say that sometimes he and Emma thought they'd do something different next year, but, when it got right down to it, they had so much fun in Reno, they guessed they'd just go right back. They really enjoyed the bright lights and all for a month, and just letting themselves go, and then he'd wink and stick an elbow in a rib and say, "Know what I mean?" Half the fun of a vacation was reliving it like that, talking about it, retelling a few of the jokes.

It was over now, and Victor Simmons let out one more yowl of laughter, topping everyone else there in pitch and intensity. Then he began to clap loudly, hoping for an encore, but it was all over. He grinned at Emma, exhausted. "I'll tell you," he said, shaking his head, "I wouldn't have missed that for anything." He finished the last of his drink and looked at his watch; it was only seven-thirty and they had already eaten. "What does my little Oregon sweetheart want to do now?" he asked, hoping Emma would solve the problem.

"I guess we could go see if there's anything on the television and maybe talk to those folks we met from Bend."

"That's an idea," Victor said enthusiastically, although the fellow from Bend was so hard of hearing that conversation with him was almost impossible. "I'll tell you," Victor said. "You go along. I may just look in on the gambling a minute, see if anything interesting is happening, and then I may just skip back here and catch this fellow's next show. I got such a kick out of it, I'd kind of like to see it again."

"I think he's going to be here for a week," Emma said.

"Well." He didn't argue with her.

24 Eddie ordered a drink and then turned around to look at the four people in the bar, the same four, waiting now for the second show. "This all there are here, these four?"

"That's about it," the bartender said, not looking up.

"Those fools are going to sit through every show?"

"Probably."

"What for?"

The bartender leaned over confidentially, resting one elbow on the bar. "That's the way the customer wants it, that's the way he gets it. The customer is always right."

Eddie shrugged and held up his empty glass.

At nine he was up on the stage and again at eleven, mumbling drunkenly at last to the bartender and one old man. By midnight he was upstairs in a small room across from the toilet, a transom onto the hallway his only source of air. He lay on the cot, suffocating. A transistor radio played in the distance, then went dead, and there was a long, empty silence. Eddie gagged; he gripped the sides of the cot, his whole body trembling and unsteady. For a moment he was afraid. Some kind of agony seemed to be tearing at his body and head, pulling him apart limb by limb while someone standing on a ladder watched from the transom, his face a moon of delight. When Eddie finally got up and opened the door, the hall was empty. He went across the way, opened the door to the toilet, and threw up. After that he was not aware of anything until a knock woke him and a voice said, "You have fifteen minutes."

Eddie pulled on his pants and shirt and then ran his hand over his face. His nose and mouth seemed to be swimming in loose flesh, not permanently placed, and his eyes watered, blurring his sight, making the cot and the door and the transom float before him. He moved slowly, grabbing the doorknob for support, then, opening the door, started down the steps.

They were all there watching again. He could see them open their mouths, wipe their eyes, stamp their feet, clap, scream. He was vaguely aware of the movement of his own mouth as well. Sometimes he imitated them, giggling when they did, applauding, stamping his feet, sitting dumbly staring back.

At the end of the week one of the old men came into the bar with pen and paper; he held them out to Eddie. "I've seen every show," the old man said. "To the old man who saw it all," Eddie wrote on the paper while the old man drooled happily nearby. "I'm quite a fan," the old man said as he retrieved the paper and the pen. "I think one of these days you'll . . ." Eddie opened his mouth; his breath smelled like vomit and his teeth were flecked with spittle. The old man retreated smiling.

When the last show was finally over, Eddie stood, puking sick, in front of the hotel waiting for the midnight bus to Ely and the Club Silver. There he spent another week not too different from the week in Tonopah, sleeping all day, drinking all night, not entirely aware of where he was or what he was doing. Not until the end of the week was he really sober; then he was scheduled for a two-minute stint at the Ely County Fair, a sobering event in itself.

At dusk the fairgrounds lit up with a fireworks display and roving lights, and two hours later, Eddie stood backstage listening to the headliner, Pard, the star of a TV western, open with the Pledge of Allegiance. Either his appearance or avid patriotism created momentary pandemonium, and the evening proceeded thereafter at the same pitch of hysteria. Pard was followed by a comic, another TV star, who could barely be heard at first over the wild enthusiasm with which his introduction was greeted. Finally he told two stale jokes and walked off-stage; his exit was immediately followed by the sound of a toilet flushing over the loudspeaker system. When he returned he was greeted with waves of hilarity. "Must have eaten too damn much cotton candy," he said, and the audience stood to cheer him, some of them standing on their seats and whistling. The comic told two more stale jokes but managed now to say "toilet" every third word, cuing hysteria each time; the audience loved it. At the end of his act, they called him back for an encore, and when he returned followed by the sound of a toilet flushing, they gave him a standing ovation.

"Wow," said a girl standing backstage beside Eddie. "That's going to be hard to compete with." He watched as she went out to do a mock striptease, parading back and forth across the stage bumping and grinding until someone in the audience called patiently, "Do it now, honey," and with the music at a crescendo pitch she ripped off the one-piece evening dress and turned to reveal a pair of bikini panties below and two police badges above, one over each nipple.

Eddie didn't get it, but the audience did, howling with laughter, applauding wildly. "Who's she?" Eddie asked a man pacing nervously back and forth.

"Are you kidding?" the man said. "That's Shelly, the new lead in 'Tough Story.' She plays a sexy policewoman; it's a natural."

Shelly ran offstage finally, her badges bouncing. "For crissake get me a fucking towel." Eddie started to hunt for one, then realized she wasn't speaking to him but to the nervous man, who held both a towel and a drink.

"You were real cute, honey," the man said, handing both to her.

"So fucking hot out there," Shelly said.

"They loved you," the man said.

"Christ," Shelly said, wiping the sweat from between her breasts, "do I ever need another agent."

"You were terrific; it was a real cute act."

210

"Another one of these cock-sucking county fairs and I quit."

"This is where the audience is, honey, and they're all going to be tuned in Tuesday night."

"Christ."

"No kidding, honey; they ate it up."

The two wandered out of hearing, and Pard reappeared, surrounded by a phalanx of bodyguards who seemed intent upon imitating his every expression and movement. Pard ran one hand over his silver hair and the bodyguards instantly assumed nervous I'm-on-next postures. "Gimme a cigarette or somethin'," Pard mumbled, and Eddie watched as a cigarette was instantly produced and lighted. "Mmm," said Pard. "O.K. let's get the friggin' thing over with." Blowing out a last puff of smoke, he trotted out onto the stage, trying to appear embarrassed and humbled by the audience's second greeting. Howls of "Pard . . . Pard . . . Pard" filled the air. When things finally quieted down again, Pard recited the Gettysburg Address in a voice of strained emotion as though he were near tears. When he was through a few people rushed the stage like converts, almost delirious, while the rest of the audience cheered and whistled, rising to give Pard still another standing ovation. He bowed meekly as though it were all too much for him and trotted back off, but when the noise continued and the screams of "Pard, Pard, Pard" began again, he returned, arms outstretched, like a holy figure. His reappearance was followed by the sound of a toilet flushing over the public address system, sending Pard into a fit of laughter and an I'm-human-too pose that was applauded vigorously by the audience. As women began to throw flowers, programs, and money onto the stage, Pard bowed for the last time and ran off. Backstage he was immediately encircled by the bodyguards, one of them massaging his back, one of them combing his hair, another touching up his tan. "That's good; that's good," Pard said, lifting his shoulders tentatively as though testing for signs of damage after a heavyweight bout.

The country western singer that Eddie was to follow came out

211

and sang the Deodorant jingle for the sponsor of his television series, and then his theme song. Eddie shuffled onstage in his wake, the first of the local entertainers to appear, his sole function to advertise the Club Silver. "The Club Silver," Eddie said dutifully; he could think of nothing else to add and was silent for a moment, then he imitated the sound of a toilet flushing, spitting and blubbering into the microphone, *"Ppppppupuplplplpl sssssshshshshshshsh."* The audience giggled nervously. "The Club Silver," Eddie repeated. "ShshShpulpulpulplplshshshshsh." He began to repeat "The Club Silver" over and over again, following each mention with a noisy flush, blowing and spitting at the audience. *"Ffff llufluflufulufulurrrr shshshshshshsh."* Then, out of the corner of one eye, he saw two of Pard's bodyguards approaching. Taking the microphone out of the socket, he began to run back and forth chanting "The Club Silver" and flushing verbally while the bodyguards moved in. At the same time the public address system drowned him out with its own toilet sound effects, which the audience applauded heartily.

Lifted by the armpits, Eddie was carried from the stage while they cheered his removal. Once outside he was held immobile by the bodyguards while Pard carefully adjusted one arm, took aim, and hit him. "Where did you learn to fight like that, Pard?" someone asked admiringly, after Eddie had lost the ability to stand and sagged slowly to the ground, his face and gut mashed and run together into one pain.

Some time later, he picked himself up and stood on two wobbly legs feeling his face. There was a crust of caked mud under his nose and mouth where dirt from the ground had mixed with blood from his nose. He began to pick off the mud and the crust of blood, clawing at his face, feeling as he did so the bruises, bumps, and still damp wounds. When he felt steadier, the night air cool and fresh in his lungs, he walked back into town, going into the men's room in the bus depot first, where he washed his face but did not look

212

at it, then he caught the first bus to Reno, sleeping all the way back, his face cradled in his arms.

"Jesus," Montana greeted him in the morning. "What happened?"

"Fight," Eddie said.

"Yeah." Montana shook his head. "Thank God you don't have to look pretty; you've got a nose like a used meatball now. You feel all right?"

"I'm O.K."

"Good, because I've got a great deal here that I don't want to lose."

"What?"

"Vegas." Montana grinned. "Yeah, every now and then the big boys have to come crawling to me—any time they have a cancellation and need someone in a pinch or want a cheap trick."

Eddie sat silent; everything about him still hurt, and this, he realized, was not helping the pain. "Where?"

"Sage Hotel. It's not on The Strip, of course, but it's not bad—downtown and they're redoing the whole place." Montana looked at him, his eyes revealing in a slight wince that he was both repulsed and amused by what he saw. "You don't want to go, just say so. Maybe you're a little under the weather or something? O.K. Fine. I've got plenty that would bust a gut to get to Vegas. Bust a gut."

"I'll go."

Montana smiled, enjoying himself, extremely entertained.

213

25 Thirty rows of slot machines clattered in ceaseless cacophony in the next room while the public address system called out keno numbers or announced jackpots in a frenzy of action. "Call for Mr. Garnett. Call for Mr. Red Garnett," the PA system screamed suddenly and insistently, as it had every half hour, whipping up the excitement and stirring the crowd into a tumult of activity. People began to wander back and forth in a hysterical herd, hoping to catch sight of Red Garnett, the headliner in the dining room upstairs, stimulated by the news that they were in the same arena with a celebrity, congratulating themselves on their good fortune, assured finally that they were momentarily, at least, in the right place, where the real action and the celebrities were. Eddie tried to make himself heard over the noise, screaming to three afternoon drunks in the downstairs bar while a crowd milled in and around, looking to see what was going on and then moving away quickly, hoping still to find something better.

By the second show Eddie was hoarse, his throat so sore he spoke in a whisper, almost inaudibly, but it made no difference. He was being paid to stand there on a platform by the front window, a living advertisement for the bank of slot machines in the other room, pulling people in from the street so that, once inside, the PA system could work on them. "Today only," the PA system chattered in a falsetto voice, "today only, five hundred Blue Chip stamps with each jackpot."

At six-thirty Eddie was finally through for the day, his two afternoon shows over. He walked past a long column of slot machines and into the crowd on the street drifting around uncertainly. It was the first time he had been here, and he fell in with the throng now, following them up and down, poking his head into other bars to look at other sick, sad comics mumbling to drunks and gapers. He watched old ladies wander set-mouthed and grim from casino to casino with paper cups full of quarters; watched hawkers in windows, at doors; heard rock bands blaring their come-ons through open entranceways; and felt a hundred air-conditioners call him in from the heat. Turning, he moved out of the crowd and started up another street, surging with traffic where huge neon cowboys blinked on and off and immense fountains sprayed the air before crystal palaces, tents, and thirty-story advertisements for themselves. In one of the glittering hotels Eddie ordered a drink and sat at the bar listening to a sequined blonde talk knowingly of the stars. "Hey," the blonde said to the bartender. "I heard Gleason died."

"Naw," the bartender said. "Where did you get that? That rumor went around all last week. It's old. Before that it was Sinatra. It's some kind of death fix."

"Yeah, two people told me," the blonde said.

"Forget it. I could call him and he'd answer."

"Yeah," the blonde said.

Eddie turned slightly; the two couples on his other side talked excitedly through bored faces, trying to top each other in quantity of fun. "Last night," one man boasted, "I saw Martin drop a grand."

"Is that all? Hell, when I played baccarat with him the other night . . ."

Turning again to look through the casino, Eddie saw a familiar face. He finished the drink, then walked over to the roulette wheel. "Hey, Crazy Eddie." It was Honey, dressed in an iridescent pink cowgirl outfit.

"Where's Charles?"

Honey shrugged. "That's over. I've got a rock group behind me

215

now and things are beginning to move. Big things are happening. Honey and the RipOffs. What are you doing anyway hiring yourself out as a punching bag? You look like you'd been run down by a Mack truck."

Eddie reached for his face, the loose bruised flesh. "Something like that. I'm working the Sage Hotel."

She looked surprised. "Yeah? Playing the bar?"

Eddie nodded.

She smiled triumphantly, naming another downtown hotel but trumping him with, "I'm in the lounge, upstairs. Come in and see me." She nodded to something in a lavender jumpsuit beside her. "Right now I'm all tied up."

As Eddie walked back through the casino, a uniformed guard followed him. In the next casino up The Strip, he was met at the door by another guard, who tailed him, flipping coins and humming. When Eddie stopped to put a quarter in a slot, the guard disappeared, only to reappear a minute later when he stood watching a line of chorus girls from a curtained doorway. "If you wanna see the show, it starts again at nine-thirty." Eddie nodded. In a minute he was back outside, lost among a million neon guides. He wandered across the street finally, bought another drink, and watched a man in drag, two-foot-long stuffed stocking tits, a crotch of feathers, parade back and forth throwing cherries that he picked from between his legs to the audience. A woman who was standing on her chair begging for the prize squealed with delight when the drag clown yelled, "You'll get yours, lady." Eddie left before it was over, continuing to move aimlessly from place to place until armored cars pulled up behind all the casinos and semitrailers of laundry moved up and down near-empty streets. It was almost morning when he walked back to the hotel alone, the only pedestrian.

After about four hours' sleep, he was back in the Sage bar surrounded by empty tables. "Hey, why don't you get your face fixed? You make me sick," someone yelled as he got up on the small

216

wooden platform. The man, a huge growth dangling from his nose, his bald head one large scab, stood unsteadily by a rear table, drink held high as though he were making a toast. "To Puke Face."

"To the Two-Nosed Scab Head," Eddie said, and when a couple at the bar laughed, he began to pick at them, mimicking their every move. "They're probably the only heterosexual couple in town; he's in drag and so's she." A cluster of sport-shirted men and lime-green-pedal-pushered women who had crowded together in the bar entrance to peek in giggled. Eddie threw a handful of peanuts to them. "Apes." They scrambled for the peanuts, then, when the PA system began its routine, "Call for Mr. Garnett; call for Mr. Red Garnett," they backed away, their attention drawn elsewhere. Eddie unzipped his pants, stopping the apes midway, then, working one finger through a hole in his pocket, he stuck it out through the open fly like a gun. "Bang," he said and wished it were real. After that, he simply stood there making obscene gestures with the hand that extended from his fly. An enormous crowd gathered to watch.

When the show was finally over, Eddie walked over to a woman at a front table, his hand still extended from his fly, to shake hands. As he approached the woman grew feverish with excitement, grabbed him, kissed his hand, and began to run after him as he moved away. Eddie lost her in a row of slot machines and started up the rear steps.

On the second floor there was a large newly redecorated dining room, THE ALL NEW BIRD CAGE. The whole upstairs had been lavishly refurbished, but since the clientele hadn't been, the place still looked like a skid row dive or a pawnshop for rejected people. Eddie went in and sat down at an empty rear table. A huge ornate bird cage was suspended from the ceiling, and inside, swinging back and forth on a gold perch, was a girl dressed in a bikini and an elaborate peacock-fan tail. Two workmen lowered her in the cage. She got out and started toward the exit and him through a

217

maze of empty tables. "Are you supposed to be a female peacock or a male peacock?" Eddie asked when she got to the rear of the room.

"Huh?" She looked about nearsightedly, finally focused on him, and smiled.

"I thought the female peacock was a drab little mudhen."

The girl giggled. "I'm not a peacock; I'm an exotic new breed."

Eddie was tempted to follow her but didn't, then two hours later, just as he had finished his second show, he saw her again, sitting at the back of the bar in a pair of old Levi's and a T-shirt. He walked over and sat down beside her. "Did you know I worked here?"

"Yeah. I heard someone talking about you the other day. They said you were a real ugly weirdo." The girl giggled. "Said they were going to have to do something about you."

"Like what?"

The girl shrugged. "Maybe we're all going to be birds." She giggled. "Hey, I missed most of your show, couldn't see, either." She waved vaguely at her head. "What do you do anyway?"

"I'm kind of a puppeteer."

"Hey, that's great. Are you from California?"

"No."

"Hey, me either. I'm from Jersey."

"A lot in common."

"Hey."

"What are you doing here?"

"I came out with these three guys. I was going to play the tambourine, see."

"And what happened?"

"One day I was, you know, playing the tambourine, just standing there in a parking lot, really grooving on the tambourine, having a wild time, and they went off and left me there. Next this guy in a Cadillac picked me up, and after we'd gone a couple of miles, we decided to get married. He drove me out here to do it."

218

The girl looked dreamily around the room. "I forget what happened next." She looked back at him, her eyes sleepy and moist. "You know, it's funny—the minute I saw you I thought, 'There's a real freak.' "

"I've had troubles like that before; a lot of people have come to the same conclusion."

"Hey, but I'm a genius, so now you know it's true." She giggled. "I have an IQ of 160; everyone in my freshman class was a genius. They told us we were the smartest class in history. That's the reason I dropped out first semester; I figured I didn't really need it; besides, I just wanted to play the tambourine—you know, jingle, jingle, jingle."

"Was the guy in the Cadillac musical?"

She looked at him blankly. "I forget all about him; he was more the establishment type or something. He was like an accessory to his car; always wanted to screw in the back seat, never wanted to do it outside in some groovy place. I believe everything should be natural. That's my belief." She looked dreamily back at him. "I bet you're a real person, aren't you?"

"I'm a magic animal."

"Hey. Hey, that's beautiful. Me too. And I'm real idealistic; I have all these"—her hand moved languidly through the air— "great ideas. I want everything to be perfect, just like Tommy."

"Tommy?"

She looked at him curiously. "The guy that owns this place. It's going to be just fantastic when he's through. I mean, you know, Tommy wants to get rid of all these crummy old people"—she pointed to a woman in white bobby socks and wedgies—"and have a really hip place. Like they're hiring a completely different kind of showgirl—like me. We're all going to be really superintelligent and great and just kind of be around, and then they're going to hire really great groups. And there'll be lots of tambourines and everything."

Eddie stared at her. "And then, of course, they're going to turn

219

off the air-conditioning and dump all the slot machines and make it really different."

"Hey," she said appreciatively. "That's great. Really freak everyone out completely. I think I'll tell Tommy." She cocked her head delicately to one side, her eyes shut. "I think it will just be beautiful. And with all the really super people here, wow!"

"What's going to happen to the people here now?"

She shrugged. "Who cares?" She looked at him again and giggled. "Hey, I couldn't borrow some money, could I?"

"How much?"

"Just enough for supper."

"Don't you get paid?"

"Tommy says if I took money for being a beautiful bird—wow —you know, that would be pretty gone. When I need money, I'm just supposed to get it from some of these old men. For spending an hour with them or something. Most of the time I don't need the money, you know, but sometimes, you know, I do it, and it's really weird, really weird. They just keep asking me what I usually do, you know, and I tell them I play the tambourine. This one little guy hit me when I told him that. When I told Tommy about it, he said I shouldn't mention the tambourine, just tell them stuff about freaks and communes and stuff like that. I make up some weird stuff. They don't know the difference; they'd believe anything weird enough. Now Tommy wants me to dress like an Indian and really freak out on them; I hate dumb suckers like that."

"Come on; I'll buy you dinner, and you can tell me more about it. I'm really sorry I don't know this guy Tommy."

"He's beautiful."

"I bet he is." Eddie led her through the slot machines to the coffeeshop on the other side. A row of bright yellow booths with tasseled canopies extended around the edge of a room filled with umbrellaed tables; they sat at one of the booths. "You order," the girl said, "and then I'll just eat part of whatever you get."

"Don't you want more than that?"

220

"I don't eat much; it's all poison."

"I once knew this old guy, Mr. K., who spooned his food into his pocket every meal—mashed potatoes and all—then flushed it down the toilet at night. He starved finally. He was very suspicious, always thought someone was trying to poison him; that's why he was in an asylum."

"Hey, that's great."

"What? Starvation?"

"No, an asylum. Once all the freaks start coming here, that's what this will be—one great big freak asylum. It'll be fantastic. Those people in asylums aren't so dumb; that guy K. was no sucker." She pointed at his hamburger. "Because I mean that really is poison."

"So what am I supposed to eat?"

"Who knows? All those dumb cows are out there eating poison. Then dumb people eat the dumb cows, and it just gets dumber and dumber."

"Is that why you're in the shucking business?"

"The what?"

"The shucking business—making a fool of yourself for the fools, all those dumb suckers with money."

"Not me; I'm nobody's fool. I've messed up my whole head and everything; I mean I'm really a whole new kind of bird—I'm competely out of this thing."

"Yeah, I'd give you odds on that."

"Hey!" The girl waved a handful of french fries at him, signaling for a truce. "I'm supposed to get paid for having weird conversations so I don't want to hassle for free. Anyway, I've got to go do my bird act now."

Eddie watched her leave, then finished his cole slaw and went down the street to a bar and finally back to his room, a cubbyhole next to the kitchen downstairs. He had no idea how long he had been asleep when he heard something jingling outside in the hall. When the jingling grew still louder, he got up and opened the door.

"Hi," she said. "I thought I'd come play my tambourine for you."

"Fine." The girl began to twist and twirl in front of him, waving the tambourine up and down, spinning languidly, slowly, almost as though she were in a trance. After a while, Eddie asked her if there was anything else she enjoyed doing.

"If you didn't want to hear me play the tambourine, you should have said so in the first place. I hate lies. People should be completely honest."

"Well, I did want to hear you play the tambourine, but now, to be completely honest, I'm tired of it and would prefer fucking or something like that. Free," Eddie added. If she was a hooker, she would be an expensive one.

"Is that the kind of thing you do?"

"What do you mean?"

"I mean I used to, but I've kind of gotten beyond that now. I used to do it all the time, but it just didn't seem to help that much."

Eddie watched as she pulled off the pair of Levi's; she wasn't wearing underpants. "Take off the shirt too."

"What for?"

"That's the way I like it."

She giggled. "You're crazy."

"Not too crazy." He rolled over her, felt her body move under him in one wave, fitting to him perfectly, the movement lasting long after the final spasm. "You know you're beautiful," he said when it was over.

"Yeah, I know," she said.

After that, Eddie went back to his room early every night to wait for her, and every night, when her own show was over, she went through the same performance with him—knocking on the door, playing the tambourine for a while, then, coaxed into bed, making love with him. Now even her tambourine excited him and, in bed, she seemed some perfect extension of his own desire, as easy to manipulate as a dream. He even liked to talk to her, enjoying her

222

fantasy as much as his own, enjoying her youth and self-assurance and conviction. She seemed to make both oblivion and action possible and about the rest he did not think much. He was extremely happy with the arrangement until, a little over a week later, he met Tommy—long bleached hair, chartreuse jumpsuit, ruffled blouse. "Wanted to have a word with you about Linda."

Eddie nodded.

Tommy bounced in on a pair of Three Musketeers boots and sat down. "She's a crazy chick; doesn't know what she's doing half the time, you know what I mean?"

"No," Eddie said.

"She hasn't been doing her bit, see, because she's been getting some interference. It's thrown her off the track, and I don't like that. Now I've set her straight, but I don't want any more interference. I don't want anyone getting confused. You dig what I'm putting on to you?"

"No."

"Look, she's my chick and she's busy; she's got her job and she does her crazy lay bit for the customers, not the hired help. I don't want you with her, that's all." He got up and started for the door, then stopped. "How's the bar show going anyway?"

Eddie shrugged.

"I'll be in to see as soon as I have some time. I'm kind of tied up."

There was no knock on the door that night, and Eddie did not see her the next day. An old half-forgotten loneliness rose in him, not the numb death loneliness he had lived with all his life but the agonizing loneliness one has for another person. Then, two days later, between shows, he saw her sitting in the back of the bar. "I guess you're back at work," he said, sitting down beside her.

"Yeah, really weird. I told this guy all about how there wasn't any brown rice in Vegas, and he said he'd send me some—all the way from Florida."

"I haven't seen you for a while," Eddie said.

"Yeah."

"I actually miss hearing the tambourine."

"Yeah? Well, it finally gets through to people." She began to hum to herself, her eyes searching through the crowd for something, then she looked up at the ceiling as though she had forgotten he was there. "I may leave." The words came without explanation.

"Why? It's going to be just perfect here."

"Yeah, I'm beginning to get bored with it. I mean it's the same old men all the time. When's it going to get better? You're the first freak. I told Tommy all about it, but Tommy said you weren't a freak or you wouldn't be working here. He said you were a hired freak, a professional, and probably blew a few in the bus depot for extra money."

"If I'm a hired freak, what does that make you?"

"Hey, are you trying to hassle me? Tommy doesn't pay me anything." Her voice dropped softly, lost somewhere in her head for a moment. "Tommy said he'd knock my teeth out if I saw you again."

"I guess that's the payoff."

"Yeah." She smiled vaguely and then drifted out of the room and was gone.

After his last show, Eddie walked up and down Fremont Street, past the winos in sandwich boards—IMMEDIATE OUT OF STATE CHECK CASHING. He drank a few beers and shot craps for a while, playing mechanically until he broke even and quit. Finally, when he had reached his tolerance for boredom, he went back to his room and listened to a quarter's worth of radio. Two hours later he heard a tambourine and the girl was at the door again.

"You're taking a chance, Linda."

"Hey, that's my name."

"I know. Your boss, Tommy, told me. Now get going before you get in trouble with him."

"I'm a free person. I'm nobody's fool." She tapped her tambourine listlessly and then sat down on the bed with him.

224

Eddie put his arm around her and felt her quivering like a small bird. "Are you afraid?"

"No."

"I won't let anyone hurt you."

"No one can hurt me; I'm a whole new kind of thing. I've fixed it so I can't be hurt."

"Let me see your arm," he said, reaching for the sleeve of her shirt.

"No." She pulled away, rolling over in a small protective heap on the bed.

"Why do you do that?"

"I don't. Just sometimes. Just a few times."

"Why do you do it sometimes?"

"Because it makes me happy."

"Happy about what?"

She moved slowly back toward him, burying her head in his arms. "I don't know. About everything."

"Where do you get it? From Tommy?"

"Yes."

For the next days their lives fit into a new and different pattern. They ate together in a cafeteria two blocks away, spent an hour together each afternoon in the bar or upstairs in the empty Bird Cage, and after she was through work, spent the early morning together, always carefully out of Tommy's sight and on their own time. Then, at the end of the week, Eddie looked out into the audience and saw Tommy and three other men dressed in identical costumes standing at the back of the bar watching him with contempt. When the show was over, Tommy said something to the bartender and he and the three others left. "Tommy was here looking for you," the bartender said, motioning to Eddie as he started to leave. "Wants to see you upstairs."

Five men waited for him, all of them lounging insolently around an opulent harem-style office—mirrored ceiling, fur pillows, chaise

225

longues—as though their at-ease positions would establish their importance in the scheme of things. Eddie stood uneasily by the door. "Vegas, this is . . ." Tommy said, introducing him swiftly to the other men, all of whom had marquee names as phony as his own. "We're in the process, as you know, of kind of redoing the place." Tommy waved his hand. "Changing the whole image. The upstairs is in good shape now, with the Bird Cage and the lounge; now we want to do something about the bar and the whole downstairs—get rid of all those five-and -dimers shuffling through with their shopping bags of crap." The four loungers laughed. "This isn't an old folks' home."

"What happens to them?"

"They die, Vegas; it's a fact of life—old people die." The four laughed in unison. "And then who's going to make all the little machines go slicketyslicketyslickety *brrrrrrr*ring?" Tommy asked, rolling his eyes in imitation of a slot machine.

"Beautiful," one of the men said.

"Cute, cute bit; we should put you in the lounge."

"We want to get the tribes in here, and you, Vegas"—Tommy eyed his nose, his shirt, finally riveting on his stomach before coming up with the words—"look like something else. This is not a truck stop." The four men were helpless with laughter.

"Oh, Tommy, Tommy. Stop."

"All I'm saying, Vegas, is that when we redo the bar, we're going to have to redo you too. The act we'll keep, but from now on you have to look like you know what's happening. Joey," Tommy called, and a kid with long hair and green eyeshades skipped in from another room. "Fix Vegas here up in something for the bar, will you, baby?" Tommy looked back at Eddie. "Joey'll fix you up."

Eddie followed the kid, glad to get away from Tommy and his audience, his objections mute for the moment. Then, once the door was closed, he heard an argument start up in the other room. "My God, he looks like a dumb prizefighter."

226

"Prizefighter! He looks like a wrestler."

"Can't you get anyone else for the bar?"

"Not that cheap."

Joey rummaged through a large wardrobe closet. "Here," he said, holding up a lace shirt. "This should fit. Try it." Eddie pulled the shirt on over his head—buttonless, the neck open in a wide V to the navel, exposing strands of curly chest hair that also poked out here and there through the lace, giving him the appearance of a baboon in a negligee. "Then let's try these," Joey said, holding up a pair of striped bell bottoms with an accentuated leather crotch.

"No. I'm not going to wear any of this shit."

"It's all that's going to fit. You should really try to reduce; you're in no shape . . ." Something monstrous in his mirror image forced Eddie into the pants while the boy stood staring at him. "Now a scarf or something," he said, coming up eventually with a leather thong and a beaded headband. "You look like . . . entirely different," the boy said, standing back.

"Yeah," Eddie agreed, "but like an entirely different what?" *Mirror mirror on the wall.*

The door between the two rooms opened again, and Tommy, followed by the others, their faces lost for an expression, entered. "Wild," Tommy said finally. "That's a sight that would blow anyone's mind."

Grabbing either side of the V neck, Eddie ripped the shirt in two. "Tell it to one of your other hired freaks."

"Look, Vegas, you've been out in the toolies too long; there's a revolution going on."

"I hope so," Eddie said, pulling his own clothes back on. "I'm going to join it in these."

"Vegas, you fifties faggot, you're going to change or you're fired."

"I'm fired."

Tommy and the four men whirled around as if on signal, then

227

Tommy called back, his voice rising in a high falsetto, "And that shirt's yours, baby. You can pay for it or be sued for destroying private property."

"Go fuck yourself."

Downstairs again, Eddie did his last show, explaining carefully to the two men in the bar that they weren't dressed like contemporary suckers and were not welcome. The two men looked at him balefully as though they found it impossible to understand whom he was talking to. They continued to drink. Eddie told them about the tribes. One of the men said, "Shut up." Eddie did; he went back to the room to wait for the girl although he was almost positive that she would not appear. Tommy would see to that. But early in the morning, as usual, he heard her tambourine.

"I'm going," he said, greeting her at the door with the news.

"Hey, great; to L.A.? I'm fed up with this; I want to go to L.A. too." Her face turned rhapsodic with the whole idea.

"L.A.? What would I do there?"

"Do?" She shrugged. "You'd be in L.A., that's what you'd do. That's where the ocean is, a lot of stuff like that." She began tapping the tambourine. "We could go swimming."

"Yeah, I guess so," Eddie agreed. "It might not be too bad. I've always thought I'd like to see the ocean."

"Waves," Linda said.

"It's supposed to be pretty nice all right. I've seen some pictures. Just cards, of course."

26 Eleanor looked out across the broad lawn to the cottonwood and the fringe of dying elm in the parking. There was only a low wall there; she could escape. She smiled to herself. Perhaps she would move to the west coast; perhaps live with bleached hair in L.A. where no one would know her. The doctor coughed, pulling her back from the window to the chair. "Let's go on," he said. "How long were you in Columbus?"

"Three years." The doctor tapped his pencil patiently, waiting for her to continue, but she stood mentally two doors down from Chittenden on Fourth looking into the laundromat. All the doors had been pulled off the dryers, the washing machines stood empty and in ruin, and below COIN LAUNDRY, OPEN 24 HOURS another sign said: FOR RENT. She picked up the bag of dirty clothes and started back to her room.

"Why don't you tell me more about it? Where did you live?"

"In a one-room apartment above a grocery store. From my window I could see the back alley and the steps that led down to the parking lot and the row of garbage cans below. There were always dogs and rats in the alley, and sometimes drunks walking and puking there, going home from the bar on the corner. In the apartment across the hall there was a couple from Arkansas with a small baby. Every day the woman hung diapers across the back porch in front of my window. She never spoke to me; later, after she had hung up the wash, I would hear her crying. Her husband was very friendly, good-natured; he did all the shopping, did the wash, played with the baby on the porch. At night the wife would

229

scream endlessly, and I would hear her crying again in the morning when I left for school. One day they were gone; a note hung on their door, and I read that note two or three times a day: 'To Whom It May Concern—I have taken the baby and gone to St. Louis. Paul.' "

"Why did you stop to read the note again and again?"

Eleanor shook her head. "Whom did it concern? It seemed so vague. So ominous. Suppose it concerned me? I could not make up my mind. If it did concern me, what was I to do? Cry? Laugh? Was it a threat? A joke? A plea for help? A statistic? Someone wrote, 'Fuck you, Paul' on the bottom of the note; finally the Scotch tape gave and the note fell to the floor, then, eventually, it faded, discolored, and disappeared."

"The couple with the baby never came back?"

"No."

"The atmosphere you lived in was quite depressing then?"

Eleanor turned her attention again to the window. Patients walked alone on the lawn, their faces masked, and the sun flooded the distance with waves of light, making the cottonwoods shimmer as though under water. "Children came in and urinated in the halls; they left turds on the front steps and on the porch. The place smelled."

"Did you have friends?"

"I had no friends; I had my work."

"Your. . . ?"

"My dissertation. I spent most of the day in the library, ate dinner at a café nearby, and then returned to work at the library until about eleven. When I got home, I forced myself to think, to reread my notes, to write a few paragraphs." Her mind wandered again. She sat in a small café crowded with others like herself— alone, books propped open as they waited for their orders. The waitress wearing a sari over long underwear brought her a basket of Indian bread, then something too hot to describe, and tea. The special cost sixty cents and she ate it every day, sometimes imagin-

230

ing pork roast and candied apples, chicken and dumplings, corn-bread and dried beef gravy, sausage and grits, food she'd eaten when she was a child and rich. Now she lived in poverty and ate Indian foods. Her mind sought rest, union, something beyond these particulars. As she walked back to the library she felt faint.

The doctor smiled, cleared his throat. "Uh uh huh. You had no time for a social life?" he asked finally.

"I had no mind for it."

"And your work . . . it was in philosophy, was it?"

Is it? Eleanor nodded her head slowly. "Logic. I'm working on 'Some Problems in Aberrant Logics and Modal Contexts.' "

"Aberrant logic? That's almost a contradiction, isn't it?"

"I once thought so, but the more I worked with the problem, the more aberrant my mind became." She smiled; it was a joke. "My mind became more aberrant than the logic." That was really funny; she should write comedy. But the doctor did not smile. She tried to explain. "The norm is itself a deviation from reality, an abstraction into fantasy. What is aberrant about logics that don't fit the norm is only that they don't fit. In other words, what is called aberrant is called so by an appeal to a standard which is itself aberrant. It is all nonsense, tricks, all a sleight-of-hand." Eleanor stopped; she was beginning to lose control. She turned back to the window, to the trees beyond. Cars passed somewhere behind the trees and the brick wall.

"Why did you choose such a field—logic?"

Eleanor smiled. "Because I love its crystal clarity. It is a mirror through which I see, my measure of the world, a yardstick held up to reality." Metaphors often drove her berserk. *Perfectly clear, perfectly clear, perfectly clear.* The hour was over.

"Logic is simply a formal language, like mathematics, isn't it?" The doctor smiled from behind his desk again, pretending a great interest. "Of course, this is your field, not mine; mine is the mind."

Eleanor smiled. "Mmm," she said. *Tearing up the pea patch in*

231

your head because my field is the mind.

The doctor waited for something, then continued coaxingly. "I wish to delve into this subject with you a little more. Addition, subtraction, that is all a kind of logic, is it not? Nothing odd about it: two plus two equals four."

"A language for what, to speak about what? If you have two oranges and two peaches, do you then have four oranges?"

"I don't understand."

"Maybe you would have four peaches. With you I suppose it's a matter of choice."

"Of course not. Mathematics is an exact science; it is . . ."

Eleanor did not wait for him to go on. "One drop of water and another drop of water when added together do not make two drops of water. That is the mathematics of life; that is the only mathematics that interests me and that is not exact; it is crazy." She was becoming extremely excited.

"Why don't you take up painting?" the doctor asked soothingly.

"With numbers?" Eleanor screamed.

"Miss Smith! I simply mean, if abstractions so bother you, why not turn to art, to nature. Why not paint a babbling brook, the Rocky Mountains, Niagara Falls in the moonlight."

Eleanor was incredulous. She giggled. "And how would I paint any of those things?"

"Many women like the delicacy of watercolor, oil; and then there are charcoal drawings. . . ."

"Yes," Eleanor said, "or I could collect garbage from the cans outside—coffee grains, used condoms, beer cans, eggshells, anything—smear the garbage on a canvas, cut a hole at the top of the canvas, hang the canvas over a faucet, and turn on the water. 'Niagara Falls this way,' I could shout from the window, scream all day, 'See Niagara Falls.'" Eleanor giggled.

"I said art, Miss Smith."

"I could frame my work in an elaborate gold frame, cupids frolicking at the top."

"A gold frame can do nothing for garbage."

"But," Eleanor said triumphantly, "the gold frame separates the garbage to which our attention is drawn from the garbage to which it is not drawn, separates the work of art from the wall. If it were not for picture frames, people might go to museums and look at peeled paint, cracks in the wall, snot buggers some kid has wiped from his nose. The frame is the context in which art exists, and it distorts, just as art itself distorts."

"If the painter is mad, but I'm afraid this conversation is getting off the track. I'm afraid that . . ."

"All artists are mad; they could not otherwise select or choose, could not otherwise create a logic of their own. The question is: how best to go mad? What are the transformation rules here? What logic governs this distortion of life?" She was screaming.

"Miss Smith! Calm yourself. Perhaps we should return to the discussion of your work."

"I am discussing my work," Eleanor said quietly. Why was everyone she met so stupid? "My work was in logic," she said patiently, prompting his memory, "in particular, aberrant logics, for I was interested in logic as a mode of distortion, not as a fanciful ideal but as a rule governing the transformation of vague notes into screaming women, threats into reality. These things I manipulated by means of argument and proof."

"Tell me, just out of curiosity; how was your work accepted?"

"My adviser said that I was completely confused, that I confused logical levels. He explained again the difference between first-order things and second-order things. Hume, he said, tortured his mind about causation; Hume saw no connection whatsoever between one object, a ball, for instance, and another, the mallet, and the movement of the ball. Nevertheless, after he had tortured his mind with these doubts, he went out and played croquet with no qualms at all. Hume knew the difference, knew that sense was to be made at one level, not another. Then my adviser explained again about Descartes, about how Descartes's doubt was philosophical, not

233

common or real. Descartes knew commonsensically that he existed; his doubt was simply a tool in his second-order research. How, my adviser wondered aloud, could I have passed the qualifying exam without understanding this basic difference in logical levels?"

"Well, then," the doctor said, "after you saw your mistake . . ."

"But I did not," Eleanor said sharply. "I did not see my mistake because I had made no mistake. I was not confused. I wanted to understand why threatening notes were pushed under the door, why every washing machine was in disrepair, why the food was always the same. I was not confused; I wanted a logic of life."

"And your adviser. . . ?"

"Said that the question 'Why is the washing machine broken?' was not philosophic. But of course my question was: 'Why are all washing machines broken?' That made my adviser laugh; he thought it was a joke." Eleanor glanced out the window, distracted for a moment.

"Did you continue your work; I mean did you continue to give your work to your adviser?"

A man on his hands and knees was picking a bouquet of grass. "Yes," Eleanor said softly. "I continued to write nonsense, to make problems where none existed, to confuse real tables and philosophic tables."

"Your adviser. . . ?"

"Said that my work was incoherent, totally unacceptable, actually stupid." Eleanor smiled. "I had come to think so myself. I began to have nightmares and headaches."

"Ah," said the doctor as though he had finally drawn a conclusion. "The rejection of your work precipitated the first breakdown, then. It was your failure to finish your degree that triggered . . ."

"No," Eleanor said wearily, "that didn't upset me. It was my experience, my mind. I experience what my mind knows is false—charades, disguises, lies, deceit—but what does my mind offer instead? What does my mind substitute for experience? Nothing

234

but empty tautologies and faith in fantasies contrary to all experience. If experience is a nightmare, faith is a form of insanity. What could I believe?"

"So," said the doctor, still drawing conclusions, "you were agitated, so agitated that . . ."

"Nothing follows. I continued to work in the library. I reread Kant; I read Hanson. I began to turn inward, to hunt for some pattern in the self or in the series of my observations, to hunt for some logic in myself. *To whom it may concern.* I saw the note on the door across the hall differently at different times; I began to record the variety of appearances and their relationship to me, the observer and distorter. How was I standing today, what was I wearing, how had I slept, how hungry was I, how depressed, where did the sunlight fall in the hallway, what was the smell? This record I turned in chapter by chapter."

"And . . . ?"

"My adviser said it was all a bad joke, that I must think myself some kind of comedian. He was incredulous; he could not wait to read sections of my dissertation to the others in the faculty dining room. I became the laughingstock of the department; people whispered behind my back, made joke upon joke." Eleanor laughed. "Actually my dissertation was quite interesting—it had action, mystery, people, funny stories, little asides, recipes for Indian foods. Once I went down to the basement of the library where the old dissertations were kept, those that had been accepted, and read through several of them. I have never been so bored. All that nonsense. What is the point? And I was the first person ever to have checked any of them out. Unread notes." *To whom it may concern.*

There was a long silence. The doctor tapped his fingertips together thoughtfully. "The attempt on your life," he said finally, selecting his words carefully. "Was that when you made the attempt?"

"Suicide?"

"Tell me about the attempt."

"I began to get threatening notes—'To Whom It May Concern: If I see you spying on me again, watching me hang up the laundry or listening at the door, I'll kill you. Believe me, I'll kill you.' They were actually trying to kill me."

"They?"

"The people next door. They had no child; they simply wanted to block my view with diapers; they screamed all night to keep me awake. I was frightened; I asked my adviser for help. I told him that my life was at stake."

"And what was his reaction to that?"

"He said that he was writing several things for publication and could not be bothered. He did not take me seriously. As I walked home through the snow, I noticed for the first time that most people in my neighborhood carried guns. At the corner of Summit and Chittenden, I asked a Negro in a black felt cowboy hat if I might borrow his gun. He refused me. I was scared witless, but I continued down Chittenden, turned on Fourth, and then went up the steps to the apartment. The hall was dark; it smelled of dirty diapers. When I turned the key, I found still another note pushed under my door—'To Whom It May Concern: Today's the day; you've had your last chance to snoop.' I went into the bathroom and bled."

"From the heart?"

"From the wrist."

The doctor coughed. "Mmmm," he said. "And do you remember what happened next?"

"Maybe I screamed, maybe I fainted. After a while they came and took me away."

"Who?"

"Strangers."

"Took you where?"

"I wasn't sure."

"Did you like it there?"

"No."

236

"What did you do?"

"I continued my work, but I no longer submitted it to my adviser. Some of it I sent to people I read about in the papers, some to various magazines. Chapters of my dissertation began to appear in various literary quarterlies, in underground newspapers; I was asked to write a comedy." Eleanor smiled. "I sent a postcard to my adviser saying that now I was writing several things for publication. I didn't say what. Let him find out for himself. He didn't answer. I wrote again to tell him that Hanson had buzzed the hospital twice in a P-47. I read about him in an old *Flying* magazine; I'm crazy about airplanes, being myself a pilot."

"Did your adviser respond to that?"

"Yes. He said Hanson was dead. He had crashed into a football stadium or Niagara Falls, I forget which. There was a war on."

"Which one?"

"Does it matter?"

"Getting tired?"

"Yes."

Once back in her room, she began to work again, carefully describing the doctor. But after dinner, when she returned to the room, her work was gone.

"Perhaps," the doctor said later, "it is your work that upsets you. Perhaps it would be best to give it up for a while."

Eleanor smiled. She was more upset by the old man who sat at dinner every night spooning mashed potatoes into his fly, but this she did not mention. Her work went on in her mind; she had hallucinations.

"This happens to a great many people when they overwork," the doctor said. "They become so intent on their work that their life suffers. They wear down psychologically. You need rest; your mind needs rest."

Eleanor became confused; she did not know whom it concerned.

"Don't you want to get well?"

237

She did not answer.

"Eleanor?"

She had forgotten her name.

"Your parents are really quite concerned."

Her parents? She had difficulty remembering anything. She painted her face and put a feather in her hair to distinguish herself from the others. She refused to eat mashed potatoes. Finally she waited in ambush for the nurse, springing upon her when she brought in the tray of pills and the selection of paper cups. "Ugphphphph," said the nurse in a muffled voice. Eleanor left a note To Whom It May Concern.

A Red Indian Thought He Might Eat Tobacco In Church

27 They watched the ducks in MacArthur Park, a long way from the ocean. No one here seemed to know about the ocean; so they contented themselves with the lake. Sitting crowded together in a long row of old men and drunks, they threw popcorn to the ducks. Eddie watched three ducks swim toward him through the slick green water, skirting tin cans, boxes, gum wrappers, soggy popcorn, and half a cheese sandwich, like sailboats on an obstacle course. "Hey," Linda said, "they really like you."

"They want to get the popcorn before it falls in the water." He arched the popcorn into the air, holding the attention of the ducks and the people for a minute. On a small rise behind the lake, a man with a Bible was screaming soundlessly, his arms waving. A small group, some of them with their own Bibles, were screaming with him. In the distance a mariachi band played, drowning out all but the loudest shouts of the Bible group. "AMEN."

"C'mon," Linda said. "I'm tired of this." Her words were a warning, a small cloud. Eddie tossed her a piece of popcorn, and she danced back, giggling, to catch it, dispelling the gloom. They walked back to the hotel, happy again. Just a block away, the hotel was set back behind three huge arched doorways. Inside there was a large open lobby filled with worn furniture, old men, and free-standing ashtrays. A clerk at the desk smiled at them as they climbed the steps, and parted a velvet curtain to the second floor. The halls were wide and dark, carpeted with an old flowered pattern; at the end of each hall was a glass door to a fire escape. Their room was at the end, overlooking the parking lot across the

239

street and Carpenters' Local 25 on the corner.

Linda pulled a plastic bag from one of the bureau drawers and rolled out two cigarettes, lighting one, drawing on it, and then handing it to him. Eddie watched her face, beautiful and abstract. She curled delicately at his side, and he could feel her silence, share it, love her. His mind filled with dreams, images of trees in the moonlight, quiet ponds. "Let's go live in the desert," Linda said, "surrounded by nothing but space. The sun will shine; everything will be yellow and bright."

The wind blew the leaves and the tall grass rustled around his feet as he stood on a hill looking down into a valley of wild flowers, yellow ones. "There won't be anyone there but us." He smiled at her.

"And we'll sleep outside under the stars." She was getting very excited.

"And there will be fruit trees all around." Eddie wandered through the glade again, the tall grass almost waist high. The house was gone now and the school, and when he slept outside, it wasn't in a car and it wasn't alone. His throat and mouth filled with smoke, and he nodded happily at her and at his own dreams, his mind a landscape. He leaned over then to kiss her, rolling over her, hearing her voice, light and distant, hearing her laugh. Their bodies began to move together. Opening her mouth against his, she blew smoke into his lungs. His body swelled, his mind swelled, and he could feel her shudder beneath him, then, warm and sleepy, he drifted away, his mind distant.

In a minute she was laughing. "Tommy will be there," she said. "I'll play the tambourine with a rock group, a really good rock group, but I'll stand on top of a sand dune and they'll be below. Everyone will be there; all these really intelligent people grooving in the desert, loving the sun."

The snow was falling, and everything was white and perfect. They were running in it, snow-covered themselves. He heard her singing to herself and smiled. How intricately they were bound

240

now, their minds one like their bodies. As he watched her mouth move, his eyes misted over, and he saw that her eyes were liquid, running red with joy. He fell asleep.

Eddie flipped through the want ads in the paper, while Linda whined at him. "C'mon, let's do something. Let's go someplace. Do something groovy."

"We don't have any more money."

"You're not going to get some crummy job?"

"Just for a while. I have to get some money before we can go anyplace."

Linda smiled coyly, curling up beside him on the floor. "We don't need money."

"How are we going to pay the bill?"

"Who cares? But I'm not going to sit around in this crummy hotel waiting for you to come back from some sordid job."

"You can go sit in the park."

"I'll pick pockets. I'll rob a bank."

"O.K. You do that while I go see about getting a job." Eddie left her sitting on the bed playing her tambourine. He took a bus first to a Hollywood employment agency and then to an unemployment office, where he stood in line twice listening to the rejects gossip about hard times and the big jobs they had almost had. "My brother-in-law killed me, right? As soon as the producer got my name, the no-sale sign came on." By the end of the day, Eddie had a small list of job possibilities, mostly commercials. He took the bus back to Alvarado, walked along the park on Alvarado, crossed Wilshire, and then cut through the park toward Lake Street. Halfway across the park he saw her. She was sitting on a bench throwing popcorn to the ducks; he stopped and watched her for a minute, then walked down the path to the lake. "Hi," she said, noncommittally. Eddie wedged himself onto the bench beside her along with the three old men. "I got a few leads, some names and addresses. Have you been here all day?"

"No."

Eddie looked at the people who lay sprawled under newspapers on the hill, at the benches, all of them filled with old men, at the crowd on the shuffleboard court. "What did you do?"

"Went to a movie," Linda said, still intently throwing popcorn, her voice a whisper.

"The one on Alvarado?"

Linda nodded vaguely. "I saw a double feature."

He didn't believe her. "Anything you want to do now?"

"No."

"We could go get something to eat."

"O.K., if you want."

They walked silently down Lake, past a long low series of prefabricated nursing homes, a teamsters' local, a cooks' union hall. At the corner of Ninth stood an old three-story mansion, still looking elegant and luxurious despite the fact that its grounds had been paved for parking and wooden wheelchair ramps had replaced the veranda; it too was a nursing home. They continued past a couple of old motels built hacienda style with adobe fronts, tile roofs, and interior gardens, the gardens now modernized to include swimming pools and additional off-street parking—movie marquee signs hanging in front advertised CLEAN ROOMS, LOW RATES—then they turned down the block to a small Mexican restaurant, with a long narrow counter, two tables, and a pinball machine. "What do you want?" Eddie asked, standing at the counter.

"I'll just eat a little of whatever you get."

"Want anything to drink?"

She nodded.

"Beer?"

She nodded again.

"Look," Eddie said, sitting down with the combination plate and two beers. "What's the matter?"

"Nothing."

"I just need to get some money for us."

She stared at him blankly. "I want to go someplace. Let's go see what Tommy's doing or . . ." Her voice wandered off.

Eddie looked at a woman sitting at the counter with two men; she wore bright green satin shoes, a tight black skirt, and a red sweater. Every now and then the woman turned to look at him, her lips, painted over the entire bottom half of her face, smiling at him. Linda leaned lethargically over the table staring at the food on his plate; he tried to think of something that might arouse her interest. "If we had some money, we could go to Hawaii," he said, and the idea, a fantasy of flamingos and tropical birds, came to him from the print on an old shirt. "We could go to the beach," he mumbled.

"Or Niagara Falls."

"Yeah."

"Entertain me."

"Huh?"

"Say something funny."

"What do you want to do?"

"I want to dance."

"All right." He watched as she got out of her chair and began to twirl around and around in the narrow aisle between counter and tables. The two men watched her momentarily, then lost interest and returned to their own sullen silences. "Linda," Eddie said quietly. He pushed back his plate and stood beside her. "Come on, let's go." She smiled at him.

Outside the sky was heavy, dark, and starless, and they walked past another series of nursing homes, where tiny birdlike people sat up in bed staring out at them. A woman, a mink coat over her evening gown, stopped before one of the homes in a Cadillac, got out with a cashbox, and went inside. Beside him, Linda danced and hummed tunelessly. They crossed the street and started down Alvarado past the peepshow arcade and the homosexual movie house where a girl with a bubble hairdo sat in the glass box office chewing bubble gum. "It's kind of depressing here."

"What?" Linda smiled at him dreamily.

"I said it's kind of depressing here." At the corner of Eighth, a boy in paratroop boots, an old army coat, and a Nazi helmet was directing traffic with a machine gun, swinging the gun out like a baton to motion oncoming traffic. Cars swerved around him, honking, speeding up at the intersection. Finally a cab driver reached out and grabbed the gun as he drove by.

"He's dancing," Linda observed. But the boy had fallen flat across the pavement and begun to cry now.

"Yeah." They crossed the street. A crowd was slowly gathering on the corner, and a siren could be heard in the distance. By the time they were a block away, an ambulance and a police car had arrived. "Let's go up," Eddie said, pushing into the hotel. The desk clerk was asleep, the lobby empty, and they went up the steps and through the velvet curtains in silence. Back in the room, Linda sat staring at her arm, intently picking at the lint on her sweater. Eddie shuffled a pack of cards in the air. "Pick a card."

"Which one?"

"Any one." He fanned the cards before her.

"That one."

"Take it." She pulled out a card, and Eddie reshuffled the pack thoughtfully. "The three of spades."

"No."

"It's not the three of spades?"

"No."

"What was it?"

"I won't tell."

"Let me see the card." She crumpled the card in her hand and put it in her mouth. "Linda, for crissake, let me see it." In a minute the card drooled out of her mouth; it was the three of spades. "What was the point of that?"

"I didn't want to be tricked."

"You can't keep from being tricked by hiding the evidence."

She giggled. "But I sure can make you mad. Card tricks are dumb. When I was little they used to hire an old clown to come

244

to my birthday parties; he did card tricks." She giggled again, her eyes lighting up. "He looked a lot like you; he had a big nose. Once I set fire to it."

"To what?"

"His nose; his was fake. Then this other kid set fire to his tail when he turned around. The clown poured Coca-Cola over the fire, grabbed the Coke from one of the kids. Then this kid set fire to his wig, and he had to pull the whole thing off. He was bald underneath. When we ran out of matches, we began to throw the cake at him."

Eddie stared at her. "What happened to the clown?"

Linda shrugged. "I don't know. He was almost nude, just standing there covered with frosting when they came and got him. Next year I had a birthday dance instead."

"I knew an old clown once."

"Did they hire him for all your birthday parties?"

"I never had any."

"You were lucky."

"I guess so." They lapsed into silence. In the parking lot across the street, lights turned on and off, and they sat like shadows in the darkness watching them.

"My parents should see me now," Linda said finally. "Holed up here with a . . ."

"With a what?"

"A lousy lunatic."

"Huh?"

"Tommy told me you'd been in an asylum once."

"That's right."

"Then why don't you act like a lunatic? Why don't you do something crazy?" she whined.

"Like what?" Eddie asked.

"Why don't you set the hotel on fire?" She suddenly grabbed the pack of matches and rushed toward the window. "If we set the curtains on fire, the whole place will go up."

"You're crazy," he said, grabbing the matches away from her.

"I'm bored." She began to cry. "Bored, bored, bored. What are you going to get a job doing? You can't even entertain me. I want to do something."

"What?"

"Who cares?" She broke into sobs.

"Don't." He held her in his arms and felt her cold and shivering. "Please don't." He rocked her, and in a minute she was asleep. He carried her to the bed, then, opening the bureau drawer, he rolled out one thin cigarette and lit it. Music played, and a block away, on the other side of the parking lot, he could see an old woman, her blond Shirley Temple curls bouncing, her arms swinging. He could see her as clearly as if she were magnified—she was standing in front of a television set dancing.

In the morning Eddie could not at first decide what to do. Beside him, Linda still slept, a half smile on her face. He made up his mind, finally, to go around the corner for breakfast, but in the lobby, the hotel clerk held up the unpaid bill. Eddie nodded distantly as though he did not quite understand what it was. Reaching in his pocket, he got out the list of names and addresses and then took the Hollywood bus again. The first place, an agency, was hunting for someone who looked like a Pekingese for a series of ads showing a man on all fours with a Pekingese eating from a dog bowl. "Bow Wow foods will make you wish you were a dog." The man in the office looked at Eddie and shook his head. "Listen," he said. "Come back in a couple of weeks when we film the boxer commercial. You've got a nice jowl line."

On the floor below, another agency was hunting for an Oriental with green teeth. After an hour's wait, a woman called him forward and told him he might as well go. "I could paint my teeth green," Eddie suggested.

"That's against the law."

Eddie tried two more agencies, one of them hunting for a midget, the other for "something different in the way of an ordinary man." At the last one he waited two hours to be interviewed. "What are your characteristic expressions?" the woman asked, looking up briefly from a notebook. Eddie wiggled his ears, crossed his eyes, drooled. "No," the woman said in a bored voice. "You could be anyone. Anyone at all." Eddie looked carefully at the others in line as he left. Six of the men had green teeth; behind them stood half a dozen midgets in body stockings.

It was now almost three-thirty. Eddie bought a paper and looked again at the want ads. One of them caught his attention: "Need comedians for original material." The address given was that of a local motel, not far away. At first Eddie hesitated, loitering suspiciously in front of the Hollywood Palm Garden, then he went in. Another line of men, a fairly small one this time, encouraged him; he stood behind them. In half an hour, a girl opened the door and motioned him inside. The girl wore a feather in her hair and had lines of paint drawn across her forehead; she seemed greatly agitated. Once inside and alone with her, Eddie began to shift nervously. "This is for some kind of a comedy," he said, since the girl seemed to expect him to speak first. "That's what the ad said." The girl wrote his words down in a looseleaf notebook and then waited for him to go on. "I suppose it's something about a Chinese midget who eats dog food?" The girl laughed and again copied his statement word for word in her notebook. "Or about a Pekingese who eats Chinese food?" The girl smiled and copied this remark as well. Eddie was beginning to feel annoyed. "What are you doing? What are you writing?"

"I'm writing a book, a thesis," she said, diligently recording his last remark. "It's a comedy."

"You mean there's no job? This is some kind of trick?"

The girl noted down his question as she spoke. "It's no trick; it's simply a matter of fact."

"I've been standing in line," Eddie said.

"Yes," the girl said, writing this carefully.

"Are you crazy?"

"Not any more; I've quit distorting. I just record."

"That's what you think. Putting a goddamn crazy ad in the paper. I'd like to . . ." He opened the door and began to run down the hall, past the six midgets in body stockings. Once in the court-yard of the Palm Garden, he slowed to a walk.

It was almost dark now. On Hollywood Boulevard he caught an empty bus and then stared mindlessly out the window until he got off at Alvarado. Some premonition of disaster forced him to run. He cut quickly across the park and ran up the lake, past a small group of men arguing outside a union hall and an old woman leaning against a car, her arms loaded with rags. When the hotel was in view, he stopped running, momentarily relieved, but up-stairs, he found the room empty. "Linda," he called softly, but she was not there; nothing was.

Eddie stood at the window looking down at the street below. Cars moved in and out of the parking lot, and men gathered at the corner and in doorways to drink. A Mexican whore called up to him, moving her tongue slowly in and out of her mouth with the entreaty, but Eddie remained at the window, waiting. Later, sev-eral dozen small explosions popped like a series of firecrackers, and a fire started somewhere in the distance. Eddie heard sirens and sensed a growing tension in the men on the corner and those sitting on the curb across the street. A few drunks mumbled under their breath as they wandered down the street in the direction of the fire, then suddenly there were several more explosions on Alvarado and angry shouts below. Eddie leaned out the window into another silence, his own mind ready to explode, drawn to the frustration and anger outside. There was no traffic on Eighth now; two blocks away, on Olympic, only the soundless hum of rubber.

Eddie went downstairs, through the empty lobby to the street. A bottle broke two feet in front of him, and then a small group of men ran out of a liquor store up the block, shouting and throwing

248

bottles. Eddie joined them. On Alvarado they smashed the window of a bank, still smeared with fading *Bring the War Home* slogans, and two little boys from a motel across the street climbed through the opening with cans of gasoline and rags. In a minute the bank was on fire. Eddie surged on with the growing crowd, meeting around the corner a larger and noisier mob. Two or three more fires were set in trashcans, and then sirens and fire trucks approached from either end of Alvarado, moving toward the bank and a nursing home on Ninth, both in flames. Eddie saw an old woman in a nightgown leaning out of a second-story window and saw a man on the sidewalk set fire to his suit, then Eddie was pushed forward. A storm of rocks and garbage hailed toward the firemen. At the corner the first fire truck stopped and sprayed water down the street, momentarily flushing back the crowd. A woman beside Eddie stripped and began to dance in the water until the force of it knocked her down. At that moment the crowd surged ahead in a new wave of anger, men screaming, women crying, children laughing.

Eddie picked up a broken bottle and ran, guided by the crowd, toward the firemen, slashing the air until, finally, the glass made contact somewhere in the blur of movement. Eddie felt blood run over his hands, and then, before he knew what had happened, he was pushed forward again. His feet were wet and he was screaming, screaming that he didn't know where he was, what he was doing, screaming with hate and impotence, screaming that nothing made sense, screaming for more blood.

Sirens whined up Eighth and Ninth, and then four squad cars blocked one end of Alvarado and canisters of tear gas hurled down the street. For the first time Eddie saw guns. Two men on the sidewalk not far from where he stood held up small pistols and began firing. A woman in front of him slid to the ground soundlessly, and Eddie saw blood trickle from the corner of her mouth and from one ear. Two guns appeared behind one of the squad cars, and suddenly the air turned acrid and unbreathable; his eyes burned, and he started running back down Alvarado in the other direction.

At Seventh a phalanx of cops, a blue army of them, marched at an angle through the park, their guns drawn, their gas masks on. Gunshots whistled and whined through the air, and panic and confusion moved the crowd in a chaos of direction. On the other side of Wilshire, still another fire started in an old movie theater; Eddie saw the marquee darken, then a bright blast of flame jet out over the sidewalk. He ran toward the fire, pushed ahead by the crowd, his momentum only partly his own. His eyes started to water again so that he could barely see, but behind him he could hear screams of pain, and he knew someone had been shot or trampled. Finally at the corner he broke away, following four men down the far side of Seventh and then along an alley flooded with water drained from a motel swimming pool. The four men disappeared in the next block, and Eddie, alone for the first time, turned into a side street. Suddenly two cops appeared just in front of him, then, just as suddenly, one of them tumbled over like a stunt man between two parked cars. Eddie stopped. From a post office parking lot, three men fired at the remaining cop; a small war was waged back and forth across the street. Eddie retreated hurriedly, running in the direction from which he had come, dropping the bloody bottle half and moving now from Seventh to Eighth, down side streets and alleys. He did not stop running until he was under the intersection of the Santa Monica and Harbor freeways, leaning against a cement pier in the darkness. Cars moved overhead, their fumes and noise making him faint, dizzy, then he heard someone running behind him. He was being followed.

He waited just an instant, listening in the darkness to the movement at his back, before he began to run again, up the hill from the underpass and then down a well lighted street in the financial district. At the corner he turned and looked back. Only two kids. He felt relieved. He walked across the street and then through an empty parking lot toward a small shack with an outsize sign in

250

front: FREE PARKING, OUT-OF-TOWN PAPERS. A loudspeaker on the roof chanted repetitiously: "Get the news, get the news, all fifty states and foreign-language papers in their own language; get the news, get the news, all fifty . . ." Then, almost as though it were a part of the announcement, the words "Templeton, Templeton" came mechanically from the distance. Eddie turned again. The two boys were still behind him, calling to him, "Templeton, Templeton," the name an accusation.

Eddie shook his head. "No," he said, "you've got the wrong person. I'm not Templeton."

"Templeton," they continued as though they had not heard. "Hey, Templeton, we've got something for you."

"No," Eddie said, "you've made a mistake, some kind of mistake." He crossed in the middle of the block and ran up the other side of the street. They followed.

"Hey, Templeton," they chanted continuously. "Hey, Templeton, Templeton."

"No," Eddie shouted back. "Fin-ninny, Fin-ninny." The name twisted on his tongue and came out in a stutter. "Finney," he said again, more clearly this time.

The two boys laughed hollowly. "That's right, Templeton, funny, very funny."

"Finney," Eddie repeated.

"Funny. Funny, funny Templeton."

Eddie looked down a side street for help. Two drunks stared back at him; the area was otherwise deserted. He continued running, then turned into a dark street lined with dingy Japanese restaurants. "Hey, Templeton. Hey, funny man; we've got something for you." Eddie began to run faster, heading down another side street, this one no more than an alley, dark, lined with empty warehouses, a Buddhist temple, more old warehouses. About halfway down the alley he felt something soft and heavy hit him from behind. Sand fell over his ears and ran down his neck. He continued to stumble forward under some terrible weight, seeing sand

251

fall around him; there was another soft thud and he fell on a dune of sand, dizzy, weighted down. He could not focus, could not for a minute see, then two strange faces grinned down at him. He saw a gun, felt something hard and cold, then he stretched out on the sand, the dark cool desert, waiting for the ocean, making faces, humoring himself, playing dead.

28 Manuel did not know exactly what he was doing. He had been running all night, waving his gun in the air, but now he was a long way from everyone else and from the disturbance. Goddamn, he was going to lose his job over this. They had been ordered to stay in tight rank, to remain with their partners at all costs, but after the first fire bomb had been lobbed into the squad, he and Jerry had started down a side street and then run into gunfire in a parking lot. Manuel could remember seeing Jerry drop, could remember shooting back wildly, overcome with anger and fear. There were three of them, and one of them had yelled an obscenity in Spanish after his first shot. "We'll get you, baby, tomorrow if not today." Manuel had been afraid, for himself, for his family. He had run, and now he was downtown standing on a corner in a gas mask. He threw down the mask and ran across the street.

He had been on the force only a year, but had already moved once and changed his phone number twice. Still they found him, made obscene phone calls, threats to his wife and baby, sometimes in Spanish, sometimes in broken English. Now whenever he saw a crowd gather, Manuel knew that within that crowd there was one who would single him out, one who was intent on killing him. One, maybe more, plotting against him. His wife wanted him to quit. "But the money," he said. "What can I do?" She cried and begged him; she didn't want him to get hurt. What could he do? He had to keep running.

He was running down a street of Mexican movie theaters now,

past a crowd lined up at one of the box offices. The men stared at his gun and called to him in Spanish. "Hey, the bandido went to see the movie. Hey, stupid, who are you chasing?" When he turned the corner, he put away the gun and began to walk casually, but as he got farther and farther away from the downtown crowd, somewhere on the other side of Flower, he withdrew the gun again, afraid of the silence and the darkness. He was in an area of deserted warehouses, running again until a sound startled him. He waved the gun, threatening, and then, when the sound came again, shot. Once, twice; he did not know. Still he saw nothing, an empty alley. Goddamn, they were hiding. He ducked into a doorway, pulling a garbage can in beside him. Somewhere in the shadows, no more than three feet away, a cat meowed. Manuel swore at himself, at the cat, and then leaned against the doorway, sick, his hands and the gun shaking, his mind out of control. He started to run again, trying to think straight, trying to pull himself together, and then something in the next block stopped him again.

A man lay, half hidden by shadows, in the entrance to a warehouse. Manuel held out the gun, unsteadily pointing it at the man. *"Usted,"* he called, his voice tight. The man did not answer. *"Usted,"* Manuel called again. He moved forward slowly, frightened. Something about the way the man lay, the way his body sprawled awkwardly across the gravel, made Manuel uneasy, then, when he got closer, he saw that the man was dead. He had caught a criminal single-handed.

29 The chief of police straightened his shoulders and pulled in his stomach as he waited for the mayor to introduce him. The mayor was making a little speech, congratulating himself on the police department, comparing himself to Christ, promising more of the same so long as he was in office, but the chief knew they were all really waiting to hear from him—he had the details, and he had carefully refrained from giving the mayor more than an outline of the case, saving all the more interesting aspects for his own use. Now he was getting impatient; he stopped listening to the mayor and smiled fixedly at his side, shuffling his feet and edging toward the microphone until finally the mayor could no longer ignore him. "And now . . ." the mayor was saying, introducing him.

The chief moved before the microphone with great authority, his body erect, his manner severe and proud but touched with the humility of a conquering hero who knows that someday he will run for office and need votes. After the first few minutes of applause, which he acknowledged with bowed head, the chief asked for silence, raising both hands and extending them toward the crowd as though he were giving a blessing. He was all business now. "As you no doubt know," the chief said over the remaining spatter of applause, "last night, months of slow, patient police investigative work"—he emphasized the word *"police,"* pausing to let it sink in; the mayor was not going to take credit for this one—"finally paid off, resulting in the capture of the man responsible, among other things, for last night's 'spontaneous mayhem.'" He spit out the last

255

two words with great sarcasm and smiled at the applause he got. A few people smirked and laughed. "The man was armed and dangerous, and we were not, unfortunately, able to take him alive. One of our finest young officers gave his life in the attempt; his partner avenged his death." There was more applause, soft, slow, heartfelt applause. "We have not as yet identified the man, but feel certain that he is also the person responsible for last summer's power plant explosions, for the unprovoked murder of two police detectives in October, for the series of mass murders in January, and for the organization of hundreds of so-called peace rallies throughout California. It is known that this man worked under the aliases Brian Douglas Jones, Huey Ordon, and Abe Lincoln, and that he sometimes disguised himself as a dentist." The chief paused dramatically before exhibiting his trump card. "The body had been stripped of wallet, watch, all identification, except for"—the chief smiled mysteriously at the press and then looked triumphantly over at the mayor, whom he was upstaging mercilessly—"except for a tattered, greasy picture postcard of Mobile, Alabama. Part of the card is torn, but the message, 'Having a wonderful time. Wish you were here,' is still legible. We are working on the code now and hope to have it broken by the end of the week. This, and certain other clues, which I cannot now reveal, should give us the break we need in this case and lead us to the others involved." The chief bowed his head humbly before the new round of applause and stepped away from the microphone.

Rushing up to lead the applause, the mayor began to clap into the microphone and then to cough into it, ready again to speak. "You can be sure," he said several times, until a tenuous quiet was established, "you can be sure that the mayor's office will continue to work in close cooperation with the police department in this investigation and that the mayor's office will see to it that the police have all the forces necessary at their disposal, including antiaircraft missiles and bombs. If necessary."

"Thank you, thank you," the chief of police mumbled, stepping just slightly in front of the mayor.

The show was over then, and the crowd rose to give both the chief and the mayor a standing ovation. One of the women screamed herself hoarse in her enthusiasm, while beside her, her husband waved a flag. "Oh, say can you see," he sang, tears in his eyes. "BAAAAALUUUUUUD. BAAAAALUUUUUUUUUD. BAAAAAAAALUUUUUUD," the woman screamed. Everyone screamed and sang and waved tiny American flags, then finally they filed outside to the parking lot, the man and the woman dragging their two kids behind them. "What happened?" one of the kids asked.

"They got another atheist nigger," the man said sharply. "One of the ten most wanted ones."

"How?" the little boy asked.

"They killed him," the man said sourly. "Now shut up."

"How how how?" the little boy screamed. "How how how?"

"Shut up," the man said. "What are you, a damn Indian?" The man got in the car and waited for his wife and the two kids to get in. "Hurry up, will you? Can't you see there's a crowd?" They waited in line to get out of the parking lot, then waited in line again to get on the freeway ramp. It was sweaty hot. The man wiped his forehead, and his wife loosened her chinchilla fur coat and began to choke quietly, gasping for air. Slowly they inched up the ramp to the Harbor Freeway. The man bit his fingernails impatiently until he drew blood; he began to lick at the blood.

"How how how?" both the children screamed.

"Shut up," the man said. "Just shut up."